A GEEK GIRL'S GUIDE TO ARSENIC

A GEEK GIRL'S GUIDE TO ARSENIC

JULIE ANNE LINDSEY

WORLDWIDE®

TORONTO • NEW YORK • LONDON
AMSTERDAM • PARIS • SYDNEY • HAMBURG
STOCKHOLM • ATHENS • TOKYO • MILAN
MADRID • WARSAW • BUDAPEST • AUCKLAND

Recycling programs
for this product may
not exist in your area.

A Geek Girl's Guide to Arsenic

A Worldwide Mystery/June 2018

First published by Carina Press

ISBN-13: 978-1-335-50663-4

For Danny, who always made me smile.

ONE

"ISN'T FALL THE BEST?" Grandma swigged the dregs of her steaming wassail and sighed. "Fall is my favorite season and not just because our sales skyrocket. There's excitement in the air. Don't you think?"

I raised a skeptical eyebrow and nodded magnanimously to passersby from my place behind Guinevere's Golden Beauty booth.

A line of eager faces joined the mass around our display case. Their cheeks were as red as living kewpie dolls in the brisk autumn air. They sampled lip balms and hand creams with more enthusiasm than I could muster over skin care and eventually handed fistfuls of cash to Grandma.

She winked. "The sales don't hurt."

Guinevere's Golden Beauty products were available decades before holistic, herbal, all-natural supplies were *en vogue*, but when the trend hit, Grandma became a millionaire. Since I was the Chief Information Officer for Grandma's company, her success didn't hurt my bank account either. Grandma loved hand selling the way she had with Grandpa before he died, so we were still a staple at the summer Renaissance Faire. And from September through November we peddled our goods at the local fairgrounds, known seasonally as Ye Ole Madrigal Craft Faire.

It was a family business and I loved being with my family, but I preferred technology, which was why I also worked as the IT Manager in the gated community where I lived. Guinevere's Golden Beauty was Grandma's baby. I had yet to discover mine.

"Uh-huh." I cast a weary gaze at the horde headed our way. To hear Grandma and the media tell it, holiday shopping was fun. Commercial images captured best friends and couples, arm in arm, sporting openmouthed smiles and jaunting along fully decorated, uncrowded streets. Wherever those pictures were taken, it wasn't Earth. There were still two weeks until Thanksgiving, and I couldn't find parking within six blocks of anything. Of course, none of that affected Grandma. She made our Christmas gifts. If not for work and the Craft Faire, I'd happily hibernate from Halloween through New Year's.

Grandma bagged another gift set and stuffed a receipt inside. Giddy in her element, she passed the package to its new owner and turned to me. "Have you spoken with Petal at Earth Hugger?"

"Briefly." Petal was the aging hippie daughter of Earth Hugger's founder. Together, they'd offered us shelf space in eleven Earth Hugger retail locations. The space was voraciously coveted and about to be ours. Petal and I were hammering out the terms. "She's finishing the marketing plan and meeting with her team to finalize our proposal package."

Grandma startled. "What do you mean by *proposal*? They proposed. We accepted. The warehouse is shipping quadruple numbers next quarter. My living room looks like a big box store. No take-backs! I shook that Earth Hugger's hand!"

"Whoa." I fetched my most reassuring smile. "Everything's fine. *Proposal* is the word they'll use until the contracts are signed. We're right on track, and we don't want to sign until Earth Hugger assures us fair amounts of marketing and visibility. We bring a lot to the table here, too. They need to do their share to make the deal worthwhile. They have to announce and celebrate the inclusion of our products in those locations or it won't even matter they're there. No one will know. No one will buy. The products will be returned unsold."

"Now who's worked up?" She relaxed against the counter. "All right. Fine. Stay on her."

"I am."

"I've always dreamed of seeing my products in stores."

We'd taken Guinevere's Golden Beauty products from the Faire circuit to online sensation, expanded to catalogue ordering and eventually landed a 6:00 a.m. spot on a shopping channel, but we weren't on store shelves yet. "It'll happen. I'm holding out for the treatment your products deserve. If she can get a solid plan together for that, I'll bring the contract to your house myself."

Earth Hugger was a globally recognized and respected maker of holistic beauty products. Their projected growth was astounding. Guinevere's Golden Beauty couldn't touch their kind of scalability. Grandma still kept half her recipes in a lockbox under the bed, and our corporate office doubled as her solarium. We needed this deal with Earth Hugger to fulfill Grandma's dream. Her products on store shelves.

Another bus unloaded shoppers and fall foliage spectators outside the gates fifty yards away.

Grandma snapped into action, loading her arms with free samples and literature about our company. "Fine. Use the lawyers. Call the accountant. Whatever you need, but let's sign those papers soon." She hustled through the booth's exit, headed for the fresh crowd.

Her trust was both endearing and terrifying.

I stacked handmade oatmeal and cranberry soaps on the counter, crunching through a mini pile of crimson leaves. The heavy fall skirt of my Queen Guinevere costume was brown at the hem after trudging halfway across creation, from the worst parking spot imaginable to the replica castle gates.

The crowd around our booth was three people deep. A smile danced across my lips. These dedicated consumers could buy our products at Earth Hugger soon. No need to wait for the Ren Faire or Craft Faire. They wouldn't have to order online. We'd make enough money to build proper offices within three years.

Grandma led another throng of smiling women in my direction. I discarded the empty soap box and pulled in a cleansing breath, preparing for the incomers.

My twin sister, Bree, popped into view, towing her husband, Tom, to the front of the crowd.

Air whooshed from my lungs. So much for my Zen.

She vibrated with enthusiasm, per her usual. A twenty-nine-year-old cheerleader without pompoms. "Are you busy? I've got someone I want you to meet. His name is Adam Clayton and he works at the brothel."

Bree and I once shared a womb and currently our looks, aside from that we had nothing in common. Bree thought sex ran the world, and she and Tom were up to their elbows in everyone's personal business, conducting research for a grant on human sexuality. Being single made me a target for their nonsense. Sex definitely didn't run my world. I was complete on my own. Like a cat.

She tapped the display case between us and gasped. "Let's go. Come on. He's there now." Her determined expression opened to a wide smile. "Are you thinking about sex?" She pulled a tiny notebook and pen from her corset.

"No." I straightened my stance. "I'm thinking of getting a cat."

She and Tom exchanged looks. His understated pirate costume was perfect, definitely more Dread Pirate Roberts than Jack Sparrow.

Bree popped her hip. "Is this about Nate? Are you two finally getting together? Where is he anyway?"

"We aren't dating. It's not like that with us." Nathan Green was a six-foot intellectual and former boxer with ginger hair, green eyes and the heart of a teddy bear. Also, my best friend. We'd never been romantically involved, but I couldn't imagine life without him. Best not to ruin that with romance.

The excitement in her eyes dimmed. "Of course not. Well, where is he? Isn't he usually at your side by now?"

"He's on his way."

She rolled her eyes. "Then you still have time to meet Adam."

"No."

Bree hacked an ugly noise. "Mia! Come on."

"Sorry. I have to stay here and help Grandma until Mom and Dad get back." I raised my palms in the universal out-of-my-control motion and shrugged.

Grandma's long gray braid swung against her backside. "Quit chitchatting and sell something."

Bree beamed. "Exactly."

I narrowed my eyes on her. "I'm not meeting a man who works at a brothel."

She sucked air, ready to implode. Bree had left the family booth to work at the brothel until her research was finished and she felt guilty for abandoning us, as if she was the hinge pin in our operation. "Merry Maidens is a theater company. You act as if it's an actual brothel." Her eyes slid shut, and I imagined her counting to ten the way Dad taught us so we wouldn't pull out one another's hair. "Outside the Faire, Adam's a highly successful CPA and a real Renaissance man. He's educated. He has dual bachelor degrees in finance and history. His graduate work was mostly accounting, but he's a dedicated historian. He's perfect for you. Just meet him. Please?"

"An accountant? He sounds exciting." I waved and smiled to passersby, feigning indifference. Protests were futile with Bree. Avoidance worked well, as long as I could keep it up. Where the heck was Nate when I needed interference?

Bree wrinkled her brows in an expression just short of pity. "They can't all be US Marshals, you know."

I grabbed a stack of flyers and coupons and walked the interior of our booth, nodding and offering samples to shoppers. Most important, leaving Bree and Tom stuck in the crowd.

"Hey." Grandma's pointy elbow dug into my ribs as I passed. "Don't mind her. She means well."

"I know, but geez." Bree had spent her life parenting me, based on the fact she was two minutes older and therefore infinitely wiser and more mature. After having her daughter, Gwen, last year, the maternal instinct had doubled. When I'd arrived stag to Gwen's first birthday party, Bree nearly lost it. I thought being single was a life choice. Bree thought it was a mental illness.

Grandma motioned to another empty display. "We need more Buxom Beauty."

"I'm on it." I set the stack of flyers and coupons on the counter and opened a stock box.

She patted my arm. "It's showtime."

Grandma waded through the throngs and climbed onto a chair out front of the booth to tout the benefits of our natural products. "Greetings!" The crowd moved in her direction, providing me with a fresh blast of oxygen. Grandma belonged onstage. She had that in common with Bree.

Cheers and clashes erupted from the jousting match across the field. I tipped my head back and inhaled. A brisk autumn breeze whipped the peppery scent of fall mums up my nose.

"Good day, milady."

I clutched my collarbone. "Marry!"

John Francis, the Faire painter, smiled coyly from his place across the counter. He shook a foam cup with paint-speckled fingers before tossing it in the waste bin several feet away. His outfit was straight out of a *Three Musketeers* movie, fitting his sassy personality. "Pardon me for saying, but ye do look lovely. That shade of green suits ye well."

"Thank you, sir. Would you care to try some hand cream? A painter's hands must get quite worn."

"Aye. They do."

I opened the sample bottle of Healer's Hand Cream and squeezed a dollop into his palm. "This will soften your calluses and work the paint loose in those rough crevices, all while making your skin as smooth as a baby's bottom."

He cocked a brow and worked the cream into his skin. "You make all these products yourself or do the elves help?" He motioned over my shoulder.

I turned, half expecting a group of rennies in elf costumes. There was only a line of small white-haired women. "No. No elves. Most of the products are made in a factory now, but they're all Lady Mary's secret recipes. Grandma's been perfecting these all her life." I nodded to the energetic septuagenarian teetering enthusiastically on a chair outside the booth.

He barked a laugh and wrung his hands. "Nice. She floats like an angel." The inflection of his voice wavered and a bead of sweat formed at his temple.

"Are you feeling okay?"

A camera crew traipsed across the jousting field, ridiculously out of place in the carefully designed Renaissance village.

John scoffed. "I know the local news has to cover local stories, but there should be a limit for preserving the integrity of the Faire. Why not visit and write a nice piece on the event instead of bringing a half dozen schmucks with lighting screens and boom mics? These are Renaissance times, for crying out loud."

I laughed. "You seem to have slipped from England to Jersey, sire."

He nodded in good humor, raising his eyes to mine. "You caught me. What can I say? It's easy to let my guard down in the presence of beauty."

My cheeks burned, stupidly. John was a relentless flirt with at least ten years on me. If I wasn't careful, Bree would spring from the ground and marry us for conversing. I checked over one shoulder. She and Tom were gone, hopefully not to retrieve Adam the accountant. "I'd better get back to work."

He cleared his throat and stroked his forehead. "I do understand, but first, may I trouble ye for a glass of water?" He rubbed his lips with freshly lotioned hands. A fresh line of perspiration appeared at his graying hairline.

I scanned the area behind me, thankful for his change

in tone. "No water, but we have wassail brewing for the even. I'm afraid it's warm. The cold cider has been consumed."

He dragged a wrist over his brows. "Aye. That'll do."

"Of course." I ladled a small cup of warm wassail from the crock on our handy-dandy, five-hundred-BTU camp stove and passed it over the counter to him. The tangy sting of cider and clove bit the air. "Mmm."

My parents appeared in the distance, swinging interlaced fingers between them. Their matching gypsy costumes were nearly as old as Bree and me.

"Hey," I called as they drew nearer. "Where've you been?"

Their smiles were bright and their hair ruffled.

"Drinking rum punch and necking beyond the privies again?"

Mom blushed and Dad grinned.

Their Ren Faire behavior used to bother me, but they deserved happiness. As a retired teacher and cop who'd survived raising Bree and me, they'd earned some lightly liquored canoodling. We couldn't all be cats.

Grandma finished her spiel on Guinevere's Golden Beauty products and the crowd applauded.

Mom's smile waffled. "I'd better help Mom off that chair before she falls."

Dad swatted her backside as she passed and turned sparkling blue eyes on me. "How's it going, darling?"

"Bree tried to set me up with a man from the brothel."

Dad rolled his eyes and turned to John. He enjoyed the idea of me dating even less than I did. "How's it going, John?"

John dotted his cheeks and neck with a handkerchief. He'd unbuttoned the front of his jacket and his cuffs. "Not too bad." He rubbed his eyes as if to clear them.

Dad gave him a long look. "Feeling okay?"

A man in an Action News-logoed polo and khakis leaned against the counter and fingered the lotion samples while frowning at John. "You don't look so good, buddy. Maybe you've got whatever the jousters had."

I frowned. "The jousters are ill?" The jousters were Ren Faire's equivalent of high school jocks. They were never sick. Rumor was they'd put their mouths on anything. It served to reason that over the years they'd probably built an immunity to most common viruses. The worst thing I'd ever seen any of them come down with was a hangover.

The Action News guy turned his attention to a bath set. "I think the jousters had too much ale, or maybe jousting is less exciting than it sounds. Who knows?"

"I think it's fun to watch."

He frowned. "Do you gift wrap?"

"Aye." I grabbed a stack of bags and arrayed them on the counter. "I can slip your items into a fine satin cinch sack for a small fee. You choose the color. I'll do the rest. Do you have any questions about the Bonnie Bath line?"

He snorted. "I think I can figure it out." He looked to Dad and John for support, as if their shared Y chromosome would somehow make them laugh at his jibe.

Dad sucked his teeth and stared.

Action News sniffed a lavender bath bomb and sneezed. "What's it gonna cost me for the set? You know you charge twenty bucks to get in here?"

I inhaled and counted to ten before answering. "Vendors don't set the entrance fee. Besides, didn't you get in free with the news team?"

"Well, yeah."

I refocused on his initial question. What would the

bath set cost him? I touched each Bonnie item, stating its name, purpose and price. "If you buy the lot you'll save ten percent and get the satin cinch bag as our gift. Just one hundred dollars."

His chin dropped. "A hundred bucks? You want a hundred bucks to put salt and oil in my wife's bath?"

Dad stepped forward, and I turned my head side to side in warning.

"Sir." I put on my sweetest smile. "I'm happy to bag them for you with a fresh sachet and a personal thank-you note from the company. Guinevere's Golden Beauty products are all-natural and guaranteed to pamper your wife. I'm sure she'd appreciate something so personal. Though it is early in the season. There's still plenty of time to visit the local shopping mall before Christmas."

His eyes bugged, and he reached for his wallet. "Make sure you throw in that sachet."

I suppressed a full Cheshire grin. He'd sneezed at one whiff of the bath bomb. "There you go, sir. All my best to your lady." I'd cheerfully filled his sack with all lavender products.

He scowled at the receipt and stuffed it in his pocket, murmuring something sounding suspiciously like, "Ye Ole Madrigal Thieves."

Dad laughed as the man disappeared into the crowd. "Mia, he was clearly allergic to lavender."

"Well, his wife will thank me every night after her bath."

John groaned. "You're quite the little fox in a fancy costume, aren't you?" His words slurred slightly, and he swooned. He covered his mouth with a fist and choked on the words. The pallor of his skin darkened and he stepped away, coughing.

"John?" Dad followed him several paces. "Can I get you something?"

I walked the length of the booth, keeping pace with Dad and John. "He asked for water earlier."

Dad set his palm on John's shoulder. "Let's find you a seat and some water."

John nodded. His wheeze grew louder and devolved into a shudder. His brown eyes glassed over. His knees buckled.

"John!" I ran from the booth, bringing the attention of the crowd with me. "Is he okay?"

Dad caught John from a free fall and settled him against the ground as he convulsed. When he grew still, Dad hovered an ear over his mouth. "I think he's had a seizure."

I fell to their side, pressing two fingers to his neck. "I don't feel a pulse, but I'm shaking."

"Call an ambulance," Dad yelled into the crowd.

I patted my sides on instinct. No phone. Grandma had collected our phones upon arrival. No breaks in the Renaissance façade. Ambiance was the bulk of the sell.

Dad pressed a hand over mine. "The pulse might be weak, but it could still be there." He laid his head on John's chest. His grim expression sent ice shards through my heart.

I steadied my breath and set up on my knees, ready to perform CPR.

"Stop." Dad pulled me back. "Not without a barrier device. You don't know what made him sick. Never put yourself at risk."

"But he's dying!" I stood and cried into the gathered mob. "We need CPR supplies. Someone call the medics."

Mom joined us and squeezed me against her side.

"They're on their way. I saw him go down and called right away."

Grandma climbed onto her chair and scolded the crowd. "Stay back. There's nothing to see. You wouldn't want to be stared at if you were ill. An ambulance is coming and the Faire medics are on their way."

As if on cue, the faint whir of sirens crept into the air.

A set of men in navy blue EMT shirts shoved free from the crowd. I recognized them from the Faire's first aid station. They dashed to John's side and set a plastic device over his lips. CPR began immediately.

I calculated the time elapsed from his collapse. Less than five minutes. If he'd been breathing during part of that time, there was a chance... My eyes stung with emotion, confusion and poignant memories of a dear friend I'd recently lost. The EMTs worked seamlessly to operate his heart until it would beat again on its own.

Mom leaned her head on my shoulder.

I fixed my eyes on the medics. "I'm okay."

I couldn't say the same for John.

TWO

"TRAGEDY AT THE Ren Faire!" The Action News reporter made a live announcement of John's collapse and, ten minutes later, his death.

The crowd grew to celebrity-sighting proportions after the Action News's second announcement. Throngs of holiday shoppers clamored for a look at the gruesome scene.

Mom stepped away. "I'm going to see if there's anything I can do to help with the crowd."

"Sure." I rubbed the chill off my arms and scanned the area for Nate.

Finally, his ginger head bounced into view. Light on his feet, he cut through the masses with the ease and skill of a trained fighter, with a presence that was impossible to ignore.

"Are you okay?" He looked me over with a frown. "I saw the cops and ambulances out front and followed the crowd to the gate. They aren't letting anyone else in and they wouldn't tell me what happened. I tried calling." He rubbed a heavy hand through his hair. "Your grandma has your phone?" He scanned the scene near my booth.

"Yeah."

I pulled back for a better look at his face. "If they aren't letting anyone in, how'd you get here?"

"I snuck over the fence. When I saw the crowd gathered at your booth…" He paused. "That was terrifying."

"You climbed the fence?"

"By the privies. First time I've ever seen that place empty." He laid his cheek against the top of my head and cradled long arms around me. "You're okay? Your family, too?"

"Yeah."

His heart pounded against me. "What happened?"

"John Francis collapsed. He stopped breathing. He died."

Mom led a group of rennies to the front of the crowd. They held hands, forming a human chain around John and the paramedics, protecting them from the morbidly curious.

Nate raised onto his toes and craned his neck. "Are you sure he's dead?"

"The medics stopped CPR right after they got here. The news crew made an announcement."

He grimaced. "I'm sorry. Did you know him well?"

"Kind of."

A white van with the medical examiner's logo parted the crowd, casting workers and spectators onto either side of the dusty path. Two police cruisers and a large black truck followed. A nondescript sedan brought up the rear.

I wrapped my arms around my middle. "Does that seem excessive to you? Four cars plus the ME? Is that normal for a guy with a heart attack or a stroke or whatever happened here?"

Nate rocked back on his heels. "Do you know what happened? Did anyone say it was a medical reason? Natural causes?"

"You think it wasn't? What are you saying?" A gulp of air lodged in my throat. "Murder?" I croaked.

"Maybe."

"No one came near him. Just Dad and me. We were talking to him half an hour ago. He was fine and now…" *How could this happen again?*

Nate and I had lost our friend Baxter in July. I'd been accused of the murder then stalked by the killer. John probably wasn't murdered, but still, any day was too soon to lose someone else.

The officers from the cruisers parked and joined local security at the gates, turning newcomers away and interviewing visitors as they left. I shaded my achy eyes and looked skyward, toward Nate's worried face. "They're talking to people before they leave. Maybe they think someone saw something."

Intrigue lit his eyes. "They think this was foul play. You're good." He turned in a small circle, inspecting the scene. "If you're okay here, I can go find out what they're asking and see if I can overhear something useful."

"Yeah. I'm okay."

"Excellent." He jogged into the crowd.

I shivered from the chill left in his absence. "Good luck," I mumbled, moving toward the family booth. A hot cup of wassail might help shake off the shock creeping through me.

A shadow fell over me. "Mia?"

I spun toward the familiar voice, heart pounding. "You've got to be kidding me."

Detective Dan Archer was several feet away and closing the gap at a clip. His open tan trench coat whipped in the breeze. Shiny black shoes carried him to my side. He looked oddly dismayed.

"Did you know John Francis?"

He pointed a pen in the direction Nate had run. "No. So are you and Nate an item now?"

Heat rose along my neck. I lifted my chin. "I never expected to see you again."

Dan's older brother, Jake, had rolled into town four months ago, accused me of murder and stole my heart. I hadn't heard from him since. My traitorous gaze drifted over the crime scene as if he might appear.

I squinted at the badge hanging from a metal chain around Dan's neck. "Why are you here?"

Dan narrowed his eyes. "I'm a homicide detective, or have you forgotten?"

"So it was murder?" I whipped my head in the direction of poor John. The word soured on my tongue. "I knew there were too many cars. I think you're wrong about the murder, though. I was talking to him when he got sick. He was fine and then *boom*. Probably an undiagnosed heart condition."

"We disagree."

I scowled. "You just got here. I was with him. I saw it happen."

Dan's cheek twitched. "I'm not sure about what you saw, but it's unlikely this wasn't a murder."

"What's that supposed to mean? Based on what evidence?"

"Based on federal marshal opinion. I'm assisting Deputy US Marshal Archer on this."

I gaped. A slew of mental curses stampeded through my mind.

"Someone call my name?" Deputy US Marshal Archer sauntered across the grass, glaring at his phone and tapping furiously at the screen.

A strangled sound escaped me.

Dan raised a hand. "Mia, you remember my brother, Jake."

Jake jerked to a stop.

"Yep."

"Miss Connors." Jake gave me a cranky look. "I'd like to say I'm surprised to see you here, but considering this is how we met last time…"

My hackles rose. "Really? You're surprised to see me at Ye Ole Madrigal Craft Faire? Working at my family booth? Maybe you should rethink your career choice."

"I'll keep that in mind. Care if I ask you a few questions?"

I squared my shoulders. "I don't know, Captain Insinuation. Planning to investigate me for murder again?"

He shrugged. "Why? Did you do it?"

I scowled. "What are you really doing here, Archer?"

Dan released a long whistle, like the sound of a bomb falling, and left.

Jake rubbed his chin. "I'm assisting Dan with his investigation."

"He said he's assisting you with your investigation. Why is there an investigation? Why are there officers stationed at the gates talking to everyone who leaves?"

"I'll ask the questions."

I shook my head. "No. You first. Start talking."

His grouchy expression wavered. "It's classified. Now, can I please ask my questions?"

I shot him a crazy face. "No."

"I can't do this with you right now, Mia. This hasn't been a good day." He motioned to the body being zipped into a black coroner bag.

The sound drew ice up my spine.

"Did you know the vic?"

I scrunched my face. "His name's John Francis, not The Vic. He's a painter. He does oils, landscapes, people. Some on commission. Some just hang in the gallery. They're all beautiful. He could've been famous."

Jake marked something in a little notebook.

I bristled. "What's this about? Why are the marshals involved? How'd you even know this happened? Why did Dan say he was murdered?"

He lifted his eyes to his brother in the distance before returning to my inquisition. "Did you speak to the v— Mr. Francis before he died? Maybe see him interacting with someone? How did he seem to you?"

"He was fine. We talked a few minutes before he got sick."

Jake's shoulders drooped. "You were with him when he died?"

"Until the EMTs arrived. Yes."

"And?"

"He came to visit around four, I think. We talked and I gave him some wassail. He tried our hand cream. It was a typical encounter for us."

A commotion turned Jake away. The Action News reporter forced her way through the reformed human barricade, calling for her henchmen to follow. She shoved a microphone between Jake and me. "Did you say you gave the dead man something to drink before he died?"

My mouth opened and closed. I looked to Jake.

"That's it." He widened his stance and braced long tan fingers over narrow hips. "Get out. This is a police investigation."

"I'm covering a breaking story. I have a right to be here."

"Cover your story from over there." He outstretched an arm in the direction of the front gates. "You're disturbing the crime scene. Get back. Get lost. Beat it."

She inched back, leaning her mic and torso in my direction. "Crime scene? Did you say the man also tried your hand cream? What was the cause of death?" Her eyes dropped to Jake's badge. "US Marshal? What kind of investigation is this?"

Jake shoved her cameraman. "Get back or I'll charge you with obstruction."

The man removed the camera from his shoulder and hustled to set up again on the far side of our booth, while the reporter repeated her new information on air. Her attention darted back to us every few moments, making me more uncomfortable by the second.

"You okay?" Jake lifted a hand in my direction but dropped it at his side.

I swung my chin left and right. "Nope." Not even a little.

"Agent Archer!" A man in gray slacks and a pin-striped button-down jogged to Jake's side. "Sorry. I guess it's Marshal Archer now." They shook hands and exchanged easy smiles.

The badge on the man's pocket identified him as the medical examiner. He'd shed his jacket and rolled both shirt sleeves to the elbows. A navy jacket hung over one arm. He could've come for the jousting and no one would've known the difference.

I stilled myself, hoping to hear something that made sense.

He handed Jake a baggie with a cell phone. "We took this from the victim's pocket. No identification. A handful of cash, small bills. The team's bagging those. You wanted the phone."

Jake nodded, wholly focused on the baggie in hand. "Anything else?"

The man turned his back to me and lowered his voice. "Cause of death looks like poison."

My tummy flattened against my spine. "Accidental poisoning? Like a prescription snafu or allergic reaction?"

Jake and the ME looked my way.

An apologetic smile lifted and dropped from the ME's lips.

Jake groaned. "Mia. Maybe you can wait inside your booth until I'm ready for the rest of our interview."

The Action News reporter popped back into place. "Poison?" Her crew adjusted cameras and boom mics from a few feet away.

Jake took a giant step in my direction, blocking me from the camera's view. "Never mind. Stay here." He returned his attention to the ME. "Any idea how?"

"Not yet. No signs of needle marks. Maybe something topical or ingested. We'll know more after a tox screen and autopsy."

Jake pinched the bridge of his nose and swore before turning anguished eyes on me. "Mia. I'll need the cup Mr. Francis used and the wassail."

I guffawed. "You can't seriously think…"

He lifted a hand overhead. "I need evidence bags over here."

The medical examiner made a hasty escape.

Shock jolted me into obstinacy. "You can't be serious. You think I did this? Are you insane?"

The reporter snapped her fingers and fluffed her oversized hair. She used my family's booth as her new backdrop. "Mindy Kinley reporting from Ye Ole Madrigal Craft Faire with breaking news. The man who died suddenly this past hour is believed to have been poisoned. Officers are talking with a representative of

Guinevere's Golden Beauty products, where the man sampled hand cream and accepted a cup of wassail moments before his death. A little wassail? A sample of hand cream? Which do you think killed him, Ohio? You can head over to my web page and vote until five."

Jake cleared his throat. "I'm going to need that hand cream, too."

I slipped into the booth and lifted the Healer's Hand sampler from the counter. Jake stayed in my way, annoying but protective, limiting the camera's access.

He stuck a sticky note on the lid. "They'll bag the product and take it in for a closer look. We need to rule it out."

I nodded.

Grandma stormed past, cell phone in hand. Her humble servant's robe and apron flapped in the wind under a fierce enough stare to take out an army.

"Uh-oh." I gripped the sleeve of Jake's windbreaker. "This isn't good."

Grandma shook her phone at the reporter. "You air that hokum and my lawyers will have you serving salads at Betty's Burgers by sundown."

"Here we go." I needed a paper bag to puff into or an oxygen mask or a getaway car. Something. Anything.

Mom and Dad rushed to Grandma's side.

"Mia!" Nate jogged into the booth. His enormous hands wrapped my wrists and pulled them to his chest. "Now what happened?" He looked to Jake when I didn't respond.

My family thundered and shrieked behind us. Grandma protested the implication that her product killed a man, while Dad and Tom tried fruitlessly to settle her.

I pressed my forehead against Nate's wool coat.

"Should I help? Should I let them handle it? I have no idea." I peeked at the chaos with one eye. "I think they're making it worse." I turned for a better view.

Nate chuckled. "No. It looks like Bree's got this."

Thank goodness.

Bree was the epitome of calm before the camera. A completely non-Connors-like disposition. If she hadn't been my identical twin and dressed as a harlot, it would've helped.

I pressed icy hands to my face. "Is this happening?"

Nate wrapped an arm around my waist and hauled me against the sharp V of his side. "Maybe you need to sit down. I think you're having a panic attack."

"Am not." I gasped through a too-tight throat.

Jake moved into our personal space. "Nate."

"Jake."

"Does she have attacks often?"

I gritted my teeth. "I. Am. Fine." My cheeks and neck burned as oxygen escaped from my lungs.

Nate slid his gaze my way. "She went through a lot over the summer. It took a toll."

"I'm fine." My dress was shrinking and the earth was tilted, but what could I do about that?

Jake's expression softened. "So you are human. You've made me wonder a few times."

"Shut up."

He parted his lips in the lazy half-smile I loved. "Can you tell me anything else about the moments before John Francis collapsed?"

"I don't think so. He was fine. Then he wasn't."

Jake lifted the plastic bag with John's cell phone. "His phone has a reminder set for three. An appointment with Surly Wench. Does that mean anything to you?"

I pointed across the dusty path to a line of eateries. "Surly Wench is a pub. Oh! Huzzah!"

"Huzzah!" A chorus rang up in echo.

Jake startled. "What the hell?"

Nate laughed. "It's a rennie thing. A custom."

"Rennie?"

I hiked my heavy skirts up and dashed the short distance to the trash bin. "Rennies are people who regularly attend the Faires or work here. Look." I hovered a finger over the trash. The setting sun threw shadows across the bin's contents. "John threw a cup away after he got to my booth. I wonder if he got it at Surly Wench?" The cup inside the receptacle seemed larger. Nondescript.

Jake poked the cup-in-question with his pen and snapped on a pair of plastic gloves. "I need those bags." His voice shot through the hoopla.

The ME dashed to meet us, professing apologies. "Sorry. Dan had some questions." He shivered. "This place is my living nightmare. Like being stuck in a circus after hours."

Jake bagged the cup and handed it to the ME.

Twinkle lights snapped on across the out-of-season fairgrounds turned temporary Renaissance village, illuminating booths and pathways around the field.

The ME looked at me. "Sorry about what I said." He motioned to my Queen Guinevere costume.

I nodded in full acceptance. "Whatever. It's my circus. They're my monkeys."

Dan moseyed back across the lawn to meet us, with a mischievous smile. "You two crazy kids get caught up?"

Jake dragged his gaze from my face to Dan's. "The vic was poisoned. He drank from this cup before talking with Mia."

Dan scratched in his notebook.

Jake nodded toward my booth. "Then Mia gave him something else to drink and he sampled her family's hand cream."

"Yeesh." Dan made another note. "Anything else?"

"Yeah, we've got a reminder in his phone for three o'clock. Doesn't say with who, but looks like they met at one of the pubs over there. Surly Wench."

Dan cocked an eyebrow. "I know who he met."

"You do?" I jumped to his side. "Who?"

He smiled. "Funny seeing you again like this. You don't believe in coincidence, but here you are. So what do you call this?"

"Unfortunate."

He winked. "Maybe."

We followed Dan to the coroner's van parked inside the replica castle gates. Nate kept one hand on the small of my back, reminding me he was still there. Jake kept his distance. Energy zipped and whirled through the air around us like The Flash trying to counteract a tornado. I couldn't pinpoint the cause, but then again, I'd never claimed to understand people. Especially not any in possession of a Y chromosome.

The crowd near the gates had thinned to a handful of curious Faire workers and a couple dozen stragglers. A pair of uniformed officers restrained a screaming woman near the coroner van. Her mix of love professions and Victorian swears stopped me short.

The officers handed the woman off to Dan and hurried away.

Dan addressed the woman. "We have a few more questions."

She smoothed her skirts and wiped her mascara-stained eyes before folding freckled arms across her middle. Her wool cape blew behind her in the nipping wind. "No."

"No?" Jake barked.

Her lip trembled. "No."

I stepped forward on instinct, a layer of padding between her and the Archer brothers. "Here." I handed her my handkerchief and tugged the cape around her shoulders.

She clutched the material to her chest and buried her head in the crook of my neck.

I startled.

She bawled.

Dan cleared his throat. "Your name is Melanie Warner. Correct?"

She took a step away from me and rubbed her face. "Sorry. Yes. I'm Melanie." Natural strawberry-blond curls adhered to her cheeks and neck, wet with tears and anguish.

"You knew the deceased?" he continued.

Her brows furrowed, and swears from every era burst from her mouth.

Dan squirmed. "Hey. It's okay." He lifted a steady hand in her direction.

She nearly broke it off. "Don't touch me!"

He snatched his hand away. "I wasn't."

Jake raised his palms. "Ma'am, we need you to answer these questions. It's not an option. You can talk to us here or we can take you downtown, let you catch your breath and you can answer when you're ready. The choice is yours."

She turned to face the coroner's van and started swearing again.

Dan reached for his handcuffs. He wasn't a time

waster, and he was all business, like his brother. Handsome, too, but that was standard in Archer DNA.

Jake glared at me and pointed at Melanie. "A little help."

"Fine." I leaned into her line of sight. "Hi. Hey. You're clearly angry with John. It's obvious you knew him. Did something happen between you?"

Melanie gripped the red cape tightly to her middle. Her freckled cheeks puffed with rage. "Yeah, something happened. The no-good scoundrel knocked me up and dumped me! I hate him!" She flung herself at the loaded gurney and hugged the bag's end. Swears turned to sobs. "I need you, Johnny! You no-good, cheating jerk!"

Well, that explained a lot.

THREE

JAKE AND DAN spoke privately with Melanie as the fairgrounds emptied, leaving Nate and me to stew.

I motioned to the officers stationed at the gates. "What did you find out from them?"

Nate dipped his head and lowered his voice. "They wanted to know who I was. If I'd ever been here before. Which shops I'd visited. If I noticed anything unusual while I was here. They took my name and contact information and said the Craft Faire would send me replacement tickets for another day." He crossed his arms and widened his stance. "Basically, everyone is a suspect and they want to know how to reach us."

I fingered the soft velvet material of my sleeve. Unfortunately, *everyone* wasn't the last person seen with him, or the one who offered him a drink and hand cream right before he died. That was me.

The officers released the final handful of shoppers and pulled the gates shut. Only workers remained.

I scanned the area for answers. For an indication I was dreaming.

Nate lowered his voice. "I climbed the fence twice today unnoticed. If I can, anyone can. I'm not exactly hard to spot."

In other words, the cops wouldn't find the killer by collecting names at the front gate. "I don't know. The killer might've hidden in plain sight."

"What do you think happened? Did you know anyone who didn't like John? Did someone here have a beef with him? Competition? Girlfriend?"

"No. Of course not."

"Poison requires a plan, Mia. Someone plotted this."

I gnawed the tender skin along the side of one fingernail and winced.

"Can you think of anyone?"

I dropped my hand to my side to avoid permanent damage. "Jake said John met someone at Surly Wench. The appointment was saved in his phone's reminders."

"Well, then. What are we waiting for?"

I stole a look at the Archers, fully engrossed in their interrogation. "Okay. Let's go." My voice cracked with uncertainty as memories of our last investigation clawed at my chest.

We slipped along storefronts into shadows cast by swinging signage and flapping striped overhangs. A storm was coming. Warning winds whipped abandoned leaves into tiny hurricanes at my ankles. Suddenly, the place I loved seemed too much like the Night Circus.

Nate slowed several yards from my family booth. "Should we check in?"

I changed trajectory, caught in the sights of my too-vigilant father. "Okay. Yeah."

Dad crossed the grass and met us halfway. "We're packing up. Meet us at home. We've got some PR work to do after those news reports."

"Sure. Nate will drive me to my car and I'll come right over."

Nate bobbed his head in silent agreement.

"Good." Dad narrowed his eyes on us. "Where were you headed just now?"

"What?" I put my giant owl eyes to use in one of their most natural expressions: *Who, me?*

Dad worked his jaw side to side. "Nate?"

"We're going to Surly Wench."

I puffed my cheeks.

"Mia!" Dad scolded. "You've got to stay as far away from this as possible. Your grandmother's having a stroke over the bad publicity. She's got three lawyers on the line and your mother's calling the Action News station to threaten them with a libel suit. Bree and Tom are on damage control. You can't be caught meddling."

"I'm not."

The Connors Clan approached with long faces, bundled to their foreheads in coats and scarves. Mom wrestled a jumble of bags in one hand. "Everyone ready?"

Dad moved to her side, unloading her burden. "I was just inviting Nate to join us at home."

"Okay. Thank you." Mom motioned us to fall in line. "You're welcome anytime, Nate."

Nate and I trudged back to the front gates under the power of my family's influence. It was the way I did most things I'd rather not do. An ex-boyfriend had once suggested I be ashamed of the control my family had over me. He didn't understand our unconventional team mentality. He saw the dynamic as a flaw. I saw him to the door.

Sure, we were different, opinionated and a little nutty, but we were family and we stuck together.

Dad kissed my cheek. "I'm going to bring the car around. I'll see you at the house?"

"Yep."

He glanced at Nate for confirmation, clearly not trusting me to stay out of this.

Nate smiled.

I waited until his silhouette disappeared into the muddy parking lot and grabbed Mom's arm. "I'm going to say goodbye to Dan and let him know we're available if he has any other questions."

She shot me a distracted smile. "Good idea."

Nate set his hand on her shoulder. "It was nice seeing you again, Mrs. Connors. If you need anything…"

She patted his hand. "Thank you, Nathan. Stop by later if you can."

I headed toward the Archers for appearance's sake, careful to stay out of their line of sight, and made a hard left at Bard's Bakery.

Nate matched my pace easily, falling into step at my side. "I think Jake saw us."

I hitched up my skirts and changed my walk into a jog. "Then we'd better hurry."

Twinkle lights and stars led the way with a little help from knights carrying torches outside various shopfronts.

I peeked at Nate as we closed in on our destination. He buzzed at my side. "What's the plan?"

"I don't know." I stuttered to a stop. "Don't they say killers hang around their crime scenes? Maybe we should make note of anyone who hasn't left yet."

"We haven't left yet."

I shook my well-chewed fingernail at him. "Excellent point. We should make this quick."

Nate held the door for me.

The yeasty scent of fried everything slapped my face. Surly Wench deep-fried veggies, candy bars, even butter. Normally I craved the junk, but a new thought occurred to me. What if John had eaten here too? Maybe the poison hadn't been in the cup Jake collected.

I hustled to the counter and dinged the service bell. "Hello?"

Pots and pans clattered in the back. "We're closed."

I leaned across the wooden counter. "It's Mia Connors. Who's there?"

Silence.

I straightened and tiptoed around the counter toward the kitchen. "Hello?"

Nate followed close on my heels.

Another earsplitting round of calamity shot from the kitchen with a peppering of curses.

I pushed the swinging doors wide and poked my head inside. "Everything okay back here?"

A young woman crouched on the floor, collecting fallen trays and pans. "We're closed."

I joined her. "Let me help." I heaved fallen items off the floor and loaded them onto the counter. "I'm Mia Connors. I work at Guinevere's Golden Beauty booth. This is my friend, Nate."

Her gaze traveled the length of Nate's body from feet to face. Her mouth fell open.

"Hi." Nate dropped into a squat beside us. He extended a hand.

She quickly accepted. "Kenna." A blush rose across her perfect olive skin.

Jeez. I hoisted the last tin and lid onto her counter. "Were you here when John Francis came in this afternoon?"

She turned dark brown eyes on me. "He's the one who...died?"

Nate tilted his head like a six-foot puppy. "Yes. Do you remember if he was with anyone?"

She wrung the material of her apron around her fingers. "Melanie. They sat at a corner table, and she was pretty upset. They drew a lot of attention. I already told the police all this." She worked her bottom lip with her teeth. Her fingers turned white under the pressure of her twisted apron.

I didn't like the implication. "I'm sorry to ask you to repeat yourself. I know how frustrating that is. It's just that John was a friend of mine, and I was with him when he got sick. The police suspect poison, and I can't understand why someone would do this to him."

Her gaze darted to the back door multiple times before stopping on Nate.

"Kenna?" His voice was so smooth I nearly didn't recognize it. "What did John Francis order?"

She wet her lips. "Same thing every time. Kale, berry and hemp smoothie. Greens salad with balsamic."

I curled my lip. Yuck. "He ordered that here?"

"Yeah. Sometimes I think Lisa only keeps that stuff on hand for him. No one comes for smoothies since Fruit Jester joined the Faire."

The back door swung open and clattered shut.

Kenna jumped.

A willowy woman in her fifties dropped empty trash bins at her feet. "Kenna?"

"Uh. This is Mina and Nate." She swallowed. "This is my boss, Lisa."

I waved. "I'm Mia." Not Mina.

Lisa glared at Kenna. "Employees only in the kitchen, Kenna. Remember?"

Nate smiled. "It's nice to meet you, Lisa. We were—"

"Leaving." She pointed to the door.

"Leaving," he repeated. He extended his hand to Kenna again. "If you want to get a cup of coffee sometime, let me know."

Her head bobbed.

I led the way out. Safely back on the footpath, I

swatted Nate. "Did you wink at her? And invite her to coffee?"

"So?"

"So?" I smiled. "That poor girl."

"That poor girl has my card now. I slipped it into her hand when we shook goodbye. Smart, huh?"

"Oh, yes. Very smooth."

"Thanks. I think Kenna has more to say, and Lisa wasn't going to let her."

I bumped into him playfully as we walked. "You think she's pretty. Be careful, big boy. I bet she's still in college. Or high school. If you guys go out, you should card her. Just in case."

"Please. She's over eighteen. Obviously. Besides, what do you think I'm going to do with her? I invited her for coffee, not a bank heist."

"Uh-huh."

"Lisa seemed angry."

I laughed. "You're like a subject-change Jedi. No transition necessary."

"The Force is strong in me."

"It is, and I agree about Lisa, but I can't blame her. Grandma's angry, too. Surly Wench and Guinevere's Golden Beauty took major hits today."

Nate followed me around a set of wooden stocks and through an employee exit in the fence behind the ticket booth. "I hate to say it, but your grandma's right to panic. A tragedy this big could ruin a business. My mom still won't buy aspirin."

"I know."

We walked in silence across the field, where my car was a tiny pink spec in the distance.

With media coverage, something like this could

snowball in days and ruin the company Grandma spent decades creating.

Nate opened his passenger door for me. "Penny for your thoughts?"

"We need to find out what really happened to John."

I PARKED ON the street outside my parents' three-bedroom ranch in the suburbs. Lights burned in every window. Voices rattled the glass.

I let myself in on an intake of breath, compiling a mental list of people to talk to at the Faire tomorrow.

"Finally!" Bree marched into the foyer, where I hung my cloak. "Where have you been? I thought you were following us? Where's Nate?" She pushed past me to check the driveway.

"He went home."

Her lips twisted in distaste. "He's the only man on your horizon. You should keep him close."

I forced a tight smile and headed for the kitchen. "I'm not doing this with you again tonight."

The heavenly aroma of percolating coffee met me in the hallway and invited me back in time. Bright white cabinetry adorned the same country blue walls I'd helped paint in junior high. Matching gingham curtains dressed the windows, and knitted cozies shaped like farm animals covered Mom's small appliances. My senior picture stuck to the refrigerator in a magnetic frame beside Bree's wedding photo and a snapshot from Gwen's first birthday.

Dad set a bottle of wine on the counter and cracked the top off a beer. "You hungry?"

Always. "Not really."

Mom had unloaded the refrigerator and spread a buffet of leftovers and sandwich components and condiments on the island. "Make a plate." She motioned to her spread. "Eat."

I scooped pasta salad into a bowl. My tummy growled in excitement. "How's Grandma?"

Dad swigged his beer. "Great. She's in the living room."

Her muffled voice ricocheted off the walls.

"Ah. What's she doing?"

"Cursing."

I smiled. "At who?"

He rubbed his forehead. "Either at her lawyer or the television. Hard to say. The eight o'clock news just started."

I followed Grandma's voice to the living room.

She pressed a phone to her ear. "They're insinuating our product killed that man! What am I keeping you on retainer for?"

I turned back for a cup of coffee. "Lawyer."

Mom made the sign of the cross and poured a glass of wine. "I'm going to check on Gwen. She was fussing when we got home, and Bree put her down in the den."

Tom rounded the corner, palms up. "No need. She's fast asleep. What can I say? I'm Houdini Dad. Some might call me The Baby Whisperer." He wound long arms around Bree and kissed her head.

Bree turned to kiss his lips. "Thank you for getting her to sleep. We make perfect babies."

Gag.

Dad nudged me into the dining room, shooing me like an unwanted cat on the front porch.

I hustled ahead of his flapping hands. "What?"

"So?" He pulled the etched glass doors closed behind us.

I used my big eyes again. "What? I don't know what you mean."

His expression turned droll. "What did Dan and Jake have to say? Your mother said you stayed behind to talk to them."

"Well, they said they're looking into it."

Dad raised his thick graying eyebrows like antenna. The air between us charged with his retired-cop senses.

The doorbell rang, and I squeaked.

A stampede of footfalls headed toward the front door. Dad shot me a look. "I'll talk to you in a minute. I have to make sure that's not a reporter. Who knows what your grandmother would do to them."

I gave Dad a thumbs-up and went back to the kitchen.

I grabbed a coffee mug and surveyed the empty bottle of wine. Mom's glass was also empty.

I pulled a fresh bottle from the rack and jammed the corkscrew in the spongy top. If I didn't have to drive home, I might have skipped the coffee, too. Regardless, Mom would need another glass tonight.

A confusing sound traveled down the hall and settled in my gut as I worked the corkscrew. It was the same deep drawl that had haunted my sleep since July. My fingers froze mid-twist.

"Mia." Mom beamed. "Look who came to see you."

Deputy US Marshal Jake Archer frowned at me from across my parents' kitchen, complete with cowboy hat and shiny gold star. "Hello, Mia."

FOUR

MY MIND RACED with possible reasons for Jake Archer to appear in my parents' kitchen. Most were troublesome. None were good. I lifted my hand waist high and wiggled my fingers. "Hi."

He nodded once, shifting his gaze across the room and down the length of me.

Bree hummed a long obnoxious note.

A rush of self-awareness stole my breath and burned my cheeks. Everyone else had changed. I was late after staying to visit Surly Wench. I lifted one hand to my head. Yep. Uncombed. Still pinned in extravagant chestnut ringlets, fuzzy and tangled from wind and wear. I squeezed a handful of heavy emerald velvet skirting between the fingers of my opposite hand. The mud coating on my gown's hem grew heavier with every breath. The plunging neckline was too revealing. The belted waist was too tight.

Jake removed his hat and rubbed a forearm across his forehead. "I'm sorry for showing up like this."

Bree and Mom ushered him forward, rambling over one another in bumbling succession. "No. Not at all. Glad you're here."

Dad made a trip to the fridge. "You on duty?"

"Not technically. No."

Mom filled a plate with everything and jammed a fork on top. "Eat."

Dad set a beer on the island before him. "She loves us with food."

"It's appreciated. Thank you."

Mom blushed.

Dad sidled up beside Jake and raised his bottle. "So, you get a bead on the killer? Someone in custody? Suspects?"

Grandma crept into the kitchen, eyeballing the badge on Jake's belt. "You're not here to arrest someone, are you?" She flicked her attention to me.

His cheek twitched. "No, ma'am. I came by to see how you're all doing. I should've been more sympathetic at the Faire. Sometimes I get focused and forget my manners."

Bree slithered to my side. "So, manners brought you here? Nothing else?"

Jake looked from my face to Bree's and back again. I squirmed. "We accept your apology."

Grandma deflated. "I'm just glad you aren't here to arrest anyone." She grabbed a beer from the fridge and knocked the cap off on the edge of Mom's counter.

Mom groaned.

Grandma shoved a pretzel in her mouth and gave Jake another once-over. "So, you came to see Mia?"

"Grandma." I gave her a warning look. "He said he came to..." What had he come to do? To say he should've been nicer earlier? At a murder scene?

Jake cleared his throat. He worked the brim of his hat between steady fingers. A network of tiny lines gathered at the corners of his eyes. "I did."

Did what? Came to see me?

He turned somber eyes on me. "Is there someplace we can talk privately?"

"Fine—" Grandma tapped the counter "—but eat

first. Gwendolyn will lose her mind if someone doesn't eat soon."

Jake forked a wad of cheese and pasta into his mouth.

I lifted my nearly forgotten bowl and joined him. He'd come to see me. He hadn't contacted me in three months and, frankly, could've been a little nicer at the Faire. Did he think I knew more about John's death than I'd already told him? Had he seen me visit Surly Wench with Nate?

The silence was palpable. Everyone stared. At me. At him. I shoved spiral pasta around my bowl, both thankful and horrified to have my family present for our bizarre reunion.

Tom poured a glass of wine and took the empty place beside Jake, opposite his wife. "How do you like the Marshal Service so far?"

Thank heavens for Tom's obsession with small talk. My shoulders dropped a bit from their positions beside my ears. I rubbed the knotted muscles in my neck, waiting for his answer.

Jake chewed thoughtfully, a little longer than necessary, it seemed, before answering. "Good."

I rolled my eyes. A real wordsmith. An open book, this guy.

Tom gobbled up the one-word answer and went hunting for more. "Yeah? I bet it's interesting work."

"It's definitely that." Jake pushed a pile of cheese cubes with his fork. "How about you? Have you and Bree finished your study?"

Tom perked up. A broad smile split his face. "Not yet, no. We're just getting started, really. There's so much ground to cover. Attraction. Flirtation. Foreplay. Coitus." He stretched a pale finger in the air for each item on his list. "We'd hoped Mia would go on some blind dates for us, provide a little recon, but, of course, she declined." He smiled sadly in my direction. "I can't say I blame her. At our age, it's hard to find many decent single people."

I shaded my face with one hand and spoke privately with my maker. *Kill me now and throw me in the river.* Why was this my life? Who were these people? How could Bree and I share DNA? DNA was a farce. That should be their next study.

"Mia?" Bree hip-checked me. "Jake asked you something."

"What?" My gaze jumped to his. "What?"

He snorted quietly, amused at something I didn't see or understand. "I said I understood your reluctance to date and asked when you moved."

"How do you know I moved?" I set my fork aside before I dropped it.

"I stopped at your apartment before coming here. A man in a unitard answered your door. At first I thought he was a friend of yours, a new roommate, significant other, but he told me he moved in August."

"My significant other? In a unitard? That's the kind of man you assume would steal my heart?"

"I didn't know, and I don't judge."

I glanced at the fork beside my bowl, and Jake pulled both hands into his lap.

Bree coughed into her fist and shook her head in a movement so tiny I nearly missed it.

I counted to ten silently. "No roommate. No lover in a unitard. I moved."

"Where?"

"To Horseshoe Falls. I told you I would when you came to see me in the hospital." I mentally added this to the abundant list of reasons I didn't date. Men were impossible, and they didn't listen.

His blank expression begged me to smack it. "I didn't forget."

"Then why did you go to my old apartment?"

He didn't answer.

"I'm sorry. Why are you here?"

A gasp rolled through the kitchen. My family scattered like mice at a cat show.

Jake wiped his fingers on a napkin and dropped it on the island. "Horseshoe Falls? Did you buy a house?"

"Condo."

"Do you like it there?"

"I'm never late for work."

He pushed away from the island and stuffed both hands into front pockets. "I just wanted to tell you I don't think your family did this thing today. I know they didn't kill John Francis."

I gnawed a stumpy fingernail. "Good."

"I don't know for sure your product wasn't used as the murder weapon, though."

"What?" I scooted around the island and dropped my voice to a whisper. "What is that supposed to mean? We make our products. You know that."

Jake's pained expression worried me. "I should go. Will you walk me out?"

"You can bet your britches." I grabbed my cloak off the rack and strode outside ahead of him. Puffs of my frozen breath lifted into the air. Steam probably rolled off my head, too. I kicked a lump of mud with the point of my boot.

Jake jogged down the drive a moment later. "Sorry. I had to say goodbye to everyone."

I bit my tongue and waited.

He opened the passenger door to his truck and motioned me inside. "Come on. I'll warm it up. You must be freezing."

"I'm fine. Talk."

He scrubbed heavy hands over his weary face and stuffed the cowboy hat back onto his head. He leaned in. "John Francis was a federal witness in US Marshal custody. *My* custody." He slammed the door and swore under his breath.

I relaxed against the closed door as I processed the news. "He was a painter."

"Yes. A painter who forged priceless works and sold them to criminals who swapped the fakes for the originals and kept or sold the real ones."

I tugged the material of my cloak tight across my shoulders. "That's a thing?"

"Yes, and this particular man was instrumental in fingering a major New Jersey crime boss. John Francis worked in the family's trust for years. He had inside information we needed." Jake shifted uncomfortably. "He was my first solo assignment and a hell of a nice guy. And he's dead."

"I'm sorry."

He lifted stormy eyes to mine. "Anyway, I know your family didn't do this, not intentionally, anyway. I suspect this was a hired hit. John was slated to testify next week in Jersey."

"Do you really think it's possible someone used our products for murder?"

"The ME's a friend of mine. I'll know as soon as he does."

I turned for the passenger door handle and climbed inside Jake's truck. Maybe I did want to sit awhile.

He joined me, rounding the hood and sliding behind the wheel. He started the engine and cranked the heater. Warm scents of cinnamon and spice filled the air. An open pack of chewing gum topped a pile of change in the cup holder between us. The soft twang of country music drifted through tiny speakers in the door and dashboard.

The street outside was dark, cold and desolate. Still, the sensation of being watched sent prickles along my skin.

I turned on the seat to face Jake. "Who was John testifying against?"

"Bennie the Bean."

I snorted. "Seriously?"

Jake scowled. "Bennie the Bean is a vicious mobster. He's evaded officials for decades and John was the department's first real break. He agreed to testify to everything he'd seen and heard while in Bennie's employ. He'd been in federal protection for a year. I got the case last month and now he's dead. I was supposed to protect him."

"Wow. John had a complete double life." His thick Jersey accent had always seemed so endearing when it slipped through the standard Elizabethan of the Faire.

I forced my scrambled thoughts into order. "What about Melanie? Maybe this wasn't some grand mob hit. What if it was something else? Maybe she announced her pregnancy and he dumped her, so she killed him. You saw her. She wasn't exactly thinking clearly today."

He raised curious eyes to mine. "I thought you didn't believe in coincidence."

"I don't. I also don't jump to conclusions. Have you spoken with the staff at Surly Wench? Did anyone at the Faire see anything suspicious? What did the cops learn during their interviews?"

"Melanie's on the short list, but she thinks it was his business partner, George Flick."

I tugged my bottom lip. "Figures. Everything comes down to money. Did you talk to Mr. Flick yet? I should give him my condolences tomorrow and see how he responds."

Jake's expression turned cold. "No. I came here to tell you I knew you didn't do this, not to push your Go button. This is a federal investigation. It has nothing to do with you. You need to stay out of it."

I straightened my spine. "Excuse me? My friend died today. You say it was murder. The Action News says my family's product killed him. This has everything to do with me. In fact, I can't think of a way that his death *doesn't* have something to do with me. You know what else I think? I think you came here to tick me off."

Jake guffawed. "That's insane."

"Did you call me insane?" I opened the door and slid to my feet. "I guess I should be glad I'm not a suspect. Again. Good luck with your investigation, Deputy US Marshal Jacob Archer." My hands shook with frustration. Something about him made me want to kick stones and him.

"Hey! You left my door open."

"Accurate."

I stormed across the lawn to my parents' home and slammed the front door behind me.

FIVE

THIRTY MINUTES LATER, I slid my Mini Cooper against the curb and stared up at my old apartment building, consumed by a clear combination of distraction and old habits. Regardless, if I was in the neighborhood I might as well see what Nate made of the things Jake had told me.

I hurried through the entryway as another tenant exited and darted onto the elevator before the door shut.

The elevator ride was excruciating and smelled like carpet cleaner. My mind flicked through today's events at warp speed and suppressed memories of being held hostage in this building by a killer. I could've climbed Everest faster than the elevator carried me up four floors. I jammed my thumb against the button a dozen times. Numbers lit and dimmed in comically slow motion. Tension bunched the muscles along my neck and shoulders. I nearly stopped on the third floor to see the new tenant in my old apartment. Why did the man wear a unitard? Fashion statement? Was he a dancer? Dramatic artist? Professional wrestler?

I pulled my hand away from the button. I couldn't exit on the third floor. Not even for a man in a unitard. Entering the building was one thing, approaching my old apartment was something else entirely. Friends, family and professionals had to move me into my condo at Horseshoe Falls after what happened last summer. If it had been my choice, I'd have collected my costume trunk and computer gear and left the rest behind.

A sharp *ding* nearly toppled me into parting silver doors. I hiked my skirt with both hands and hustled to Nate's place, keeping an eye out for the small crowd of hipsters living next door. I liberated my cell phone from the satchel on my wrist and texted Nate before knocking. You up?

Somewhere beyond the door, his phone chimed.

His response arrived seconds later. Yeah. You ok?

I hovered my thumbs over the tiny screen. Was I okay? Not remotely.

Nate's door sucked open and I yelped.

"Hey." He took my arm and pulled me inside. "Come here. What on earth?" He looked me over as if the answer was hidden on my cloak or in my hair.

I huffed. "How'd you know I was there?"

"I heard your phone crow."

Nate led me to the couch. His cutoff shorts had seen better days, and his Fighting Irish shirt clung to angles and planes of his well-defined chest like a sticker. "Did you run into Carl and his crew in the hall?" His teasing tone lifted a smile on my face.

"No. Why? Because they love it when I walk around dressed as a medieval queen?" I patted my skirt. Why on earth was I still in this outfit? I puffed air into overgrown bangs and accidentally steamed my glasses. "I don't understand hipsters and their dull, underenthused lifestyle. Excuse me for having fun."

I dropped into my spot on Nate's sectional and tipped over, face-planting into the neighboring cushion.

"Are you having fun now?" His footsteps retreated, thudding softly against kitchen tiles. "Can I get you something? Coffee? Wine?"

I waved a hand overhead. "No, thank you." The muffled words heated my face. I forced myself upright, adjusting my glasses. "I don't know why I stopped here. I guess it was the unitard."

He chuckled. "Who doesn't like a unitard?" Nate returned to my side with a cup of coffee. "Your life's blood, milady."

"I don't suppose you have an outfit I can borrow?"

"Yep."

"Really?" I sipped the coffee, enjoying the bitter steam swirling around my nose.

"Give me a minute." Nate disappeared into his room, sliding drawers open and shut. "Ah-ha." He rounded the corner, back to my side, with a broad smile and pair of capri pants dangling from his fingertips. "You left these after the ice cream-eating contest of 2012. Do you remember? You wore a pair of my basketball shorts back to your apartment." He dropped the pants onto my lap.

A laugh bubbled through me. "I couldn't button them. I totally forgot they existed." I hugged them to my chest. "What about a shirt?"

He flipped a knot of cotton at my face. "I want that one back."

I shook the knot into shape. "You kept your middle school boxing shirt?"

He shrugged. "We were champions that year. Anyway, how'd you know about the unitard guy? Also, it's called a singlet. He's a professional wrestler."

Knew it.

I took another gulp of coffee and settled my nerves. "Jake told me." I carried the outfit to Nate's bathroom and shut the door slightly. "Any other reason you asked if I saw your neighbors? Did they say something about me?"

"There's a Furry Convention tonight. I saw them hauling in costumes yesterday, and I know how you like it when the Furries come out."

"Jeez." I'd had a childhood run-in with a Furry at a Renaissance Faire in Maine. The experience turned me off to costumed characters for life. I was eight and some stoner in a fox costume had assaulted me with nuts from a tree. When I ran, he skipped along behind me, drawing attention from Faire visitors. Everyone thought we were adorable. Me running for my life and him bounding along beside me in the giant smiling head. After the lunatic grabbed my arm and forced me to dance with him, a group of merry minstrels surrounded us. Apparently, they thought the fox was entertaining with his animated moves. I thought I'd die in a shallow grave wearing his fox head. Bree barreled in, as usual, with Big Sister Mode initiated. She kicked his shins soundly and knocked his head off. I burst into tears and the minstrels got a clue. Adults had dragged the fox-man away and Bree had comforted a hyperventilating me.

The pungent scent of pot on his fur came thick with the recollection. I shook off the memory and shimmied free of my heavy velvet dress and lung-crushing corset beneath. Delicious oxygen rushed in. "Ahh."

"Feeling better?" Nate's voice carried around the unlatched door.

"Yes." I pulled on my twenty-first century gear and frowned at the ratty condition of my hair. "Can I use your brush?"

"Um. I have a comb, but yeah."

I opened tidy drawers until I found a perfect comb. No hair stuck in the teeth. No giant hair creatures rolling alongside it. The comb would be lost in my nest of fuzzy curls. I put it back and sighed.

Nate's bathroom was immaculate, like the rest of his place, minimally furnished and only in the best pieces. My apartment, on the other hand, was jam-packed with memories of everything from Girl Scout Camp to old retainers. I liked vintage stuff, flea markets and sentimentality. Granted, I kept most of the clutter crammed into pretty boxes and bins, but no one would ever accuse my place of immaculacy or minimalism.

I emerged carrying the old ensemble.

Nate leaned against the couch. Arms crossed. "How did Jake know about the wrestler?"

"He didn't. He called it a unitard."

"But he knew about him. Was he here?"

I bit my lip, sorting the important from the not. "Yep."

"Looking for you?"

"He showed up tonight at my folks' place to apologize for not being more congenial at the Craft Faire today. He said he stopped here first. I guess he wanted me to know he didn't suspect my family of killing John, but they haven't ruled out the possibility our products were used to that end."

Nate slouched. "Well, that's horrible. Your grandma must be sick."

"There's more."

He patted the seat beside his.

I perched gingerly on the edge. "John was in federal protection under Jake's care. He was due to testify next week against a mobster in Jersey. I'm probably not supposed to repeat this, but if I don't, my brain will explode."

Nate's green eyes twinkled. "I knew it."

We'd looked up the marshals' function after Jake left the FBI. Witness protection and fugitive apprehension were part of their gigs.

Nate seemed proud of himself for guessing correctly. "I figured John as a fugitive, but I expected he was some old tree hugger hiding out after releasing test monkeys from a lab twenty years ago or something."

"That's very specific."

"It was a long drive home." He set his big hand on mine. "Don't get involved in this, Mia."

I hated disappointing Nate, but I wouldn't lie to him. "I don't have a choice."

"Yes, you do. We always have a choice."

"Then I choose saving Grandma's company. We're in negotiations with Earth Hugger, and the local news is undoing all my hard work with every salacious update."

He curled long fingers around my palm. "Then focus on the PR not the crime. How about that? Can we compromise? Let the Archers do their thing and I'll help you with PR. I'm great with people. You know that. Let me help."

"Fine. You can help."

"And you'll focus on the company? Not the investigation?"

I pulled my hand free and shifted on the couch.

"Mia."

"PR is first."

"Mia."

I cracked under the interrogation. "I've already researched poisons at my folks' place."

He flopped against the backrest. "Why?" He lifted both hands overhead before clamping them on like a hat. "I'd planned to ask you to stay out of this when I thought John was a lame former activist. Now that we know he was involved with the mob, you can't seriously pursue this." He plunged forward, landing elbows on knees. "You'll be the next target for the Jersey mob."

"I don't think it's a statewide thing."

His eyelids drooped. "'You're killing me, Smalls.'"

I smiled at his quote from *The Sandlot*. He posed a good argument for keeping my distance, but the bottom line was he'd never fight with me and we both knew it, so I was going to do what I wanted.

"I'm going to help the company first, but I plan to do a little more research on John. You're welcome to help with both."

"Fine."

Knew it.

I pushed my phone between us and brought up my most recent search. "According to this site, poison's a good choice for covert killing. If you think about it, poison's been taking lives, by accident and otherwise, since the beginning of time."

He scoffed at the little screen. "Poisons for Beginners."

"Yes." I rotated on the cushion, cocking a knee between us. "There are a ton of ways to deliver the dose. Some toxins work really fast, others take days. In spy movies, villains use a syringe, but victims can also ingest the poison, breathe it or have it rubbed on their skin. Look at this." I scrolled the screen with the flick of my finger. "Arsenic. Hemlock. Cobra bites. Mushrooms. Methanol. I could read all night and only learn a portion of what there is to know."

"Uh-huh." He pressed the heels of both hands to his eyes. "I think if he was bitten by a cobra, he might've noticed."

"Exactly, but what if someone put something into the

Healer's Hand Cream tester or our wassail? I don't think that's possible, but I'm eliminating worst-case scenarios first. I wonder if he stopped to talk with anyone after he left Surly Wench, but before he spoke with me."

Nate uncovered his eyes and stared, helpless. "Last time nearly got me killed." His voice was low and weak, a last-ditch effort to bring me to his side of the debate.

Gooseflesh rose on my arms. "Last time, I caught a killer who was in the process of ruining dozens of lives." My counselor said so.

"Yes, and for that, you're a hero. A hero with nightmares, a new apartment and no tech support. You still haven't replaced Warren and I know why. You're not over the last murder investigation you got involved in."

I ground my teeth. If he kept going, he'd just piss me off, and he knew it. "I'm fine. In fact," I improvised to prove my point, "I'm calling a temporary agency tomorrow and hiring a woman to fill Warren's position." A very tiny, feeble old lady, preferably.

My phone buzzed and my heart stopped. I'd chosen "Flight of the Bumblebee" for Bree's ringtone for good reason. Scary how one sound could encapsulate a person's personality so perfectly. "Hello?"

Bree's voice blasted through the phone. "When are you sending the email? Grandma's on her fourth beer and threatening to call the news station again. You need to do something."

"Calm down. I needed to see Nate. I'm heading home now."

"You need to smooth things over with the public. Squelch these ridiculous accusations against the company ASAP. We need to get out in front of this train before it runs us over."

Technically, getting out in front of a train was the perfect way to be run over, but Bree hated logic.

"Are you there?" She tapped the phone against something hard. "Mia. You're the face of this company. I suggest you get busy before we're all ruined."

I opened my mouth to silent scream. "I told you. I'm on it. The letter will go out in the morning. I don't need to be reminded to do my job."

Bree covered the phone and repeated my promise to Grandma in muffled words. "Hey?" She switched from her shrill boss-of-me tone seamlessly to something more like we're-still-besties, right?

"Hmm." I buttoned my cloak over the T-shirt and capris.

"Did you tell Nate about Jake stopping by?"

"Yeah."

"What'd he think?"

I shrugged, only half caring she couldn't see me. "I'll talk to you after I finish the letter. Tell Grandma to hang tight and try to get some rest. I've got the letter half-drafted in my head. This is my thing, and I'm on it." I disconnected.

Nate was on his feet pacing. "Who was John testifying against?"

"Bennie the Bean."

He typed on his phone. "New Jersey crime boss. Holy mobsters, Batman. There are a thousand entries on that guy."

"Too bad we can't use facial recognition software with a security feed to match someone at the Faire with one of Bennie's known associates."

"I think you should drop this."

"Duly noted."

Nate opened the door for me. "The county fairgrounds doesn't have security cameras with face recognition software. They don't even have Wi-Fi."

"It's too bad. With the right technology, every case would be closed by dinner."

"Don't get me started. This conversation will go all *Minority Report*, and I'll need a beer. I'm watching my carbs."

"Whatever." I stepped across the threshold. "I bet this wasn't a mob hit. These things are never what they seem. I bet the killer didn't even know John had mob ties. He couldn't have been here longer than he's been in custody, which was only a year according to Jake. How could anyone really know him? Wow. Wait. Was John Francis even his real name?"

"I have no idea."

I forced my thoughts into focus. Business first. "I've got to go home and do some fire stomping for the company. I'll research later. Please don't worry about me. Okay?"

He huffed. "Forget about it."

I bobbed my head and tugged my collar. "Fuggedaboutit."

"Stop." He held my giant dress and corset over one arm. "Not funny. You want me to carry this to your car for you?"

"Nope. I'm good." I loaded the costume into my arms.

Snuffling and ruffling sounds stopped me from accepting my things. Seven costumed animals, complete with giant heads and paw-covered hands and feet, stopped outside the elevator doors, posturing and fluffing their coats.

Furries.

The silver doors parted and the people-sized menagerie crowded inside.

"Call me." Nate shut the door to his apartment and outright laughed inside the safety of his home.

I stared at a six-foot pink bunny waving me into the crowded elevator.

"No, thank you. I'll catch the next one." I tugged my velvet cloak tighter over my short pants, Victorian boots and twenty-year-old middle school boxing T-shirt.

The elevator doors began to close, and I exhaled in relief.

A brown paw struck out from the stuffed car, stopping the motion. The bunny summoned me again.

I shook my head.

The other animals extended their arms, bending their wrists and elbows, silently insisting I join them. Giant brightly colored eyes and wide cartoonish smiles stared back at me. My feet hit the steps at a runner's pace. I burst through the door into the lobby as the elevator dinged behind me.

"Dear Lord." I hugged the heavy gown to my chest like a protective shield and ran for the car.

I had an email to write.

SIX

I SWIPED MY keycard at the Horseshoe Falls guard gate and motored into the lot outside a new set of condos. Per my new routine, I double-checked that the gate shut behind me and waited for security lighting to register my arrival before exiting the car. Thanks to Horseshoe Falls' obsession with green living, motion-sensor lighting was everywhere. The idea being why light the place if no one's there? Reduce costs. Save energy. Save the planet. Unfortunately, there was a two-to-four-second delay on occasion that made me edgy. I could fix the problem, but the lighting company had refused my offer. Rudely. As a result of their "policy" allowing only members of their team to make changes to the system, any cash the community saved through our new lighting system was subsequently spent on maintenance calls.

The light snapped on, and I hastened to the elevator. I poked my key into the penthouse hole on the interior panel and the car bounded upward, delivering me seconds later on silent authority. No obnoxious *ding*. No creak, rattle and roll like the jalopy at my old building. Just the little whoosh of air as my entranceway came into view. A giant blue letter C, hand-painted and hung by Bree, swung and jostled at eye level as I unlocked the knob and zipped inside. Good grief. Everything was silent in this building except me. I was a marching band of heeled boots on marble and enormous crafts on doors.

I dead-bolted the door and dropped my keys into the glass dish Bree gave me as a housewarming gift. It was meant for candy, but when you lived alone, there was no one to share with. Four bags of caramels and a dress size later, the dish had been repurposed from trough to key holder.

I hung my cloak on a hook and stared at the expansive space before me. Even I didn't have enough stuff to fill the place. My book collection barely filled one side of the floor-to-ceiling built-in shelves. My furniture was too small. The space was too big. Bree had suggested I adopt a pet, but she was the maternal one. Grandma understood. She bought me a thumb-sized cactus at the drugstore. Thelma had a tiny terracotta pot and little pink bow. So far so good with Thelma.

The lights flicked on as I moved through the rooms. I grabbed the remote that controlled everything else, including hidden speakers, and powered on my favorite station before turning it down to a whisper. My boots landed in a pile near the door, and my pants hit the hamper on my way through the bedroom. I wanted to soak in the tub until today ended, but I had work to do.

I stepped into the shower and let the water knock the tension off me. My tiled bathroom floor busily heated outside my marble oasis. I curled my toes in anticipation of their next treat and pressed both palms against the wall, greedily soaking in the hot water until my skin was red and my toes were white and pruny. My mind whirled, despite every effort to unwind. An endless loop of Jake's face and John's death kept peace at bay. Sheer speculation and an elevator load of Furries made relaxation an impossibility. Worst. Day. Ever.

Twenty minutes later, I padded to my computer wrapped in fleece jammies and fuzzy socks. The letter, reassuring consumers about our company, was solidly formed in my head. I opened a blank document and ran a quick search for press releases from other companies who'd faced similar allegations. They read like political statements and campaign promises. Guinevere's Golden Beauty wasn't like that. We were real. Our consumers were family.

I made a pot of coffee and got to work.

Three cups later, caffeine percolated in my veins. I curled shaky fingers into a fist and stretched them wide. Time to switch to decaf or ice cream. I went with ice cream. Honestly, in a situation where ice cream is an option, there really isn't a choice.

At five minutes before three, I jumped to my feet and punched the air a few times. Done. I knocked it out of the universe. The letter was gracious and reassuring. Honest and forthright. I pledged the company's continued dedication to pure, natural ingredients, holistic and handcrafted products and emphasized the careful inspection process, making it impossible to tamper with anything at our small family-run facilities. Anything inside our product was carefully listed on the outside label. Nothing more and nothing less.

I couldn't be positive the sampler hadn't been poisoned while I was distracted by the crowd, but my gut said the odds were too slim to mention. I'd sensed John wasn't quite himself from the moment he approached. Besides, no reason to increase public fears and perpetuate the crazy. For good measure, I offered a full refund to anyone who had a change of heart about our products, and I promised responders to the email a love package in time for Christmas. Anyone willing to contact the company with their thoughts, worries or words of encouragement would be rewarded. I'd post the positive comments online and hopefully nip the negative ones in the bud.

I arched my back and stretched. Much as I wanted to crawl into bed, something itched my restless mind. Something I'd wanted to research since Jake said the name.

I opened a new window and typed Bennie the Bean. I marveled at the number of entries, though most were speculation, blogs and alleged sightings. It seemed Bennie dabbled in everything from money laundering to racketeering. The guy was practically an urban legend. The most recent photograph of Bennie was outside a courthouse in the 1970s, based on attire. No accompanying article. Apparently, he hadn't made a public appearance in ages, increasing to the man-myth-legend persona.

One article became two dozen as I devoured information on my subject. How could John have been tied up with this guy? Weren't there better choices for a painter with his talent? What about art school? Teaching? Anything other than working for the mob.

Hypotheses whirled in my addled brain, mixing with coffee-laced adrenaline and fear. John had died in front of me. How close had the killer been at that moment? Chills swept over my arms. I flipped through more articles on Bennie. Murder. Shootings. People found in the river. Crushed in cars at junkyards. If there was a theme, it was that Bennie's known associates met untimely deaths by the busload.

There was also an anomaly. None of his alleged victims were poisoned.

I rubbed tired eyes and set my glasses aside. Maybe he'd gotten bored and wanted to switch up his MO. Who knew what went on in a mobster's mind? Then again, maybe this was more complicated than a mob boss locating a guy in witness protection and taking him out. Though, that scenario seemed complicated enough. Maybe I'd been right when I told Nate it probably wasn't a mob hit at all?

Melanie's wild outbursts came to mind. She'd been livid, but would she have killed him? She'd whacked his body and screamed professions of undying love. Unstable? Maybe, but who was I to judge? Was she a killer? Not likely, but not impossible. She had motivation and opportunity.

I pinched the bridge of my nose. My elbow slid over the cool desktop, and I rested my head on my arm. Everybody loved John.

Maybe it was his business partner. Money was a powerful motivator.

A wide yawn split my tired face.

Poison was so unusual. So specific and personal. Wasn't it? Not a crime of passion or a typical mob hit. People weren't poisoned in the heat of the moment. Someone had planned his death, boldly placed the poison in his way, and moved on as if nothing had transpired. Would they have stayed to watch? To be sure it worked?

The crowd in my mind's eye had pitchforks circa *Frankenstein* and unruly expressions. They were different than today, ready to charge on me at any moment.

"It wasn't me." My voice barely rang above their rage.

The feral crowd snarled and lunged.

I ran.

They chased me into the forest outside the Faire. My bare feet caught on twigs and branches, spearing my skin and hobbling my movement. The trees were tall and barren. No way to climb and nowhere to hide without summer's bushy foliage.

Torches tossed orange flames into the sky, casting shadows over the world. Heavy feet crushed leaves and insects in a stampede to find me.

Panic mounted in my heart and head until I screamed. A bloodcurdling wail that burned my lungs.

I jerked my head off the desk and groaned. "What on earth?" When had I fallen asleep and what was all the racket? I wiped drool from the corners of my mouth and acclimated myself.

My phone buzzed and vibrated on the desk, inches from where my head had lain. A British squad car siren blared from the tiny speaker as it shook. I slapped it. "Stahp."

The nuisance ceased.

"Thank you. Yeesh." I stood on rubber legs and grabbed the phone. There were still two hours before I had to get up for work, and a soft warm bed called to me.

Shuffling toward my room, the blasted alarm began again.

"What?" I barked into the phone, steps from my beloved bed, still reeling from the wretched dream.

"Mrs. Connors?" An unfamiliar voice opened my eyes, ripping me back to the present.

Unease crawled over me. "Yes?" Normally, I made a big deal of being addressed as Mrs., but the snap in this man's tone warned there was no time for that.

"Your name is on the contact information at 1121 Portage Street. Ye Ole Madrigal Craft Faire. Booth 12."

I leaned against the wall for support. "Yes. What's wrong? Were there vandals?" With all the negative publicity today, I wasn't surprised.

"Yes, ma'am. An arsonist."

"Arson?"

"I'm afraid so. How soon can you get here?"

Bugger.

SEVEN

GNARLED SMOKE FINGERS clawed the night sky above my family's booth. A smattering of firemen chatted near the truck, content with their efforts, while a few scattered embers smoldered in defiance. The booth was toast.

Grandma was going to have a thousand consecutive strokes when she heard about this. I focused on the positive to keep from screaming. At least no one was hurt. At least it was the middle of the night and would be cleaned up before the Faire reopened in the morning.

"Miss?" A hand landed on my shoulder.

I whacked the interloper free of my person and spun.

A man twice my age lifted both palms in the air. His blue jacket and badge stopped my racing heart. "I didn't mean to startle you, but you can't be here." His expression softened, as if he'd read my flailing thoughts. "You okay?"

"I'm fine, and I'm supposed to be here." The weight of the situation settled over me. My shoulders sagged and my feet ached. "This is my booth. My family's booth. Someone called and asked me to come down."

The man rocked back on his heels and looped stumpy thumbs behind his belt buckle. "Well, I suppose that was me. You're Mia Connors?"

I nodded sharply and batted my eyes against acrid smoke in the changing wind. "Do you have any idea how the fire started?"

The officer turned toward a knot of firefighters and trench coats and motioned me to follow. "Detective Archer wants to handle this personally. I'll introduce you. He's the one in black."

I speed-walked past the officer. "I know who he is."

Dan raised his chin, mid-belly laugh. His gaze met mine, and he excused himself and came up to me before I reached them.

I shoved hair off my wind-battered cheek. "What's happening? Who would do this?"

He shifted his weight. A look of dissatisfaction crossed his normally amicable face. "We have a confession from Melanie Warner. The lady you met earlier."

"I remember her." How could I forget?

"She thinks you killed John Francis, but she's not in her right mind at the moment." He tipped his head toward the cruiser ten yards away.

Melanie sobbed behind the backseat window.

"You're kidding. She did this?"

"Yep. Grief does things to people. She's going to need time and a little counseling, but she'll get through this."

I gave him my best crazy face.

"Hey, she was careful not to harm anyone. Waited for the grounds to clear."

"How thoughtful of her."

"If she really wanted to hurt your family, there are plenty of ways to do that."

I hacked an ugly noise. "Gee, thanks." I turned to appraise the smoldering wreckage. "She burned it completely down. Do you know what it will cost to replace or what people will think? There's no telling how much business we'll lose as a result. I'll never be able to clean up this mess. It's a PR nightmare. People will assume our product killed John and this was retaliation for that crime. Consumers won't come within a hundred yards of our booth if we rebuild."

"I know."

I dropped my head back. "This is horrible. This whole day. Total crap."

"I agree."

"Well, stop. I'm trying to be crabby."

He chuckled. "The fire was unfortunate, but I'm sure it's not as bad as you think."

"You're clearly not a businessman." *Whose grandmother was going to lose her mind when she heard about this.*

"Thank God."

I righted my head and braced frozen hands on my hips. "You don't think Melanie killed John."

"I don't."

"Despite the fact she's the most obvious suspect? She has motive and she was the last one seen with him before he came to see me and dropped dead."

Dan dug the toe of his shiny shoe into soot-covered grass. "That makes you the last to see him before he died, and I remember having another 'obvious suspect' this past summer. I didn't think she did it either."

"Right." That suspect had been me. I scanned the scene and lowered my voice. "Jake says John died from a mob hit."

Dan smiled. "He came to see you, huh?" A sly grin spread over his mouth. "Well, for what it's worth, I'm not convinced on that theory, but it's my job to be skeptical."

His job. I straightened. "You're a homicide detective. Why are you here if no one was hurt?"

"This is still the scene of my murder investigation. I

need to know if the two crimes are related." He glanced back at the cruiser. "She's a mess. I can't get her to eat anything. That can't be great for the baby, right?"

"You're worried about her?"

His troubled expression answered my question.

Melanie's head rested against the window. She looked like she could use a friend. "Do you think they'll let her out on bail?"

"She's broke. Had a tough upbringing. Ran away. She found comfort at the local Ren Faire and made it her family. She's scared and angry, but she's not a killer and she sure doesn't have money for bail. There's a good chance her record will be enough to get her some immediate probation with time served."

"Maybe I can swing the fire story as faulty outlets?" It would never work long term, but I could start a rumor that didn't scream "poisoned products"!

A commotion drew my attention from the cruiser to the front gates. Bright lights beamed into the night. A familiar silhouette floated toward us.

I squinted, unable to adjust my eyes to the spotlight.

"Set up here," the voice snapped.

My tummy churned. "Oh no." So much for my rumor.

Mindy Kinley and her crew were back. A pair of officers corralled the trio as much as possible, enforcing crime-scene preservation and securing proper distance from our booth, but it didn't matter.

Mindy shook her long hair over one shoulder and stood directly before the charred remains of Guinevere's Golden Beauty booth. She held three fingers in the air. The cameraman gave a thumbs-up and the third leech hoisted a boom mic over her head. "Tragedy strikes again at Ye Ole Madrigal Craft Faire. As you recall, I was the first to report a murder at this very location yesterday. Now I'm back at the scene of the crime where fire broke out, consuming a Faire staple. Guinevere's Golden Beauty."

I rubbed both temples. "If I kill her, can I get off on temporary insanity?"

Dan chuckled. "No, and you shouldn't have told me. It's premeditated now."

"What if you forget I asked?"

"Not going to happen."

Mindy overacted her way through the report. "Is it a coincidence a local man died of poisoning after sampling Guinevere's Healing Hand Cream? Could someone blame these products for his death?" She turned a wrinkled nose back to the camera. "Maybe it's time they change the name of that hand cream."

"It's Healer's Hand Cream." I stalked through frosty grass toward Mindy, intent on removing her forcibly. My arm snapped back, snared at the wrist by steel fingers before I could get my hands on the microphone-wielding opportunist. I shook hard against Dan's grip.

He raised an eyebrow.

"Fine." I jerked free. "But I hate that woman."

A dark form in the distance seemed to move with human qualities. I squinted, trying to force the shape into something ethereal, a shadow or trick of the moonlight. It blended into the dark trunk of a tree and didn't budge. Clearly, I needed rest.

"Who doesn't? She's a regular at every car accident and town hall meeting."

Figured. "Anywhere she might have an opportunity to say 'You heard it here first.'"

He nodded. "How about I buy you a cup of coffee?"

"Sure." I had a long day ahead of me. "Make it two."

BERNIE STEPPED OUTSIDE the guard gate at Horseshoe Falls, wearing a fringed coat over her usual park ranger-esque uniform. A replica—I hoped—coonskin cap covered her cropped black locks. She waved.

I stopped to swipe my card. "Hi, Bernie."

Bernie was at least twice my age, with a round face and kind eyes. Her parents had named her Bernice, after a Hawaiian princess, and she kept a blog, *Aloha from Ohio*, about growing up on the Big Island. The blog served as an unofficial Horseshoe Falls who's who and gossip guide.

She sashayed to my window. "Nearly seven. You're just getting home? Oh, Lord." Her face dove toward mine.

I leaned away. "It was a long night."

"Heaven have mercy. Doing what? Grave-digging? You're filthy." Panic seized her features. "Are you hurt?"

"I'm fine. It's ash from the wind. I'm going to clean up, read your morning post and get to work. What's today's topic?"

The look she gave bordered on lunacy. "Pioneer Days."

I dropped my forehead against the steering wheel and contemplated an impromptu trip to Peoria. I lifted my face. "Right. Have a nice day."

The road to my apartment was closed, forcing me to travel the entire perimeter of Horseshoe Falls to get back to where I started. My building sat beside the guard gate, unfortunately. The community blocked the area during Pioneer Days. Making room for festivities jammed up modern methods of transportation in favor of horses and carriages.

Despite the early hour, people filled the roads and

sidewalks dressed like everything from Pocahontas to Civil War soldiers. The Native American costumes were borderline offensive, and the trio of retired judges in saloon girl garb was enough to send me under the blankets until Wednesday. Clearly, I wasn't myself.

My soot-covered hands and cheeks earned unending stares as I walked from my car to the building. I scared an older couple exiting the elevator. "Sorry."

I rode to my apartment on tiptoes, hoping not to spoil more of the pristine floor than necessary with my mud-soaked sneakers.

Thirty minutes later, I stuffed freshly shampooed but still-damp waist-length hair under a blue bonnet and covered thoroughly exhausted legs with the white ruffled knickers and a matching blue hoop skirt of my Southern Belle ensemble. Costumes were an upside of Pioneer Days. I tucked in the blouse and rolled my eyes at the purple crescents and puffy lids of sleep deprivation. Time for work.

On the street, I inhaled history. Fresh bread baked in stone ovens near the waterfall. Eggs scrambled over open fires beside newly erected pup tents. My tummy tried to eat itself as I hustled to Dream Bean for a triple-shot café au lait and pain au chocolat. I measured my gait, careful to maintain the balance of my hoop skirt. Nothing screamed *amateur* like a swinging hoop.

The clip-clop of horses' hooves added to my morning trip through time. Slowly, my pace settled into a casual stride. Music and laughter energized the cool autumn air. Maybe Pioneer Days wasn't the worst thing ever. Maybe I was a grouch in need of sugar and caffeine treatments.

"Morning, Mia." A man on horseback tipped his hat.

"Hi, Mark. How's it going?"

Mark was the head of Horseshoe Falls' security. He'd taken a leave of absence over the summer when the FBI contacted him about an outbreak of identity thefts centralized around our community. They'd thought I was a criminal mastermind and sent Jake in to play temporary head of security in Mark's stead.

He slid off the horse and tied him at a bicycle rack. "Not bad, yet. I'm checking in on the Kubickas."

"Uh-oh." I glanced at the side-by-side doors behind us. Dream Bean and Sweet Retreat. The Lindseys owned Dream Bean and sold the best coffee and pastries in town. The Kubickas owned the Sweet Retreat and served the most delicious ice cream and gossip around.

The shop owners had a long and colorful history of feuding.

Mark sighed. "Pioneer Days started two hours ago, and I'm already here to document a complaint. I believe this is a record."

"Good luck." I tried to smile but couldn't manage without more coffee.

I tugged the door to Dream Bean open and suppressed the immediate urge to twirl when warm scents of caramel and brown sugar climbed my nose. I leaned against a stool at the end of the bar and shoved my skirt under the counter.

The soft pink-and-white décor reminded me of a French candy shop, complete with white twisted-iron chairs and small round tables. The best seats, though, were along the beautiful glass counter.

Stew Lindsey winked at me. He filled a display with fancy pastries, éclairs and macarons in every color. "Can I get you something, Mia?" He leaned an elbow on the case and dusted his palms.

"Café au lait, triple shot, please."

"Okay. Can I get you something sweet to go with that?"

My mouth watered. How could I choose? He might as well have asked me to pick a favorite book or pair of shoes. "I came in for pain au chocolat, but everything looks amazing. I can't decide."

"How about I surprise you then?" Stew turned to prepare my coffee.

His wife, Darlene, dumped a load of empty cups into the sink. She dried her hands and headed my way. "Morning, Mia."

"Good morning." I beamed. The promise of coffee and surprise treats had completely remedied my earlier disposition. Today was a good day.

Darlene stopped moving. Her gaze fixed on a smudge, she grabbed a fancy cloth from her apron and scrubbed the glass display case.

Stew hummed behind her, cheerfully filling a plate with a rainbow of assorted sweets. He delivered my order with a flourish. "Surprise."

"Thank you." I gripped the cup with both hands.

Darlene shoved the cloth deep into her apron pocket. "Enjoy." Her smile seemed somewhat counterfeit.

Mine, on the other hand, was born of pure bliss.

Stew tapped her shoulder. "Honey? Everything all right?"

"There was a smudge." She turned for the prep sink without another word.

Stew raised his gaze to mine. "I guess she's a neatnik now?" He laughed and gave the counter another wipe. "I left powdered fingerprints again?"

I sipped the heavenly drink and imagined floating above the stool. "Something gooey. Butter maybe."

Stew was always covered in the fruits of his labor—powdered sugar, flour, butter. He lifted each arm and examined the white material of his smock.

I pointed to a greasy mark on one sleeve and swallowed a pastrygasm. Bits of flaky croissant filled with melted chocolate clung to my tongue and lips.

He stripped off the soiled chef's coat. "Ready for a refill?"

How'd my cup get empty? "Yes, please. In a to-go cup?"

Stew returned with fresh coffee in a cup I could take with me, and bagged the remaining treats with a handful of monogrammed napkins. "Enjoy your day."

"The bill." I laughed. "Nothing this delicious is free."

"On the house." He disappeared into the back room. Darlene followed.

"Okay then." I stuffed a ten into the tip jar and headed for the clubhouse, where I worked as Horseshoe Falls' IT Manager.

I barely had both feet on the sidewalk when Bernie rounded the corner. She barreled in my direction, pad of paper in hand, crazed look in her eyes.

I braced myself for impact, but she whipped open the door to Sweet Retreat and disappeared.

A handful of costumed residents took notice and followed, gathering at the shop window and speculating about the scoop big enough to drive Bernie from her post.

Mark and the Kubickas stood akimbo inside the shop, glaring into the window display, transfixed by a mound of cream-colored goo that roughly resembled a melted dog.

Bobbie Kubicka pointed frantically at the slop. Her face turned pink, and her voice rose to penetrate the glass. "They melted our butter sculpture! Do you have any idea how long it took Steve to carve an authentic-looking Civil War horse from solid butter? Fine them! Close their shop! *Do something*."

I took a baby step away and spun on my heels, vividly recalling the smudge on the Lindseys' countertop and their combined reaction. I hustled toward the clubhouse at a clip, before the butter started flying.

EIGHT

My office in the Horseshoe Falls clubhouse was a tomb, albeit a gorgeous one, decorated by Bree and designed to simultaneously stimulate and relax me. Soft shades of gray for peace and tranquility. Punches of yellow to keep me awake. A reed diffuser that smelled like vanilla and cinnamon. Bree had exacted Feng Shui on the space, and it was a long and expensive process. One I'd adored until I found my best friend dead in my office chair. Now it gave me the creeps. It was too quiet and full of sad memories. Unfortunately, I couldn't change offices the way I'd changed apartments. I'd tried.

I set my coffee on the desk and carefully maneuvered my hoop skirt underneath without sending it over my head. The pile of papers awaiting my review was mind-boggling. Office memos. Flyers for Pioneer Days events. An office birthday calendar for November. I tapped the days for free cake into my phone and threw the calendar in the trash.

Coffee scented the air and warmed my mood. I booted up my computer and logged into the work email, expecting ten to twelve emails had appeared overnight. Instead, I found nearly thirty. "Good grief." A quick scan of subject lines left me spinning. *Can we cut off Wi-Fi until after Pioneer Days?*

Can you create a Pioneer Days app for our phones?

Can we order a green screen for souvenir photos?

Yep. Let's turn off that modern-day Wi-Fi and haul in

a green screen. Have to keep Pioneer Days as authentic as possible.

I responded to those with messages of hope for next year. If they wanted it, I could make it happen, but not with zero hours' notice.

I moved on to the things I could fix. Residents with new devices needing to be networked to the community Wi-Fi. Residents needing help creating or maintaining their clubhouse accounts. Others with spyware or viruses slowing their speed and threatening their work systems via remote sessions.

I gave the empty desk beside me a weary glance. I needed to fill the tech support position. It wasn't fair to make residents wait while I went door to door on my own. We'd always had two bodies in IT. I had to face my issues.

I pulled up the resumes sent from a local temporary service and gave them a once-over, skipping the male names and focusing on the most interesting applicants. The ages weren't listed, thanks to the Equal Employment Opportunity Commission, so I couldn't make the feeble old lady request I wanted. I chose my top three from the list and shot an email to the company, asking if any of those workers were available for a trial run. With any luck, none were homicidal, roofie-wielding maniacs.

Another email popped into my inbox. Then three more. I cracked my knuckles. Time to start putting out fires. I stuffed earbuds into my ears and set my playlist to shuffle. One benefit to a lonely office: I could sing to myself without being judged.

After I tackled the email, I grabbed the black file seated atop my paperwork. The attached business card was my calling card. Someone needed information. Carriers of the card knew my secret. For a small fee, I would retrieve or redact online information as needed. More often than not, the card showed up when a middle-aged resident wanted proof their significant other wasn't a gold digger or long-con artist. Dating in the millennia was complicated. Personally, I avoided it at all costs.

The card was intentionally blank except for one small embossed almond leaf, to keep my anonymity. The leaf signified a mutual promise. The customers trusted me to keep my digging on the down low, and I trusted them to return the favor.

"Whose secrets will I unearth today?" I asked the folder before flipping it open. Ah. Mr. Fillmore wanted to know about Daisy Evans.

As it turned out, Daisy was a human rights attorney and standup citizen. I printed several sheets of information and stuffed the empty folder. Sorority photos. Credit report. Speeding tickets. Nothing of interest if Mr. Fillmore didn't mind a little boob flashing circa Mardi Gras 2001. Seemed harmless enough to me, and it hadn't stopped her current employer from promoting her twice in the past four years.

By early afternoon, I'd responded to all company email and set appointments to visit the residents who needed me to stop by for assistance. Shockingly, not everyone owned a laptop. I still made house calls to those with desktop computers and outdated towers.

"All About That Bass" boomed through my earbuds, and I spun in my seat, caught up in the sass. My hoop skirt popped loose from beneath the desk and I pumped both arms as I twirled, singing along, quietly but enthusiastically.

"Mia?"

My eyes popped open.

Marcella, the community relations head, smiled sweetly across the desk from me. Her cheeks were as red as poison apples. "You didn't answer when I knocked. There's someone here to see you." Her thick Latina accent clung to every word.

Jake Archer leaned against the doorjamb behind her, thoroughly amused.

I nearly swallowed my tongue. I jerked earbuds from my ears and shoved the hoop dress back into position under my desk.

Marcella ducked out before combusting with laughter.

Jake lumbered to the guest chair and took a seat. "You can finish the song if you want. I told her not to interrupt you."

"Shut up."

His brilliant smiled disarmed me. "I'm not joking. You can sing, too. I suppose I shouldn't be surprised. Is there anything you can't do?"

"I can't seem to get rid of you with any permanence. Does that count?"

"Funny." He rubbed his palms against jean-clad thighs and surveyed my office. The marshal badge on his belt shone under fluorescent lighting.

"Why are you here?" Impatience bubbled in my tummy as I waited for the answer he wasn't in a hurry to give.

He leaned forward. "I spent the morning at the Faire."

I matched his body language in my best you-can-trust-me-with-your-secrets move. "Is this about my booth? Did Dan send you? Was there a break in the John Francis case?"

Jake averted his eyes.

"This isn't about any of that?"

He didn't speak.

"Jake, please. I don't understand why you're here or why you haven't made that clear, and you know I'm terrible with social cues and small talk. So, at the risk of sounding rude, I'm begging you. Why are you here?" I enunciated the last four words. Politely.

He rolled his head to one side, a mixed look of defeat and aggravation in his eyes. "The vendors weren't very forthcoming with me."

I imagined a lasso around his tongue and how much effort it would take to physically remove the information from his mouth. "Yeah, and?"

"I think they took one look at my badge and decided they weren't talking."

"Are you sure it wasn't your personality? I'm just throwing that out there."

He worked his jaw. "They don't want to talk to a lawman, and I don't know why."

I shrugged. "It could be anything, or you could be imagining it. How should I know? Go back and try again without your badge."

He was swinging his head in disagreement before I finished speaking. "That won't work. They've already seen me and decided they aren't talking."

I huffed. "Fine. Don't. Why are you here?"

He rubbed the back of his neck.

Why wouldn't he answer me? The proverbial lightbulb flickered on, and I slapped my desk. "You need my help! You came here to ask for my help and then chickened out."

Jake flinched. "I don't need your help."

I leaned back in my chair and smiled. "Oh. Okay then. It was nice seeing you. Thanks for stopping in."

He glowered. "I could use some advice. That's all. Just advice."

"Can you say that again?" I lifted my phone in his direction.

"Are you recording this?" A little pulse beat in his temple.

"Not yet. That's why I need you to say that one more time. Please. Go ahead when you're ready." I wiggled the phone between us.

Jake growled and sprang to his feet, mumbling about women being impossible and other ridiculously misogynistic things.

"Okay."

He froze. "What's okay? You'll help?"

"Yes. I'll help." I set the phone aside and folded my hands on the desk, very businesslike. "Did you talk to the business partner?"

Jake dropped back onto his seat. "Yes. I compelled Mr. Flick to talk. He said the company is fine and he and John Francis got along well. He didn't know him long, obviously, but they were well-suited for a seasonal business. He said a woman was a more likely suspect."

"What woman? Melanie?"

Jake shook his head. "He didn't name anyone, but he called John a hussy."

"He was a flirt." Melanie's face came to mind, sopping with tears and locked in the back of a squad car. "I saw Melanie last night. She's a little cuckoo, but I don't think she's a killer."

Jake scoffed. "She burned your booth down. I'd say that stands as evidence of impulse control. She might regret it now, but she still did it."

"She was slippery too. Dan said he'd been keeping an eye on her all day, but she still annihilated my booth."

Jake chuckled. "Nothing like allowing first-degree arson on your watch."

"That's what I thought." I scooted to the edge of my seat. "Last time we talked, you were certain this was a mob thing. Now you're looking at Faire employees and John's business partner. What changed?"

"Poison."

I nodded, immediately on board with his line of thought. I'd had it too. "Poison isn't a normal mob MO. I read about it last night. Also, Melanie might have issues with her temper, but poison takes time to plan. She'd have to decide what to use and how to administer it. She didn't look like someone who'd expected him to die when she was pounding on his body bag."

"I agree." Jake balanced on the edge of his seat, matching my body language. An obvious attempt to connect with and manipulate me. I'd read about that after we met. Whatever his intentions, I wasn't going to be managed, and he should know better.

I shook it off and engaged in the puzzle. "I researched poisons while I was at my folks' house. There are plenty of slow-acting things John could have ingested earlier in the day. The killer could have been miles away by the time he died. It's like I told Nate. This is probably unrelated to the mob thing."

"The possible time delay is another reason I'm still convinced this has everything to do with his testimony in the Bennie the Bean trial. One of Bennie's guys could get in and out before anyone knew the deed was done. I'm willing to concede Bennie might have used someone outside the family, especially with all the publicity on the case. He wouldn't want a known associate to be seen within a hundred miles of John Francis."

"I accept that premise."

Jake lifted his cheek in a lazy half-smile. "Good. Now what?"

"Now we try to disprove it."

"You mean prove it."

"No."

"That's not how criminal investigation works, Coffee."

"Well, it's how science works, and it's how *I* work." I ignored the pet name. He'd called me Coffee once or twice the last time he blew through my life. I didn't hate it.

"So you're helping?"

"I'm helping. Jeez."

He leaned back in the chair, stretching long legs out and digging in one pocket. "Here." He set a thumb drive on my desk.

"What is it?" I turned it over in my fingertips. The US Marshal emblem was painted on the back.

"It's a thumb drive. You know. For your bowl." He waved a big hand over the glass dish on my desk. My family competed with one another, buying me silly novelty drives I never used. It had started in college and stuck. "It's official. You can't get that without credentials."

My heart softened and my bottom lip poked out. "Aww. Thank you."

He pulled his hand back and put his grouch face on. "Don't thank me. It was bribery in case you didn't say yes."

I wrinkled my nose. "You didn't think I'd help you?"

"You said you told Nate your theory. Should I assume you told him everything I told you?"

I pulled my guilty lips to one side. "In hindsight, I probably shouldn't have done that, and I might owe you an apology." My tummy knotted with regret. "You don't have to worry about Nate repeating anything I've told him. He can be trusted. You know that from the summer. He won't cause you any trouble."

Wow. Apologies were hard.

He lifted his brows in wait. "Am I getting the apology now or in a birthday card next spring?"

"Funny."

Jake rolled his head over both shoulders and sighed dramatically. "At least tell me the classified identity of my witness isn't typed out forever in an email or text message somewhere?" A vein in his neck throbbed.

"Of course not. I went to Nate's place on my way home."

Jake's steady expression faltered momentarily. "I see."

"No, you don't." Why did everyone assume there was something physical between Nate and me? Repeatedly? "We're friends. He wanted to help."

Jake made a face.

"Why do you care either way?"

"I don't."

"Good."

"Fine."

I pulled in a deep breath. "Can I ask you something?"

He rolled tentative eyes in my direction but didn't agree.

"Why didn't you contact me after you left?"

"I told you. You had everything you needed, and my case on you was closed."

I pursed my lips and nodded.

"What? What's that face?"

I waved him off. "No. It's nothing. I misread people. No big deal."

"Can I ask you something now?" He didn't wait for my permission. "Why on God's green earth are you at work dressed like Little Bo Peep? I mean, I know you love costumes, but this is a little over the top, isn't it? Don't tell me it's for Pioneer Days. Not another soul on this staff is dressed like that."

I patted my bonnet. "Bernie has a coonskin cap."

Jake shook his head. "You're not normal."

"Thank you." I moved to the office door. "I'll meet you at the Faire after work and go with you to talk with the vendors. They'll see you mean well and open up."

He moved to meet me at the threshold. "You think so?"

"Yeah, but come in costume." For clarity, I added, "Not as Harry Potter." As far as I knew Harry was his only costume and better suited to Comic Con than Ye Ole Madrigal Craft Faire. "Wear something that shows you get it and you aren't judging."

His eyes bulged. "I'm not dressing up. I'm a Deputy US Marshal. They have to answer my questions. It's a murder investigation."

I crossed my arms. "Excuse me. You asked for my help because they wouldn't talk. What are you going to do? Arrest the whole place for obstruction of justice? Just wear a costume. Jeez."

Jake opened his mouth, probably to complain some more but didn't. "I'll wear my hat."

Footfalls thundered down the hall. Mark, the head

of security, swung through the open doorway, nearly crashing into Jake. He pressed a slimy hand to Jake's chest to stop himself.

"Sorry," Mark panted. "Thank goodness you're here."

Jake examined the greasy stain on his gray cotton shirt. "What the hell?"

Mark doubled over at the waist, gasping for air. "Detective Archer. I could use your assistance. There's a problem at Sweet Retreat. The Lindseys and Kubickas are in an all-out butter battle and civilians are being hit. I need your badge. They won't respect my authority."

Blobs of melted butter dripped from Mark's sleeves, pant legs and nose.

I giggled and grabbed my clubhouse ID and jacket. This, I had to see. I patted Mark's back. "Detective Archer is a US Deputy Marshal now."

Mark sputtered and spun, grabbing my hand and towing me toward the clubhouse door. "Thank you."

"No problem." I pushed the front door open so Mark wouldn't leave a butter print for maintenance to clean off.

Jake tipped his chin back and spoke to the ceiling as he passed. "I hate this place."

NINE

"Ow." I PRESSED a finger to the large red knot on my elbow. My workday had ended thirty minutes ago, and I still ached from the afternoon butter battle.

The brouhaha was certain to make Bernie's morning blog. I dumped ice into a towel and rested my elbow on top. The worst was over by the time Jake, Mark and I arrived, but the aftermath was gruesome. Residents caught in the crossfire were doused with handfuls of the melted civil war horse and raging with indignation. By the looks of both shops and the sidewalk outside, it had been the over-fifty equivalent to a cafeteria food fight.

While the Kubickas chased the Lindseys across the street with fistfuls of what was left of their civil war horse, I tended to the injured. Two eye washes, a twisted ankle and lots of bumps and bruises from spills at the hand of one hundred pounds of melted butter. Luckily, Horseshoe Falls had enough retired medical personnel to settle nerves and help bandage scrapes.

I pulled the sleeve of my ice-blue Queen Guinevere dress over the bruise and rested my arm back on the towel. If I hadn't tripped over Bernie on the sidewalk, I'd have made it out safe and clean. As it was, I'd spent my lunch hour deep-conditioning my hair and disinfecting butter-basted scrapes.

I tugged black knee-high socks up both legs and brushed my freshly dried hair, thankful I hadn't seen Jake after my fall. Mark sang his praises all afternoon.

Apparently, Jake was fast on his feet and his scary law-man voice had settled the fight before anyone ended up in the lake.

My phone vibrated on the counter. Jake's number glowed on the screen. "Hello?"

"Hey, I'm downstairs. Can you buzz me up?"

Panic shot through me. My condo was ridiculously expensive, the building was brand new, sterile looking and everything about it screamed money. I'd bought it on a whim after a near-death experience, mostly for the twenty-foot walls and twenty-four-hour guard stationed outside the private community, but Jake would only see the cost. He had issues with money—and I wasn't in the mood for defending mine. "I thought we were meeting at the Faire."

"I thought we could ride together."

Jeez. Presume much? Arrive unannounced. Put me on the spot. "How will I get home?"

"I'll bring you," he huffed. "Are you going to buzz me up or not?"

I deliberated. "I'll meet you in the lobby."

"Buzz me up."

I pulled the phone away from my ear and glared at it. "Rude."

Silence.

I pressed the phone back in place. Nothing. "Jake?"

"Buzz me up."

I disconnected and buzzed him up.

"Shoot." I made a wild crisscross through the living room, loading discarded socks and unfolded laundry into my arms. I threw them onto my bed and pulled the door shut.

Jake knocked.

I shook a fist at the ceiling and ran for the kitchen.

"Just a minute," I called, sliding on socked feet through the apartment. I swept a half dozen dirty dishes off the counter and jammed them into a full load of clean ones inside the dishwasher.

"Mia?" He knocked again. "Everything okay in there?"

"Yes. Hang on. I'm coming." I dragged out each response as I kicked wayward shoes out of sight and gave myself a couple mental blows for being an enormous slob.

It was Jake's fault. The place was fine until he demanded to come in.

"Mia?"

I yanked the door open and worked to slow my rapid breath and pounding heart. That was more exercise than I'd had in weeks. "Yes?"

He peered over my shoulder in full marshal mode. "Are you going to invite me in?"

I moved out of his way and let him pass then pressed my forehead to the door behind him.

"Nice place."

I spun and made a beeline for the living room, searching for any errant bras or panty hose. "Thanks."

"Penthouse."

"It seemed safest up here. The hardest apartment to get to and all that."

He strolled around the living room at a snail's pace, stopping for a look through floor-to-ceiling windows. "Do you like it?"

I slouched against the kitchen island. "Not really."

"No?" He scanned the vaulted ceiling and leaned around the corner, taking a long look down the Italian marble-floored hallway to my oversized bedroom and master bath. "Seems cozy."

I laughed.

He smiled. "It's safe, so I like it."

I rolled my eyes. "Right. It's lavish and obnoxious. Can I get you something? Water? Coffee? Hot cider?"

"You have hot cider?"

"No." I had plenty of nervous energy, however, and that made me stupid. "You're my first guest, besides the family and Nate, I mean. They helped me move. Them and the movers." *Stop talking!*

Change the subject.

Talk about him. I pressed the ice pack to my elbow and winced. "Do you think John could've had a nemesis at the Faire?" Maybe he was part of another dueling vendors set, like the Lindseys and Kubickas.

"I'll ask around tonight. It's a stretch, but I'm not counting anything out until after the interviews."

The ice wasn't helping. I shook it into the sink and turned to Jake. "Time to get our interrogation on."

He didn't look impressed by my enthusiasm.

That was his standard response, but something else was off. I focused on the costume, absorbing details and realizing I'd missed the obvious when he walked in. "What are you wearing?"

"You told me to come in costume. I'm a woodsman."

I circled him, taking in the green hood, brown boots and gloves. "You're Link from LEGEND OF ZELDA."

"So. I found it in Dan's closet from a high school Halloween party. I left the pointy hat at home. What's the difference?"

I dialed Nate.

"Who are you calling?" Jake lifted his palms into the air. As if *I* exasperated *him*.

I covered the phone with one palm. "Nate. You need help."

"Do not."

"Hey, are you coming to the Faire tonight?" I asked Nate.

"Yeah," Nate answered. His voice echoed through the receiver. "I've got a coffee date with Kenna from Surly Wench."

Jake gave me a look, clearly overhearing.

I turned my back on him. "Can you bring your brown cloak and meet me in an hour?"

"No problem. See ya." Nate disconnected.

I turned to Jake. "You're going to wear Nate's cloak and be the Sheriff of Nottingham. Take off that quiver."

He huffed but got the job done. He raised his arms wide like an airplane. "Better?"

"Better." I stuffed my feet into black boots and grabbed my keys and leather satchel. "Let's go." The Craft Faire ran until seven most nights, nine on the weekends. Working full time at Horseshoe Falls meant I felt perpetually guilty for not spending enough time on the family business. Everyone else was retired and waiting for me whenever I arrived. Bree's day job involved human behavior studies, so even when she was at the Faire, she was working. I couldn't win, and I was always in a hurry.

"Nate can bring me home. You don't have to." The elevator was smaller and slower than I remembered.

"What about his date?"

"It's just coffee, not a hookup."

Jake's reflection watched me in the shiny metal walls. "No need to get defensive."

"I'm not defensive. You're nosy."

"Kind of my job."

The doors parted, and I jumped out. Jake's mammoth truck was parked across two spaces five feet from the door. Dual wheels and giant side mirrors reached for the cars on either side.

I pushed the power unlock on my Mini Cooper. "You know, on second thought, we can take Stella. Save the ozone. Park in one space."

"Nah." He marched to the blue beast and opened his passenger door.

I beeped to relock Stella and climbed dutifully inside. We'd had this discussion more than once. I always lost. He always drove. Like chauvinists did.

The interior of Jake's truck was spacious. I felt like a child in my dad's big chair. Country music CDs lined the sun visors. Mud caked the floor mats, and everything smelled like camping.

Jake drove like a maniac.

I ignored it as long as I could. "Must be nice not to worry about speeding tickets or anything that jumps out in front of you. Is that why you added the grill cover? To keep the things you demolish in this behemoth from scratching the paint?"

He took the exit to the Faire and slowed to normal speed. Barely. "I would have turned the radio on, but I thought maybe you'd like to sing."

I glared. With any luck, the flush of embarrassment didn't resurface on my cheeks. "No, thank you."

"What was that you were crooning about this morning? Bass?"

"Stop it. New subject."

He flipped his turn signal and steered into the line outside the Faire parking lot. "How'd Nate meet the Surly Wench girl?"

"He's at the Faire all the time. He knows everyone."

"That's good to know. So, he didn't meet her while nosing into my case on John Francis?"

I scoffed. "Please. Don't be nuts."

"I'll take that as a yes." He flashed his badge at the parking attendant and rolled into the grassy field without paying.

We bounced over grooved and pitted earth to a place not meant for parking, just outside the castle gates.

"You know this isn't a parking space, right?"

He got out and opened my door. "You're awfully concerned about the rules until they apply to you."

Accurate. "Fine. Who do we question first?"

Jake shut the door behind me and tapped his marshal badge. "*We* aren't questioning anyone. You agreed to introduce me to the vendors. I'll do the rest. I figure if you can walk through the Faire with me once, make some introductions, smile, look like you like me, then you're done. Services rendered. I'll make another lap and talk to everyone on my own."

I adjusted my glasses and pulled a foot of brown curls over one shoulder. "Whatever." I had plenty of time to talk to vendors when he left. "Have you looked into the financials for John Francis and George Flick?"

We moved toward the gates. He flashed his badge.

A pair of lovely damsels in soft blue velvet gowns and floral headpieces curtsied as we passed. I nodded magnanimously.

"You said Flick wasn't worried about their finances, but did you check?"

"I've got that under control."

"So, not yet?" I waved to my family gathered at the new Guinevere's Golden Beauty display. "I took a look last night. The business is fine. It's not making fat rolls, but it's doing better than plenty of others. The partner's personal finances seem legit. He's comfortable. Here's where it gets weird. John's financials were a mess. His business and his partner are okay, but he was barely paying his bills. What do you make of that?"

Jake waved to my fast-approaching sister and her husband. "Did you get all that information legally?"

"Mostly."

Jake dropped his head forward.

Bree skipped the last few steps to my side and grabbed my hands. Her lavender-and-vanilla perfume took me back ten years. "You're brilliant. Anyone who says differently is a liar."

"Who says differently?" Probably her.

"Never mind." She tugged me toward Dad. "The gypsy carts are a hit and you know how Mom and Dad love gypsies. They were upset when we walked in. They saw the wagons and poof! The frowns disappeared."

Tom met us halfway. "Like panties at a brothel."

She whacked his middle. "No more brothel jokes."

Tom raised an eyebrow and wrote something in his notebook.

Jake closed in on the gypsy wagons. "You did this?"

Brilliant afternoon sun obliterated the autumn chill and warmed my cheeks. "Yeah. They're rentals for parties, but I figured we could use them as storefronts until the booth is rebuilt." As an added bonus, they came dressed for Christmas.

The largest of the wagons had three wooden stairs and windows on either side. Shoppers could walk through the wagon for an authentic gypsy experience. The two smaller wagons flanked the large one, creating a crescent. The smaller wagons were strictly for displays. No one allowed on board. All three were lined in twinkle lights, adorned with thick scarlet curtains and dusted with a shimmery coat that resembled a winter's frost. The wrought-iron luggage racks mounted on top were decked in holiday greens and red faux berries.

Grandma had set up a table as her point of sale in the center of the semicircle. I'd hired a stage setter to cover every inch of the display surfaces with silk scarves, arrange the products and hang an array of crystals on fishing line. The company also painted a new sign for the display and mounted large golden flags with our logo. Stage setters were my new superheroes.

Nice as the wagons looked, something was missing. "Where are the customers?"

Bree released a sigh. "It's a little slow, but that's to be expected after yesterday's bad press. We'll be fine."

I wasn't convinced. A scan of the area showed a hearty crowd of eager shoppers, nearly all of which had bags.

"Never mind that for a second." Bree pointed to Dad. "What do you think of him?"

"Dad? His gypsy costume finally coordinates with the display?"

"No, silly." Bree smiled. "What do you think of Adam?"

"Who?" Jake asked.

Bree's eager expression waned. "It's nice to see you, Jake. You're here because of what happened to John, right?"

"Yes, ma'am."

Satisfied, she turned back to me. "Adam is the accountant I told you about. From the brothel. I met him last year. You must remember him. He's the man talking to Dad."

Jake chortled.

Man was a generous interpretation. The fellow talking to Dad was my height with excessively curly white-blond hair and freckles. "Is he twelve?"

Tom leaned his head over my shoulder from behind. "He's twenty-six. Graduated top of his class in business finance and makes a nice living at Wade and Thomas. He's smart. Funny. Travels."

"He's tiny," I whispered. "Not that I'm judging, but he's really small. I bet I could wear his pants. Young, too. Does he know I'm pushing thirty?"

Jake stepped closer. "You don't look thirty."

"You only think that because you're over thirty."

He shrugged. "You want me to run a background check on him?"

"Like I can't do that on my own?" I glared into his pompous face. "You have such a hero complex. Are you so desperate to rescue someone today that you'd resort to internet research to get the job done?"

He matched my hostile stare. "Are you so determined to not need help that you'd yell at people who try?"

"Yes," Bree butted in. "That. All day. That."

I glared.

She and Tom stepped away, whispering heatedly.

Adam looked in our direction. "Hi, Mia."

I walked the other way. "Tell Grandma I'll be back in a few minutes, Bree. I'm introducing Jake to some regulars first." I grabbed his hand and pulled. "Come on."

He shook me off when we hit the dusty path along storefronts. "Hey, I wanted to see you meet Adam."

"Mia! Jake! Wait up." Nate's voice carried over lively minstrel music in the courtyard where merry maids and men bowed and bobbed. He handed a brown cloak to Jake. "I believe this is for you."

"Thanks. I think." Jake buttoned the cloak around his neck. "You're meeting the girl from Surly Wench for coffee?"

Nate glanced my way. "Yeah. Why?"

Jake clapped him on the back. "I think I'll join you. Nate can take me from here, Mia. No need to keep your family or Adam waiting."

Nate stared. Conflict rumpled his forehead. "Uh. Umm. I don't know. It was kind of a date. Not really a three-person sort of occasion."

Jake pushed Nate forward, steering his too-tall frame away from me. "Feel free to report back to your captain later, but this isn't my first rodeo, and I know exactly what the two of you are up to, so let's get moving. You can introduce me around the Faire when we're done with Kenna."

Nate submitted with a helpless look over one shoulder.

I hiked my skirt off the ground and headed back to my family.

Dismissed like a peasant.

TEN

I MARCHED TO Grandma's checkout table and hooked a basket of product samples over one arm. Who asked for someone's help, then dumped them before they started helping? I took a few steps before a new idea hit me.

Jake wanted to play games with me? Well, I had news for him. I wasn't having it. He had a shiny badge and questionable attitude. I had chutzpah.

I freed my cell phone from my pocket and texted Nate. "Who, by the way," I informed the phone, "is *my* accomplice, not Jake's." Try to record the conversation so we can analyze it later.

I sent the message and looked up in time to see Grandma materialize in front of me. "Ah!" I stopped on one foot. "Hey! I almost tripped over you."

Grandma glared while I fumbled for a reason.

"You wouldn't even be the first person I fell on today. Ask Bernie."

Grandma stretched and curled thin wrinkled fingers. "Hand it over."

I dropped my cell phone into her waiting palm. "Fine."

The phone crowed.

"Wait!"

She whirled away. "After we're finished here."

Dang it. "How are sales today?" I asked her retreating figure.

She turned her head in the direction of charred grass

where our booth had stood yesterday. "We need a re-covery plan. Fast."

I lifted my chin and put on a happy face. "On it like a bonnet." I'd work on the murder investigation while drumming up business. I could mentally multi-task like no one else. Obsessive overthinking and a lifetime of painful introversion were occasionally useful. "I put a call in to Petal this morning."

She spun to look at me. "And?"

"She was in meetings all day." Though her assistant may have lied about that. *Uh-oh.*

This could be worse than I'd thought.

"I'll try her again first thing tomorrow."

A pair of tree faeries peeked around a wide oak and waved. Their faces were painted in shades of green and blue, like leaves and the sky. Body shimmer coated every inch of exposed skin which, considering the weather, was extensive. Their iridescent wings reminded me of Tinker Bell. I waved back. I'd always admired the faeries, unafraid of showing their figures like that. Even if I was a size zero in a training bra, I wouldn't be caught dead in body paint and a few strategically placed leaves. Inhibitions were the building blocks of my life.

Mom hated the faeries on principle. She thought they lurked and ought to put some clothes on.

I made a circuit through the Faire, offering samples and planning my next move on the case.

"No," shoppers said as I extended the free products they'd gobbled up twenty-four hours before. Every answer was the same. "Uh-uh. No thanks. Get away from me with that!" They shook wide-eyed faces. Waved their palms in big "Don't even come over here" warnings when I made eye contact. Their whispers crawled over my skin as I passed by like the town leper. My stomach knotted at the implication.

Our company was going down if I didn't get the newswoman to re-cover the story with facts. First, I needed facts. Otherwise I'd look like someone trying to cover up her crime. Negative public opinions spread like wildfire.

Nate better have a ton of information to share. I didn't see his big ginger head anywhere.

Across the common, Bree rushed from the brothel carrying a bright orange flower.

I pointed at her. "If you stick that in your cleavage, I will pull it out."

She stopped a foot away and locked both palms in the curves of her waist. Her black satin corset and boots were topped off with a red ruffled miniskirt that opened in the front. The giant scarlet plume in her hair danced happily in the breeze. "It's for you."

"Oh?" I accepted the pretty rose. "It's gorgeous. Why orange?"

"Coral." Her sudden cat-that-ate-the-canary look tamped my enthusiasm.

I'd said something wrong, or right, depending on which side of the mirror you were standing. I waved the flower at her. "Why are you giving me a coral rose? Be specific."

"It's a secret message." She rocked her hips, as if she was an actual showgirl.

"Why are you doing that?"

"Don't you want to know the secret?"

"Can you stop shaking your ass first?"

Her perfectly sculpted brows rammed together. "This is a message in the language of flowers. A coral rose means desire. Adam sent it."

I leaned around her for a look into the building she'd bounced out of. Inside, Adam waved.

Bree added a tiny toe tap to her bouncing hip. "Isn't it romantic?"

"No. It's weird and a little forward." Desire? Really? "I haven't even met him." I followed Adam's gaze across the dusty path to Bree. "Oh. Yeah. He's staring at you." Typical. Basically my life story.

"What are you talking about?" She turned in a circle. "You met him last year when I did. I'm almost certain I introduced you. I've told him all about you, and he wants to get to know you, but you're being a pill."

"Adam is inside the brothel watching you shake your assets out here in that teeny tiny outfit. This is high school all over again." I handed her the creepy rose and headed away.

"Wait!" She caught my arm. "I think you're wrong, but we can talk about it later. Come to the magic show today. Please?" She used her giant eyes on me. False lashes dusted her brows. "You won't regret it. Mom and Dad are going. It'll pick up everyone's spirits after a dismal day of sales."

"Maybe. First, I have to get people to trust we won't kill them with hand cream and ask around about John's death. I may also have to rescue Nate from Jake's evil clutches."

She bobbled her head. "Great. Bring them too, but come, okay? Promise."

"I'll try."

"If you come, I won't try to hook you up with any man for the rest of the month."

"Fine. I'll stop by the show, but I can't promise Jake or Nate will join me."

She bounced on her toes and wiggled her way back to the brothel.

A month? Either that was a bold-faced lie or the magic show was going to be phenomenal. I went back to the wagons and exchanged samples in the basket. Maybe they'd go for the full-sized lip balms we gave away at conventions. "I'm making another round."

Grandma drew a curved line in the air above her mouth. "Smile."

I smiled my way along the path outside shops and vendor booths, ignoring the charred rectangle where our booth had stood. A few looky lous snapped photos of the wreckage with their phones.

Adam's lust rose circled my brain. Who couldn't appreciate a message in the language of flowers? It was a cute gesture for our setting. Too bad his effort had nothing to do with me.

I stopped outside the Tilted Tulip florist. A painted sign announced half-price roses.

Cheapo.

I went inside and leaned on the counter. Tilted Tulip had a regular retail setup and rented the spot all year around, weather permitting.

"Good even, milady. May I be of some assistance to ye?" A burly man with a handlebar mustache and pointy beard sat on a stool arranging asters and Russian sage. His name badge said Duff.

"Hi. I'm Mia Connors. I'm also Queen Guinevere at my family's booth, Guinevere's Golden Beauty. Did you hear about what happened yesterday?"

He stopped working and gave his crowded shop a cursory scan. "Aye. I saw your booth on the news."

"I meant what happened to John Francis."

"The reporter said it was poison." His cartoonish

red facial hair and over-the-top Scottish accent were a bit much. Like interviewing a pirate living abroad.

"That's probably right. I wish I knew who would want to hurt him. Did you know John?"

He scooted back on his stool, suddenly playing it cool. "I might've seen him around."

According to Jake, Mr. Flick thought he was seeing more than one woman. Maybe he sent them flowers. "Did he ever shop here? Did he order flowers?" If I had the names of women John courted, I'd have an instant suspect pool.

"Nay. He never ordered anything from me."

"Does anyone else work here? Are there records of purchases I can see? Maybe you could check the last month for me and let me know if John was here."

Duff crossed stubborn arms over his chest. "Nay."

A couple with heart eyes and armloads of wildflowers joined me at the counter.

I patted the edge and excused myself. "Okay. Thanks for your help."

I offered lip balm samples to shoppers as I moved along the path toward the back of the fairgrounds. No one accepted.

Maybe John wasn't a flower-sender, but he was definitely a flirt, and Duff seemed like he was hiding something.

A couple stumbled away from the privies with red cheeks and unkempt hair.

"Bingo."

The privies were always busy. Aside from patrons in need of a restroom, Faire regulars and workers used the area behind the port-a-potty trailers as a place to get out of character, have a smoke and drop the Elizabethan speech.

"Hi, Larry." I leaned against the fence where Larry the privy keeper spent his days.

"What's up, Queenie?" Larry had heavy eyelids and spoke like a stoner. His brown shirt and vest hung on his skinny frame; both needed a good washing. His pant legs dragged the ground.

"I wondered if you've seen John Francis back here with anyone lately."

A knowing smile crept across Larry's narrow face. "A jealous queen."

"No. I was his friend, and I'm trying to figure out what happened to him."

"Right." He nodded. "Sure. Well, this place ain't the most romantic, so it's a hard sell when you've got a picky woman, you know? Probably why I never see you back here. Royal tastes and all."

"Yeah, that's probably why. Did he come here with a woman or not?"

"Mostly the blacksmith's daughter, but sometimes others, not too often. John was a classy guy."

"Apparently."

Larry produced a cigarette from his pocket that looked suspiciously like marijuana. "You got a few minutes?" He lifted it toward me.

"Sorry. I have to get back to work."

I shook off the heebie-jeebies and headed back to the wagons.

Nate locked eyes with me from a few yards away. He stood with Jake, who was yacking on his cell phone. Jake raised his eyes in my direction.

There was no one I wanted to see less than Jake, and I surely didn't want him asking why I was talking to Larry. I dashed back to the privy trailers and tried every door. Locked.

Larry fired up his questionable smoke. "I thought you were headed back to work?"

Desperate, I climbed onto the set of crates by the back fence and hoisted one leg over. "I was, but now I'm avoiding the Deputy US Marshal headed this way."

Larry's mouth fell open, the little white cigarette stuck to his bottom lip.

I flung myself over the fence the way Nate had snuck in the day before. A large Dumpster positioned opposite the crate pile made the process ridiculously simple, even for a shorty like me in twenty pounds of crushed velvet.

I trudged around the periphery of the fence, back to where I started, and prayed the ticket takers didn't give me a hard time about arriving twice in an hour.

The merry maidens at the gate gave me a look. The taller one curtsied. "Did ye leave by this pass, milady?"

"Yes." I inclined my head and hustled back through the gate, sample basket swinging. I had a long walk ahead of me.

THE BLACKSMITH SHOP was at the top of the hill, opposite the front gates, strategically positioned beside the stables where jousters tended their stallions and local farmers sold everything from chickens to alpaca wool. A sign on the front door said the shop was *Closed until noonday on the morrow.*

My thighs burned from the hasty climb. I pressed the back of one hand to my nose as the wind changed and stink from the barn overwhelmed my panting senses. "Marry!"

A steady clanging of iron called me inside the dark shop and guided me through the narrow halls where foreboding sharpened the air. The continuous pounding of iron on an anvil slowed my pace and increased my heart rate. Dark walls groaned with the weight of horseshoes, weapons and chainmail on display. A shiny sign hung overhead, forged, no doubt, from the same deadly material as the product it protected. *Touch ye not, lest ye be bludgeoned.*

My tummy knotted. What if the blacksmith was the killer? Or his daughter?

What if I was alone in a closed shop with a killer and surrounded by weaponry I wasn't allowed to touch?

"Hello?" My voice cracked.

The clanging stopped.

Signs be damned. I grabbed the nearest thing I could and clutched it to my chest. "Hello?" I gave my weapon a quick look. The crooked broom was made from a sturdy limb and broomcorn. I angled it out in front of me like a sword.

"Closed!" a woman snarled.

The clanging resumed.

Curiosity forced my feet forward, dragging my scared body along.

Inside the next doorway, a curvy woman with sweat on her temples and grief on her face stood over an anvil.

I cleared my throat to announce my presence. "Hi there. I'm Mia Connors, I'm Queen Guinevere from Guinevere's Golden Beauty." Did I always have a baby voice or was that new?

The woman's sculpted arms made mine thankful for long sleeves. Her green-and-black corset and skirt were simple and marked with soot. The blade on her anvil glowed red with heat. "I'm Adele Nash, daughter of Eli. What do you want, Guinevere, Queen of Camelot?"

"I'd like to ask you about John Francis. I was with him when he died."

She bared her teeth. "You, too? Did the man ever

sleep?" Her voice roared through the building. "John was a filthy man-whore, and I hope you get syphilis."

"Hey!" I snapped. "I never touched him. My family got to know John over the summer at the Ren Faire. I wasn't *with* him when he died. He was speaking to my dad and me at our booth before he collapsed."

"Oh." She gave me a long look. "Sorry. I don't hope you get syphilis."

"Thanks." I pulled the broom back to my chest. "I want to know what really happened to him. I thought you might want to know, too."

She turned glassy blue eyes on me. "Yeah?"

"Yes." Finally, she seemed to have come to her senses. For a moment I'd worried what she might do with the blade on her anvil. "Can you think of anyone who wanted to hurt him?"

"You mean besides me?" She went back to pounding the blade, which was no longer orange. "He got Melanie pregnant. Did you know that? He told me he loved me, but I overheard them at Surly Wench yesterday. He knocked her up." She whacked the blade hard enough to knock it off the anvil. "He'd promised to break it off with her!"

The outpouring of curses that followed were enough to raise the rafters.

Apparently, John had a thing for foul-mouthed women.

I set the broom aside. "Did he ever mention anything about money problems to you?"

She deflated, rounding the anvil to retrieve the blade. "Are you kidding? That was his mantra. Too broke for this. Can't afford that. He never had the money to take me anywhere, or so he said. Probably why he kept a sugar mama." She clamped the blade with a pair of metal pincers and stuck it into her nearby fire.

"He had a rich girlfriend? How do you know?"

"I don't know," she said. "I just *know*. Every time I visited his house, there was another ugly bouquet on his table. Shrubs, carnations, geraniums. I suppose they were meant to be masculine, but they all looked like horse crap to me. Then again, I'm not a dainty-flower type of woman."

Agreed. "Do you know who sent the flowers?"

"No. You think he'd tell me about his other women? Even if I'd caught him red-handed, he'd have said it wasn't what I thought. The card stem was always in the bouquets but the card was always missing."

I chewed my bottom lip. If I didn't get any new information from her, I'd be at a dead end. "Any guesses?"

"I don't like to think about it." She went back to smashing the blade.

"Really? You seem like someone who isn't easily fooled. You must have some idea of who sent the flowers. Do you think it was Melanie?"

"Pft. Melanie couldn't afford to pick grass for him. I say it was the apothecary. I saw the way they looked at one another. There was something there. I guarantee it."

Just like that, I gained two new suspects. An angry blacksmith's daughter and a possible flower-sending apothecary.

ELEVEN

I'D WATCHED ENOUGH television to know the guilty party was always quick to throw shade on someone else, so Melanie, Mr. Flick and Adele the blacksmith's daughter stayed on my growing suspect list. Playing with peoples' hearts was mean and dangerous business. How many more women would make the cut, thanks to John's promiscuity?

The apothecary shop was a small wooden structure painted pale pink with a teal door and shutters. Colorful flowers spilled from oversized boxes at the windows. Delicate black script on a wide white sign spelled Closed.

Figured. "Plenty of that going on today." I pressed my ear to the door and knocked. "Hello? Anyone home?"

"She's out for the day." A man's voice shocked me upright and away from the window. A pretzel vendor wiped sweat from his brow.

"Aye? All day? You think she might be back?"

He rested the butt end of an enormous wooden pole against the grass at his feet. The pole was slashed through with cross bars, much like a wooden television antenna. Hot pretzels hung in swinging rows on every bar. "Nah. She hasn't been here since last even. Day's done soon. Wouldn't make sense to come in now. Try again on the morrow."

"Thanks."

Nate and Jake stepped through the soap shop doorway beside the apothecary.

Nate hustled to my side. "We're finally done. I think we've met everyone on staff, plus vendors and a handful of pedestrians."

Jake shook Nate's hand. "It was insightful. I appreciate your help." He plucked invisible lint from the material of his costume, clearly uncomfortable.

I stepped away from the apothecary, unsure I wanted to share my findings. "Any luck?"

Jake nodded absently. "Some. Nate greased the wheels and folks warmed up. I can't believe how many women John Francis was involved with. How'd the man have the time to meet them? He's only been in town a year. He just partnered up with Flick at the start of the summer Ren Faire, but everyone knew him. Everyone loved him."

"Literally," Nate joked.

"Yuk." I choked on a laugh. "John was a nice guy, and rennies are open, welcoming people."

Jake snorted and slid his eyes my way.

"Got something to say about my people?" I asked.

"What did the women see in him? None of them could've known him more than a few months. I only knew the man a few weeks, but I've got to say, I didn't see the draw."

I lifted and dropped a shoulder. "To each his or her own, I guess."

"I wonder why you weren't you attracted to him."

"Am I supposed to answer or was that hypothetical?"

Nate rubbed my shoulder. "Men always want information on how women think. I know the answer to this one, though. Mia's on the hunt for brains and brawn. John fell short in both departments in my opinion."

I shoved Nate's arm. "Excuse me. Is it too much to ask for both? You have no idea how difficult it is to find someone who'll open a door for me because it's a chivalrous gesture, not because he thinks I'm a delicate flower, or someone who can take me riding and not assume I want to be treated like a cowboy. I enjoy being a lady. I want a man who behaves like a man. None of that gross stuff, though. And he has to have a brain or what would we ever talk about?" I jerked a finger in the air. "I almost forgot. Did you find out if any of the vendors had an ongoing beef with John?"

"Nope," Nate answered. "Everyone seemed to like him. He flirted indiscriminately."

Jake eyeballed a kid with vinegar fries. "I'm hungry. Can I buy you guys something?"

Nate answered first, patting his flat stomach. "Yeah, man. I can eat. How about you, Mia?"

"I promised Bree I'd watch the magic show."

Nate checked the time on his phone. "We've got almost fifteen minutes. Why don't you save us seats, and we'll run for the food. What do you want?"

I checked Jake's face to see if it worked for him, but who could know what that blank expression meant? "Okay. Turkey leg and cider. Maybe some popcorn?"

"On it." Nate pointed Jake in the direction of the food vendors and they took off at a jog.

I saved a generous chunk of the front row, spreading my long skirt out on either side. Seating consisted of logs split down the center and sanded smooth on top. Sturdy legs held the logs a foot off the ground. The stage was constructed of wide weathered planks and backed with a tall handmade fence. Red curtains hung from a clothesline and pulley system across the front.

Ten minutes later, the guys returned with enough food for a small army. I took my turkey leg and got busy.

Nate sucked on a large mug of ale. "Why are we watching a magic show?"

Grease slid down my chin. Hazards of the feast. I wiped my mouth. "Who knows? Bree couldn't stop shaking her business earlier. Maybe she scored a role as the magician's assistant. She promised not to try to hook me up for a month if I came. Apparently this is a show worth seeing."

A familiar commotion rose behind me. I smiled as it drew closer. Mom and Dad popped into view at my side and squeezed onto the bench beside me. I shoved the guys down to make room. Dad grumped softly, ending the argument they'd entertained on the way to their seats.

Nate passed a hot pretzel across my lap to Dad. "Hey, Mr. C. How's it going?"

Dad ripped off a chunk. "This family's nuts. Get out while you can."

"Stop." Mom shoved Dad forward and looked over his back at me and Nate. "Don't listen to him. He's a party pooper."

Nate nodded, completely serious. "Every party needs one."

Dad sat upright, forcing Mom from our view. "All I said was she should be careful parading around like a teenager." He bit into the pretzel like he had a grudge against it. "All the PDA is unsettling. I'm sorry, but it's true and heaven forbid I have an opinion on what any woman does in this family, never mind I raised two of them."

"Preach." Nate raised his beer in toast to the comment.

"Watch it," I warned.

Dad turned to Nate. "Thank you." He looked at me. "Let's hope your mother never acts that way. You Potter women are killing me."

"What?" I forced a hunk of turkey down my throat. We were collectively in trouble when Dad referred to us as Potter women, Mom's maiden name. "What's Bree doing now?"

Mom tipped back until she caught my eye. "She's calling the sitter to check on Gwen. She and Tom will be here in a jiff."

"So what's Dad all worked up about?"

She shrugged.

Dad growled. "I'm sitting right here."

"Well? What's your deal?"

"Nothing." He pretended to zip his lips and lock them with an invisible key. Nate passed him a beer.

The announcer strode onstage dressed as a court messenger and unfurled a scroll from which he pretended to read. "Good even, gentlefolk. Tonight we have a treat for you. A feast for your eyes. An experience for your soul. A show guaranteed to end your search for magic among us."

Tom and Bree scooted onto Jake's end of our log, pushing everyone down by two people-widths. Mom nearly ended up on the grass. Nate wrapped his arm around me and stretched his legs out in front of us to make room. He wedged a box of popcorn between his thighs to share.

I leaned across his lap, infringing on Jake's space. "Hey." I waved my hand at Bree. "What are you doing?"

She stopped whispering into Jake's ear and feigned innocence. "Shh." She pointed to the stage.

The announcer boomed, raising both hands overhead. "I bring you Merkin the Magnificent."

Jake and Nate choked on laughter with the crowd around us.

Dad tugged my sleeve. "What's so funny?"

I took another bite of turkey. "A merkin is a pubic wig."

"A what?"

"You know, for period shows when hair down there was still *en vogue*. They make wigs for that."

Dad paled. He rubbed his chest and turned to my mother. "Gwendolyn."

Mom swatted at me and missed. "Stop that. Merkin is Marvin's last name. Don't upset your father."

Twinkle lights blinked on around the fairgrounds.

The red curtains parted, and a man dressed as a wizard took center stage. He opened his arms and his cape fell from his shoulders, revealing a dainty assistant behind him. She curled the cape over her arm and took a bow. He thanked her with a kiss. A long one.

Nate gripped my knee. "Do you see that?"

Dad groaned.

I smiled.

Grandma pulled away from the magician's kiss. Her face was bright enough to light up downtown. Her costume was charming. White billowing sleeves and skirt, black corset and boots. She'd arranged pounds of gray hair into a pile on her head and adorned it with brightly colored plumes.

"She's beautiful," I whispered.

Merkin the Magnificent threw his cape into the air and a bird flew out.

The crowd clapped and whistled.

Grandma put seventy years of attitude to work onstage, selling every trick Merkin performed and hanging on his every word. She laughed at his dumb puns and kissed him twice for luck before the grand finale.

Nate shoved a fistful of popcorn into his mouth and applauded. He put on a singsong voice. "Your grandma's got a boyfriend."

Bree muttered something likely directed at me, but I let the crowd drown her out.

I focused on Grandma's performance and sheer delight at being onstage. I hadn't seen her so happy in years. Merkin was adorable in a little-old-man way. The crowd loved him, and clearly Grandma was smitten. Seeing them together should have put Dad's pessimistic mind to rest, but there was a joke about her breasts during a card trick and he nearly stroked out.

When Merkin slapped her backside and called her cheeky, I feared for his life.

Mom patted Dad's back and cooed to him. Grandma was Mom's mom, after all. If she wasn't worried, he needn't be either.

Nate dusted his palms and whistled with two fingers. "This is the best magic show ever."

The announcer pounded a drumroll on a nearby bongo.

Grandma climbed into the dreaded wooden box, ready to be sawed in half. The crowd droned to a hush.

I set the bare turkey bone aside and gripped the log beneath me. If Merkin hurt my grandma, he'd have a full row of Connors to deal with, and we were ruthless when it came to defending family. My knee bounced erratically. This wasn't some well-tuned Vegas illusion act. This was a seventy-year-old man with a cape, saw and slight tremor.

Grandma looked at the sky, arms dangling through tiny holes cut into the box. He hefted a lumberjack saw and beat it on the ground to confirm its authenticity.

I leaned forward, ready to storm the stage and intervene if Grandma so much as grimaced.

Jake's phone rang and someone threw popcorn at him. It might have been me.

He slid away for a private conversation.

My heart raced, torn between what was happening onstage and Jake's phone call. Was the call about the case? His expressions were impossible to read. Why hadn't I learned to read lips? I made a mental note to research that.

Applause burst around me and Nate was on his feet whooping and throwing popcorn at the stage.

The magician liberated Grandma from the box, spun her, dipped her and kissed her then positioned her on his lap for a final pose. Mixed emotions brewed in my chest. I'd missed her grand finale, and I hated myself. On the bright side, she seemed unharmed, so I didn't need to commit a crime tonight.

Jake waved goodbye from a few yards away.

I gave chase. "Wait."

He turned back. "I've got a lead on Bennie the Bean. Can Nate still take you home?"

"Yeah. Of course."

He looked past me, presumably at Nate. "Right."

"You never told me if you got any useful information today or if Nate was a good guide."

"I said he did a good job. Everyone seemed to trust him." Emotion flickered in his eyes. "Hey. I'm sorry I ditched you earlier."

"It's fine."

He flipped the phone around in his fingertips. "I don't know what you thought of me taking Nate instead of you but, for clarity's sake, I'm attempting to distance you from this. I don't want you more involved than you already are. It killed me to ask for your help today, so when I saw Nate, I knew he was the answer. You can stay out of Bennie's crosshairs, and Nate will point me in the right direction here if I have any more trouble navigating."

I bristled. "What if I'm not done looking into things?"

"You are."

"No. I'm not, but in the interest of full disclosure, I'm willing to tell you the blacksmith's daughter and the apothecary were involved with John. That gives them both motive and opportunity since they work here with him."

Jake's face turned an angry shade of red. "Did you question them both already?"

"No."

"Good." He blew out a long breath.

"The apothecary was out today."

His mouth opened, but his phone rang again, effectively stopping him from ranting about how hardheaded I was, or whatever other complaints he had.

He barked into the phone. "Archer."

"Talk to you later." I hurried back to my family without waiting for a proper goodbye. I needed all the information Nate had gathered while helping Jake, and I needed it now.

TWELVE

THE INSIDE OF Nathan's Navigator was roomy and warm. I pointed a vent at my cheeks and relaxed into the soft leather seat. Nathan's ride always smelled like aftershave and shampoo. Stella smelled like coffee and crullers, which made me hungry for more of those, thus creating a vicious cycle and legit explanation for my growing waistline. Soft music droned through hidden speakers as we crawled down John's street.

I chewed the tender skin around my thumbnail, fixating on one stubborn question. Why was John broke if his business was doing so well? Even if his partnership with Flick was new, shouldn't he have made some money by now?

Nate paused at a stop sign before rolling through another desolate intersection. "Do you see it? I can't read these house numbers. Doesn't anyone use a porch light anymore?" He craned his neck and leaned over me for a look at the dark houses on my side.

"I think that one was an 800. We must be close."

Nate slowed under the next streetlight. "I can't see anything. Why didn't we use GPS?"

I shook my hand and stuffed it under one thigh before I drew blood. "I know the street. I didn't think finding the house would be a problem."

"How do you know the street?"

"My Girl Scout troop had meetings at the church on the corner."

"Of course."

The neighborhood was old but quaint, exactly as I remembered it, minus the daylight. Tiny Tudor homes sat beside brightly colored cottages and mini craftsman designs. Narrow walkways led to porches with flowers and swings. The variety had impressed me in grade school. Our neighborhood was composed of nearly identical split levels in varied shades of tan.

Nate stopped at the next sign. "Plug the address into your phone."

"Fine." I tapped my phone screen and shook my head. "Two hundred feet ahead on the right."

"Figures." He crossed the intersection and slid into an open space at the curb. "Here we are. Now what?"

I peered at the unsuspecting yellow cottage with its little blue shutters snuggling every window and a red rocker on the porch. The house number was painted in calligraphy on a matching mailbox at the curb. Charming. It was the kind of house bluebirds roosted on and squirrels frolicked over. Not the sort where criminals hid from other criminals. Emotion pitted my stomach. He hadn't hidden well enough.

Nate opened my door. "We're here, so we might as well have a look around, milady."

"Shut up." I'd been in too big of a hurry to stop at home and change. If John had nosy neighbors, they'd find Queen Guinevere of Camelot skulking through his yard with a really tall ginger.

I hefted my skirt and hustled onto the porch for a peek in the window. "I can't see inside. The curtains are closed."

Nate dragged his fingers over the doorframe and checked under the rug. "No spare key. I could check the rocks for a fake."

"I'll go around back."

He twisted the doorknob and grabbed me as I passed him. "Unlocked."

"What?" I scurried through the door behind him and closed it tight. "Why hasn't anyone locked the door?" John lived alone, but he had been in federal protection. "Surely, someone would have checked on his house and locked the door after his death."

Nate accessed the flashlight app on his phone and pointed the beam around the room. "What are we looking for?"

I scanned the sparse décor. Wide planked floors and simple white walls. A Jersey Devils hat hung on the coatrack beside me. Nothing screamed money. Everything screamed temporary. As if he'd never really moved in. "There's nothing personal here. Jake said he'd been in custody a year. Do you think he still expected to move without notice?"

"Maybe he just wasn't into decorating."

"It doesn't make sense that his business partner was financially secure and the business was stable but John was broke. Right?"

"Depends."

"He had to earn some money with those paintings. They sell like crazy at the Faires. I see tons of people carrying them out. Do you think he had money but stopped using a bank because someone hacked his account? That stuff happens."

Nate tipped his head left and right. "I don't know. Maybe he had a gambling problem or some kind of addiction like drugs, prostitutes or those gentlemen clubs."

"Ew. Why'd he have to be gross with his money?"

"Okay. Maybe he gave compulsively to a charity."

"Thank you."

"Like a cult."

I examined all the wall art and framed photographs. The home was staged. It looked like the apartments people got to see before they signed the lease and ended up with the one downstairs that had mold and shag carpet. "Maybe he was blackmailed."

Nate swung his light through the room. "Why? He was already scheduled to testify against Bennie. Besides, if someone wanted him to back out, they would have paid him, not the other way around."

I motioned Nate to get moving and inched through the rest of John's first floor. It was a simple square. Four rooms, all connected to the next. Foyer and living room up front. Kitchen and dining room in the rear.

A pungent stench whacked me in the face as I entered the kitchen. "Ugh." I covered my nose with one sleeve. "Do you smell that?"

Nate toed the trash can and stepped on the pedal, popping the lid. He waved the air. "Just some flowers." He shone his light on a stack of dead bouquets in the kitchen trash. "The top ones don't look half bad."

"They smell like roadkill." I pulled a plastic stick from the top of the pile. The card it had once held was missing, like the blacksmith's daughter said it would be. I poked through the flowers with the stick. "The ones on top are still fresh. They get grosser the farther down I dig."

"Compost?"

"Not in the kitchen trashcan. Maybe he really didn't like flowers or he had a fight with whoever sent them." I shoved the stick back where it came from. "They're ugly, too. Do you like them?"

"Decomposing flowers? Not really."

I scoffed. "I mean do you like these types of flowers? The blacksmith's daughter thought another girl-friend sent them. She thought they were supposed to be masculine. Do you think these are masculine? Like bouquets for boys?"

"That's an oxymoron."

I rolled my eyes and turned in a circle. "This place is as neat as a pin."

Nate opened the cupboards and picked through the canned goods. "None of these cans sound hollow. No secret diamond stash under the guise of a baked beans can."

"Gross. He has baked beans?"

"Tasty O's, too, and sauerkraut."

I contorted my face. "Who was he?"

"A man with stinky breath, if I had to guess."

I shoved Nate and smiled. A little red dot appeared on my wrist. I pulled my hand away, but the dot stayed on Nate's chest.

He swiped at his shirt. "What is that?"

"Hold it right there." A man with a gun trained on Nate motioned toward the wall. "Move it. Hands where I can see them."

"Uh." My tongue swelled to fill my mouth. My feet were cement blocks. Panic worked through my limbs. "Uhhhh."

A familiar tenor echoed down the hallway. "All clear."

Nate cursed.

Jake walked into the kitchen beside the man with the gun. He cursed, too.

JAIL WAS SCARIER than it seemed on television, especially after an angry marshal made me ride in the back of the gun-cop's car wearing handcuffs. The station bustled with activity and smelled like my old dorm room—stale beer and popcorn. Gun-cop walked us inside and stood us at a large desk, where Desk-cop collected our personal things and Other-cop handcuffed us to a bench.

Across the room, Jake muttered to Gun-cop until his face was the color of an eggplant.

Nate whistled. "He looks pissed."

"Stop talking." I elbowed him. "You're going to get us in trouble."

"We're handcuffed to a bench. What else can they do? Do you think we're being arrested?"

"No one read us our rights. This is a flimsy ploy to scare us."

Nate tented his eyebrows. "We trespassed in a murder victim's home. The same guy the local news implied you killed. We interfered with a homicide investigation the US Deputy Marshal told you to stay away from. All I'm saying is be prepared for the worst."

Heat blasted up my neck and into my face. I tried to stand but ended up back on my can. "Excuse me," I called. "This is a mistake. I get a phone call."

Nate tugged my arm. "Now you're going to get us in trouble."

The heavy fabric of my dress flattened my lungs. "I'm having an attack. I think I'm…" I gulped air and gripped my chest with the uncuffed hand.

Nate rubbed my back and shoved me gently forward. "Head down. Breathe."

I shook my head but couldn't get enough oxygen to argue.

"Those flowers were really ugly," Nate mused.

I fought the constricting pain in my chest. What would the media report if I died cuffed to a police bench? Grandma's business would never recover.

"Really ugly." Nate prattled on, as if I wasn't two puffs away from a blackout. "I would've thrown them away, too. One of them had a black ribbon." He smoothed figure eights over my spine. "You asked if the bouquets were masculine, but the black ribbon might have signified a threat. Did you see any cards in the trash?"

The panic retreated like a wave pulled back out to sea. I lifted my face, mental wheels spinning full speed ahead. Images of the black ribbon and ugly flowers barged into my thoughts. *A threat.*

"Do you think he could've known he was in danger? Maybe that's why he broke up with Melanie." I straightened and let my head fall back against the wall. "He wasn't a jerk who left her to raise his kid. He was trying to protect them, not abandon them."

"You took that a few steps further than where I was going, but okay. Feeling better?"

"Yeah." I nodded too long, and spots floated through my vision. A tremor played over my fingers.

A putzy cop wearing fifty extra pounds and pants above the ankles rolled into view. He tucked chubby sausage thumbs beneath his belt and chomped his gum. "Green. Connors. You're up."

"Thank goodness." I tried to stand but was yanked back to my seat. I fought budding panic.

"Can she get some water?" Nate asked. "She's not well."

The cop uncuffed us. "Right this way." He left me in a small room with a mirror on one wall and a camera on the ceiling. "Take a seat. We'll be right with you."

He led Nate away.

I glared at the mirror and rubbed my sore wrist. "I know my rights. I get a phone call."

The door swung open and Gun-cop moseyed inside as if he had all night and no one else to deal with. "You're not under arrest."

"You took my things."

He set a bottle of water on the table and made wide innocent eyes. "That must have been a mistake. I'll get those back for you. How about a little water?"

I gulped thirstily, then pressed the half-empty bottle to my forehead.

"Do you know why you weren't arrested for breaking and entering?"

I set the bottle aside, inspired and motivated by his sneering tone. "Was it because the door was unlocked and I had a standing invitation to stop by anytime?" I slid the lie through my best look of indifference, making mental notes to go to church on Sunday for repentance.

He raised a brow. "Really? You were close with the homeowner, then?"

"Yep." I twined two fingers. "Like this."

He tapped a rhythm with his fingers on the tabletop. "I think you're lying and I don't like it when people lie." He leaned on his elbows and leered across the table.

I leaned away.

"The man who lived in that house was a federal witness. We watched him and the house. You've never stopped by before. I know you're lying."

"You couldn't him watch every second. You've never listened to us talk. You can't know every person he invited to stop by."

"We think we do."

"You're wrong. Obviously. I'd like to go now." I stood and he mirrored my movement.

"Sit down."

"No. Arrest me or release me." I made it to the doorway before Jake appeared.

He made eye contact from several feet away, apparently leaving another interrogation room, probably Nate's. "Where are you going?"

"Home. I'm taking Nate with me. Where is he?"

Jake brushed past me in the doorway and pointed to my chair. "We need to talk." He addressed the cop. "Can we have a minute alone, please?"

Gun-cop left in slow motion, eyes hard, jaw clenching. "Watch it, fruitcake. That guy's the only thing keeping me from arresting you." He turned his heated glare to Jake. "And I have every right."

"Sit down, Mia," Jake ordered.

I accepted his offer. "Sorry."

He pulled the door shut. "For?"

"For going inside John's house, but the door was unlocked and we didn't touch anything, not even a light switch. Just the doorknob." I kneaded my hands. "Nate might have looked in the cupboards, too, and we peeked in the trash, but that was all. I swear."

A little vein pulsed in Jake's neck. "Why were you there? I told you I wanted you as far away from this thing as possible. I confided in you so you'd comprehend the complexity and danger level involved. What did you do with that confidential information?"

My shoulder hunched under his stare. "I considered it at length and formulated a series of rational questions which I followed up on?"

"No." His voice boomed through the room and my head. "No. What you did was ignore my warning, misappropriate the information I entrusted to you and enter the home of a murder victim. What were you thinking? Have you learned nothing since we met? I thought you moved to Horseshoe Falls to be safe? I thought you finally had some sliver of understanding that this world is a bad place, and pixie-sized women shouldn't go dive rolling into murder investigations."

My blood boiled. "Excuse me. I am not a pixie, nor am I helpless. I'm allowed to ask as many questions as I want about anything I want. Maybe I shouldn't have gone inside John's tonight, but that's not a crime." I waved my hands in the air like a maniac. "The door was unlocked! I touched *nothing*. Excuse me if someone forgot to lock his door. Who might that have been, anyway?" I made a winner face. Answer *that*.

He gathered dark eyebrows over his nose and huffed until I thought I smelled smoke. "It was a stakeout. What kind of crappy marshal do you think I am? You think I just walked off and left the house unlocked? We were waiting to catch Bennie's guys snooping for evidence John might've had in his possession."

"Oh." I adjusted my skirt across my thighs. "I see."

"I doubt it." He rubbed heavy hands over his face. "I didn't mean to yell. I shouldn't have." He dropped fists lightly onto the table. "Stay out of this, Mia. I mean it. You could've run into a much bigger problem today than a couple of marshals."

"You were waiting for Bennie's guys, not Bennie. Is that because he's still staying away from this or has something changed? With John unable to testify, it seems like Bennie could come if he wanted."

"The family's not stupid or reckless. They'd send goons to do their work."

The inconsistency plucked at me. "You did it again. I said Bennie, you said 'the family.' What happened to Bennie?" I lowered my voice. "Is he sleeping with the fishes?"

Jake smirked but quickly hid it away. "We learned Bennie had a stroke two years back. His sons and grandsons have been running the show. They're not new to this life, and they wouldn't come in person either."

"Interesting. I bet things are running smoother now than when Bennie was in charge. New minds for new problems. The same thing happens to big companies. The old guys who started the business lose their market footing and blame the economy, but as soon as they retire and people half their age take over, money's back in the game. I imagine Jersey mob life isn't much different. It can't be what it was in the pre-internet years."

"You're not wrong. The sons are cleaning things up. They're still criminals, but they've streamlined. It's strictly high-end laundering these days."

"See? Streamlining. I'm not in any danger. No one's coming down from Jersey to break my legs or burn down John's house. He's dead. Bennie's free to live the rest of his impaired life at home. I just wanted answers for why he's dead, and if I'm being honest, I don't think it has anything to do with Bennie."

Jake grimaced. "I think you're probably right, but it's better to be safe."

I grabbed the water and tossed it palm to palm, reasoning through the new information. "If you agree, then why are you staking out his place? Who on earth would want to go in there?"

He rocked back in his chair, exasperated. "Gee. I don't know. Someone not too bright, I guess."

"Have you heard from the ME yet? What kind of poison killed John?"

"Mia Connors." A familiar-looking man in a five-thousand-dollar suit and a watch I could retire on stood inside the doorway. "Don't say anything else."

He handed his card to Jake. "I'm Marvin Merkin, Miss Connors's attorney. Since she's not under arrest, she's leaving now. Nathan Green is coming, too."

I hustled to his side, utterly relieved. "Look at that! Merkin the Magnificent is my new lawyer."

THIRTEEN

I was late to work the next day, despite living close enough to throw a stone and hit my office. Thanks to the unfortunate butter incident, I was out of genteel lady ensembles suitable for Pioneer Days, so I had to get creative with the contents of my costume trunk and skip my trip to Dream Bean before work. I'd check on the Lindseys and Kubickas later. Meanwhile, my head pounded from two nights without sleep and a long evening of interrogations. First by the marshals and then my grandmother. There honestly wasn't enough coffee in the world to reanimate me, but a girl has got to try.

I stopped at the concierge desk and patted the tabletop blindly in search of my precious. I shoved the largest to-go cup under the caffeinated coffee pump and flipped the glorious spout open. A few sips later, I felt more like myself.

Sunlight twinkled through floor-to-ceiling windows on either side of the clubhouse foyer, inviting the outdoors in and enhancing the rustic commune-with-nature vibe the community adored. Dust motes twinkled in the air over a giant inlaid compass on the marble foyer floor. I smoothed wild hair behind both ears and tucked it neatly into my white bonnet.

Marcella sashayed in my direction with a giant smile and a crisp white clipboard pressed to her chest.

"Morning, Mia." She tapped crimson nails on the counter. Her thick Latina accent made everything sound wonderful. She was in charge of public relations for the community, so she basically had a degree in how to manage people. "Where's your gorgeous costume from yesterday? I loved the hoop skirt."

"It's at the dry cleaner."

"This outfit is cute. Are you a pilgrim?"

I forced a congenial smile and pointed to the red letter on my chest. "Hester Prynne." I sipped liquid energy and motored away from the desk to barricade myself in my office until lunchtime. I pulled the door shut and relaxed into my chair.

My phone buzzed to life with an incoming video call from Nate. I propped the phone against my laptop while I booted it up.

Nate's face appeared on the screen. Twinkling green eyes and bushy red hair, way too happy before my coffee. "Hey! How's it going? TGIF, right?"

"Right." The weekend was upon me. John had been murdered two days ago, and I wasn't any closer to finding the killer than I was before Jake told me it was murder. In fact, my suspect pool had quadrupled, which seemed the opposite of progress. Angry girlfriends and mobsters, money problems, who knew what I hadn't uncovered yet.

"Have you heard from Jake since we left the station last night?"

"Nope."

Nate leaned close to the screen. "Do you have any theories about John, yet? Did you find what you were looking for while we were there? Do you think the marshals are still watching? We could go back. Now that we know they're out there, we can be stealthier about it."

I smiled, imagining Nate as stealthy. "Like what? Ninjas?"

He made weird chopping hand movements. "Exactly."

"You're like eight feet tall. I think you can prune ninja from your list of potential professions."

He kicked back in his seat and locked long fingers behind his head. His office came into view. A white board covered in nonsense, probably math, peeked above his head in the background. "Fine. It doesn't come with dental anyway. How's the new temp working out?"

My tummy curled. "I completely forgot about the temp." I checked the calendar on my computer and the time on my screen. "She'll be here in a couple hours. You want to meet me for lunch? It's Pioneer Days."

"Ah. Fresh ears of corn, kabobs of unnamed animal chunks, tiny chickens on a spit. Not today. I have a date with Kenna."

"You have a second date? That's not like you."

"I didn't get a first date. Your boyfriend tagged along."

I bit back an objection to him calling Jake my boyfriend. Clearly, it was Nate's intention to irritate me. I smiled. "Well, have a nice time and call me after." I reached for my screen to disconnect the call.

"Wait!" Nate jumped forward. "Wait. Hey. What do you think about the apothecary for John's killer? The blacksmith's daughter, what's her name?"

"Adele."

"She said they had a thing. The apothecary shop was closed all day after he died. Maybe she's guilty and making a run for the border."

"Mexico is kind of a haul from Northeast Ohio. I think we can relax."

"Canada, goofy."

"Whatever. She's on the list, but I'd like to meet her before drawing any conclusions."

"When you talk to her, keep a couple things in mind." He lifted fingers to tick off his list and blocked half his face from the tiny screen. "An apothecary has knowledge of poisons. This apothecary had intimate access to John. If she was like the others, she was tired of the infidelity. Means, motive and opportunity."

"I'll visit her shop before I get started at the booth this afternoon, but she's not a real apothecary any more than I'm Guinevere, Queen of Camelot. She might not have the first clue about poison."

"Booth? Do you mean the wagons you rented?"

"Yes. Not that we need them. Sales are dismal. We did a thousand dollars less yesterday than the same day last year." Which reminded me I hadn't heard back from Petal at Earth Hugger. "I've got to get public opinion turned around before we go under. I seriously hate opportunist reporters. Mindy Kinley made this so much worse than it had to be."

Nate gave me a limp smile. "If anyone can fix this, you can. Keep me posted on the apothecary. I'll let you know about Kenna."

He wiggled his eyebrows again, so I hung up.

I placed another call to Petal. This time her assistant put the call through...to voicemail. I left a message and focused on my day job. With everyone outside enjoying Pioneer Days, there was little to do in the office. My inbox was clear by noon. I had no research cases waiting on me. By one, I needed fresh coffee, something to eat and a good stretch.

I opened my door and squeaked.

Marcella and a fashion model wearing a bright pink minidress stood outside the door. Marcella lowered her hand. "I was just going to knock. Mia Connors, this is Fiona Wise."

The young woman's mouth fell open. Her wide-eyed expression startled me. She smoothed long, poker-straight platinum locks over each shoulder. "Call me Fifi. Fiona's my grandmother." Fifi gave me an exam from head to toe.

I stepped back to take in her perfect coed figure and adorable shoes. Fiona was an old lady's name and part of the reason I'd chosen her from the pile of temp applicants. "Nice to meet you." The words warbled on my tongue.

Marcella wrinkled her nose. "Can we come in?"

"Oh." I stepped aside and let them pass.

"This is the IT office for Horseshoe Falls," Marcella explained. "Mia spends most of her time here, unless there's an issue on a home PC, then she makes a house call."

Fifi seemed to recover from her initial shock. "Awesome."

Marcella swallowed a chuckle. "Indeed. I'll let you two do your thing." She did a little wave and ducked out, pulling the door closed behind her.

Awesome. Being alone in the office with her made me uncomfortable for no good reason. "I was just on my way to get something for lunch. Would you like to come with me?"

"No." Fifi shook her head purposefully. "I don't eat lunch. Is there something I can do while you're gone?"

I looked at the empty desk beside mine. Unease slipped up my spine. "You can stay and get acclimated, I guess. There's a notecard beside the keyboard with generic passwords for your email and employee intranet.

Are you sure you don't want to come along? I can show you around the community."

She looked hesitant. "Okay, I guess, but don't you want me to get to work?"

"I think better with food." Besides, I wasn't ready to hand over the keys to my castle just yet. Until I got to know her, those generic passwords and supervised desk time were all she could have. "It's the perfect time to see Horseshoe Falls. You can come with me to get some food and we'll check out your skills when we get back, figure out which tasks you can take over."

She nodded sweetly. "Okay. Sounds like a plan."

She sounded surprisingly annoyed, which made me wonder if she had an angle.

I led her to the foyer and pointed out a bunch of things she could see for herself. "Derby is the restaurant. There's the salon. The Spa. Gym. Groomers. Pro shop."

What was I thinking? Volunteering a private tour? Small talk and new people were my kryptonite. I'd jumped headlong into both. "Staff offices are in the hallway with IT. Conference rooms are there, too. Out back you'll find the tennis courts, pools and café. There's no smoking here. We recycle or repurpose everything, and we walk or take a golf cart when we leave the clubhouse for a destination inside the community."

Fifi watched patrons and staff with suspicious eyes. "Do I have to dress like an early settler? Is there a uniform or dress code?" She pulled in a sharp breath. "Is this place…" She hesitated. "Is this like a cult or something?"

I scanned the groups of people in period costumes. "No. We're a community that values green living, limited carbon footprints and nature. This week is Pioneer

Days. They do lots of neighborhood things together here. It's all part of the charm."

She blushed. "Sorry."

"It's okay. Don't worry about it." I headed for the front door.

She shuffled along behind me. "I didn't mean to be rude. There's nothing wrong with cults, if that's what you're into. I mean, it didn't work out for me, but they found my trunk of shoes, so I had to choose, you know?"

I stopped in the parking lot for another look at Fifi. "I'm going to get a salad at the Dream Bean. Can you drive a golf cart?"

"I think. I've never tried."

"I'll show you. You drive and I'll eat my salad. First I have to check on the shop owners. There was a bit of a brouhaha here yesterday."

"Mia?" Fifi looked at me with concern in her eyes. "Thank you for giving me this opportunity. I don't always fit in. Maybe I try too hard because I'm so accustomed to ruining things with people. Then new people see me trying too hard and push me away. Somewhere along the line it became a vicious cycle. I don't know why." She took a deep breath and shook her hands out at the wrists. "Sorry. I just thought maybe if you understood upfront how much I need this job to work out, maybe that would help."

"Come on. I'll buy you a water."

A FEW HOURS LATER, Fifi and I'd had lunch, mingled with the residents, enjoyed a square dance and explored the community via employee golf cart. Much as I'd hoped for an old maid of an assistant, Fifi wasn't bad. A terrible driver, but a nice enough person, and if she lost her mind like a former colleague of mine, I was almost certain I could take her down.

We stopped beside the waterfall where Tennille King, our resident photographer, had staged a number of sets from wine barrels and plastic grapes to rifles and—hopefully fake—animal skins. She threw her arms out like an airplane when she saw me. "Mia!"

I gave her an awkward one-armed hug and smiled. "You look perfect."

She bounced her hip, jostling a line of feathers in her hair. "I'm a saloon girl."

"I love it."

Fifi cleared her throat and extended a hand to Tennille. "I'm Fifi, the new IT girl."

Tennille's blue eyes narrowed. "Why?"

"No." I jumped in. "I'm not leaving. Fifi is filling Warren's position, temporarily."

Tennille trailed something in the distance with her gaze and smiled. "Well, Fifi, how about a photo with the waterfall?"

Fifi bounced onto a stump, hoisting an old musket against one narrow shoulder. She crossed her long legs and leaned into a pose. Apparently, this was not her first photoshoot.

"Nice." Tennille settled in for a few dozen snaps.

I plotted a path back to work by way of my favorite dessert stands.

"This is interesting." Jake sauntered to my side. He crossed grumpy arms and nodded at Fifi. "Where'd you find her?"

"She's my new Warren."

"Why are you dressed as Hester Prynne? She wasn't a pioneer."

"That depends on your definition of *pioneer*. Maybe colonists were the original pioneers."

He sucked his teeth and stared. "No."

I shot him a fake but cordial smile. "Did you stop by for some campfire chili or have you come to arrest me again?"

He made his usual cranky face. "I've never arrested you."

"Came to haul me downtown for more threats and questions, then?"

"You had no business in that house."

I lifted my palms. "And yet, you didn't arrest me."

He scrubbed both hands over his face. "I came to see how you are doing. You were pretty upset last night when you left."

"When I left the police station? Gee. Do you think?"

"Hi, I'm Fifi." A thin arm poked into view as she encroached on Jake's personal space.

"Deputy US Marshal Archer," Jake grouched at her.

Tennille bumped into my side. "How about a picture, Jake and Mia?" She grabbed our wrists and pulled us forward without waiting for a response. "Here." She positioned Jake beside a small wooden fence and adjusted his fingers around the back of one slat. She moved me in front of his arm. "Look shocked, Mia, like a pinup girl."

I made an O with my mouth and opened my big eyes.

"Perfect!"

She stuffed a pilgrim hat on Jake's head, ignoring his protests, and placed his hands on his hips. Grouch pose. His usual. She put my hands in prayer pose and asked me to kneel before him as if begging forgiveness.

I knelt and bowed my head.

She moved behind me and snapped a round of shots.

Fifi roared with laughter.

"One more." Tennille raced around, gathering props. She sat Jake on the bench and stood me beside him. "Put your foot on the bench by his hand, Mia, as if you're going to tie your shoe."

I obeyed. "But I'm wearing heels."

She clucked her tongue. "And hose, not very pioneer-like of you. Look over your shoulder at me."

I twisted at the waist, holding the pose. "Like that?"

"Yeah. Hold that. Hey, Mia? Are those panty hose or thigh highs?"

I finally caught on. Heat rose in my cheeks. These were naughty poses. Jake would hate them. I flipped back the length of my pilgrim skirt to reveal the line of lace above my knee.

Snap!

"Good Grief." Jake was back on his feet. "This place is bananas." He headed for the clubhouse.

Tennille winked as I passed her. "I'll email the shots to you."

"Thanks!"

Jake waved a hand overhead, without looking back. "I can see you're fine. I have to go."

"Where?" I jogged to catch up. "Can you stop, please? Your legs are like twice as long as mine."

"Work. I have more folks to interview at the Craft Faire."

"Do you need any help? Have you considered the apothecary?"

He puffed air.

"Hey." I whacked one of his hands as they swung at his sides. "Stop walking."

Jake froze. "I'm considering every angle. You aren't. You promised."

"I did not."

He glared, probably expecting a pinkie oath from me. A pledge of my fealty to his will. Fat chance. His phone rang and he pressed it to his ear.

I stepped closer, listening to the deep tenor rattling across the line.

"Kent Logan, from the medical examiner's office... confirmation on cause of death..."

Jake narrowed his eyes and turned his back to me. "Just a moment." He took several long strides away before telling the man on the other end to go on.

I tiptoe-jogged behind him.

"...Poison. Belladonna."

"Thank you." Jake stuffed his phone into his pocket and turned so quickly he almost stepped on me.

"I heard that. We should go check it out. The apothecary would know all about belladonna."

"What the—?" He tossed his arms open to balance himself as he avoided my toes. "That was a private conversation. I walked away to take the call. Wasn't that clear for you?"

I waved to Fifi, who'd stayed behind to talk with Tennille. "Can you meet me in the office Monday at nine? I have to leave now. Official police business."

Jake groaned. "What are you talking about?"

Fifi prowled forward. "Will I see you again?"

"Uh." *Didn't I say Monday?*

She stopped at my side and touched a button on Jake's shirt with one bright pink nail. "Deputy US Marshal Archer?"

Jake gave a slow reptilian blink.

Ah geez. "We've got to go." I pushed him toward his giant truck. "See you Monday, Fifi."

Jake opened his passenger door and smiled. "I think she likes me."

I climbed inside. "Just drive. You'd better bring me back for my car this time. Last time you lied and left me at the Faire."

"I told you I was sorry about that." He shut my door and dodged around the hood to climb behind the wheel. "Besides, Nate took you home. It's not like I left you there alone."

A retort about manners and idiocy came to mind, but I squelched it. "Odds are the apothecary can get her hands on belladonna without any trouble. Nate suggested the same thing this morning, and I blew him off. I should be used to him being right." I pulled my phone from my pocket and typed *belladonna* in a search engine.

"You're forgetting she's not a real apothecary. It's all make believe, Hester."

"That's exactly what I told Nate, but the fact someone used belladonna and not rat poison makes me think it's someone in the mindset of another time."

"Or someone trying to point the finger away from themselves."

"Did they finish testing the hand cream and wassail? Our company should be cleared now, right? There isn't any belladonna in anything we make, products and hot beverages included."

"He's faxing me the full report."

"I want a copy." I scrolled through the site of natural poisons. "This says belladonna is also known as deadly nightshade, and the name literally means 'beautiful lady.' Well, that's creepy. It's also known as the devil's herb, witches berry and love apple. Gross. Symptoms include dilated pupils, hallucinations, confusion and agitation."

Jake blew down the road toward the highway at

seven miles above the speed limit, ignoring my rapid-fire questions on the toxicology reports and their relevance to my company. "How did you get in here?" He motioned to my phone. "Put that away."

"Maybe you've had a dose of belladonna. You asked me to come with you."

He shook his head and muttered something unintelligible.

I beamed. "Time to visit the apothecary."

FOURTEEN

GRANDMA WAS ON a chair near our rented gypsy wagons demonstrating the pore-shrinking powers of her Lemon Refresher Splash when we got to the Faire. Mom wandered aimlessly around a space devoid of customers while Dad whittled a knotted tree branch into a smaller knotted branch.

Bree and Tom fussed with the product displays. He was dressed as a knight. She was still a harlot.

"Hey, you!" Bree waved Jake and me closer. "When will our booth be back? I think these wagons are confusing customers. We always have a booth."

Yeah, that was the problem. I smiled. "I'm working on it. I'd like to get an exact replica of the old booth and that means getting my hands on the original specs. The builder's been busy, but he's coming when he can."

She huffed and grumbled. "We need our booth back."

Tom shook Jake's hand. "Back for business or pleasure?"

"Business."

Tom beamed. "Putting Mia's IQ to work for you?"

Jake barked a laugh. "No. I don't even know how she ended up coming with me. One minute we're arguing over a B&E and the next minute she's spouting theories on my case and we're halfway here."

"That sounds about right. How are her theories?"

Jake slid his eyes my way and frowned. "Not terrible."

Tom grabbed Bree into a bear hug. "Connors women are crazy smart." He kissed the top of her head.

Bree snuggled against her husband. She lifted an accusatory finger in my direction. "What are you wearing? Where's your Guinevere costume?"

"This is my Pioneer Days costume. I'm here on marshal business. I'll change into one of my Guinevere gowns and come back later."

She scrutinized me. "Any particular reason you chose Hester Prynne, a sexual deviant? You know what Freud would say."

"That my sister's obsessed with sex?"

"Says my doppelganger."

I grabbed Jake's sleeve. "We should go, so I can get back here and help out. I'm sure Bree's needed at the brothel soon."

He followed without further prodding. "Where's Gwen?"

"With their manny, Linus. A manny is a guy nanny."

"I know what a manny is. What do you think of Linus?"

"He's okay. A drama major, so a little flaky. Draws pictures on their sidewalk with chalk and sings show tunes. Gwen loves him."

"You want me to run a background check on him?"

I puffed air. "Like I didn't do that the minute Bree introduced him."

"Right. Sorry your family business is taking such a hit. I'm going to get this wrapped up soon and clear your company name."

"I know." If not him, then me for sure. I tilted my chin to absorb the sun's warm rays. The thermostat on

Jake's dash had said seventy-one, more than Ohio could ask for so close to Thanksgiving.

We turned in unison down the path to the apothecary shop. The sign on the door hadn't moved. Closed.

I shaded my eyes from the sun with one hand and squinted at Jake. "Well, she's either in mourning or she's made a run for Canada."

"What?"

"Never mind."

An army of kids ran past us whacking a ball with sticks and screaming.

Jake's phone rang.

I got busy. First, I walked to the soap shop next door and asked about the apothecary.

I asked the same question to several vendors pushing carts and four with shops nearby. No one had seen her since Wednesday. All complained a pair of men came by earlier asking about John.

Jake loitered outside the candlemaker, still on the phone.

I bobbed in front of him until he paid attention. "No one has seen the apothecary since John died." What could that mean? Where was she? Who was she?

He covered the bottom of his phone with one hand. "I'm on the phone."

Obviously. Try as I might, I couldn't picture her face. Melanie was a redhead, and Adele had coal-black hair. John didn't have a type. I chewed the edge of my thumbnail.

I tapped my foot to an approaching minstrel band and swung my skirt in time. The musicians were all in kilts, though only one had bagpipes. Grandma loved men in kilts. She called them her weakness, and it was true. Clicking kilted men ads had given her laptop more than one virus, and guess who had to fix that problem?

Jake disconnected his call.

"Finally. What'd you learn?"

"Not much. You want to go back to work?" He moved in the direction of the parking lot.

"Not really. No one's seen the apothecary since Wednesday. Don't you think that's worth looking into?"

"I can take you to your place so you can change and grab Stella."

"Fine, but then we should stop by her house. Did you get her name? Why can't I remember her? I thought I knew everyone here."

Jake kept moving. "Her name's Agatha Bellsbury."

"Well, that sounds like a fake name."

We climbed into Jake's woolly mammoth-size truck and polluted a serious strip of ozone up I-77 North.

I fingered a stack of country music CDs on the visor. "That trip was a bust."

"Most trips are. That's how it works. One thing leads to another until you get where you're going."

My intuition perked. "Hey. Where are you going?"

"I'm taking you back where I found you."

"And then where are you going?"

He concentrated on the road, glancing into his rear-view mirror in regular intervals. "Work."

We rode in silence the rest of the way to Horseshoe Falls.

Bernie winked as we passed through the guard gate.

I fidgeted with my skirt as Jake maneuvered around piles of road apples left by horses and knots of distracted residents ogling the festivities. "Can you take me to my condo?"

"Sure."

"And can you walk me up? I get nervous sometimes after what happened over the summer." I averted my face when he turned to analyze me.

He escorted me, silently, into my apartment and did a thorough run-through of each room, checking for boogeymen.

I did a costume change quick enough to impress Katy Perry's handlers and waited by the door.

He startled when he found me. "What?" He looked around. "When did you change?"

"Just now." I huffed, out of breath.

"Here?" He pointed to the living room.

"No. Behind the kitchen island. My Guinevere gown was on a hanger in the front closet. Are you ready to go?"

Recognition dawn on his face. "To work? Without you? Yes, I am."

"Okeydokey." I gathered my things and jumped in the elevator behind him. The sweeping material of my ice-blue gown clung unapologetically to my body. Why hadn't I chosen one of the more casual A-line options? I forced my chin up and promised myself to get back into running when the weather improved, or to donate this dress to a worthy cause in the morning.

He moved away from me in the small space. "You're not coming with me."

"Or maybe you want me to tag along."

"No, thank you."

"Well, then. I'll just walk you to your truck."

"What are you up to?" He shifted his stance and rested long fingers on his shiny marshal star.

"What do you mean?"

The doors parted, and we split ways, each toward our own vehicle.

I waved goodbye as I beeped Stella unlocked. "Have fun at work."

He trailed me with his gaze, unspeaking.

I pretended to talk on my phone until he pulled out of the parking lot. He watched me in his rearview mirror as I followed him through the community and the guard gate, then onto the highway, off at an exit I'd never used before and down a street I didn't know.

My phone crowed on the seat beside me. Jake's face lit the screen.

"Hello?"

"Stop following me."

I huffed. "I'm not. Jeez. You're so paranoid."

He hung up.

I parked behind him along the curb outside a turn-of-the-century saltbox home.

He climbed the steps to the front door, without a look in my direction. He rang the bell.

I drove a ChapStick around my lips and waited behind the wheel.

Jake peeped in the front windows and tried the doorknob. He went around the side of the house, doing the same. The side door opened under his touch, and he drew his sidearm.

I hefted my skirts and hauled tail to meet him inside the door. I stopped short, knocked half-silly by the pungent sent of dead flowers. "Ugh. I know this smell."

Jake motioned for me to be quiet and wait outside.

I shook my head. Negative.

He frowned.

I motioned him ahead.

He made a mean face and crept into the house. "Miss Bellsbury? I'm a United States Marshal." He put one silent boot in front of the other, swinging his gun left and right inside each doorway.

"It's hot in here," I whispered. "And it smells like dead plants and something else."

He swore and holstered his gun.

I peeked around his ribs while he dialed his phone.

Agatha Bellsbury was facedown in her salad, surrounded by dead plants and open books. "Now we know what the other smell is." I dug a pair of gloves from my pockets and paged through the books, careful not to look at Agatha. If I looked, I'd have another attack, be overcome with memories of Baxter, and probably throw up, ruining the crime scene.

Jake contacted the medical examiner and his team while I nosed around.

He shoved his phone back in his pocket. "Don't touch anything."

I produced another pair of gloves. "Here."

"Do I want to know why you have plastic gloves on you?"

"You didn't have any when John died, so I brought these in case we needed them. All these books are on poisonous plants. I think that salad is the murder weapon."

"You think she read about poisonous plants and then killed herself with them?"

"Maybe. If she killed John, it could've been a murder-suicide, or good old-fashioned guilt." I hefted an open book in one hand and a wilted bundle of something resembling parsley in the other. "Look at this. Is this hemlock?"

"I don't suppose you've got any evidence baggies in your costume."

"Sorry."

He poked through the kitchen and uncapped the blender for a sniff. "Ah. Puke. This smoothie could've done the job."

Everything about her home was normal, except the body. She had family photographs on her refrigerator and open cereal boxes on the counter. My tummy squirmed.

I snapped a few pictures with my phone.

"Hey. Stop that."

I put my phone away. "I'd better go before your team gets here and thinks you're unprofessional for bringing me along." I slid past him and took the short path out the back door to Stella.

Jake called after me. "You'd better delete those pictures."

"Will do." I waved overhead as I drove away.

John also had a smoothie before dying, and I didn't believe in coincidence.

FIFTEEN

I HUSTLED THROUGH the crowd at the Craft Faire. After inching along the highway from Agatha's house in five o'clock traffic and waiting behind a line of tour busses to find a parking space, I had to hike across the entire field and wait in another line at the gate where employees were bottlenecked by newly hired badge checkers. I tried waving and making eye contact with the maidens at the gate, but no one recognized me. Friday night meant bigger crowds and added staff, half of whom came from the local high schools and theater troops. None who knew me from Merlin.

By the time I got through the castle gates, my feet were sore and my disposition was shot. Offloaded bus riders wore matching shirts and some pulled wheeled trollies, like the lady who slept outside my old apartment. I wiggled around the slower ones and drafted behind the speedy ones. I was a big step closer to clearing our products' reputation, saving Grandma's company. It wasn't even too late in the season to save Christmas sales. I chugged along, pumping my arms like a mall walker and chanting the *Little Engine That Could* theme. *I think I can.*

I think I can. Get out of my way!

When Guinevere's Golden Beauty wagons came into sight, I dipped an arm into the crowd and nabbed a sample basket from the counter. I could pass out promotional materials while asking tough questions. I'd keep smiling. Keep representing. Keep selling. And seeking truth.

"There you are!" Bree clamped icy fingers around my wrist before I could get the basket back to my side. "I need to get to the brothel, and Tom has to relieve Linus. He's got some kind of stomach flu, and I don't want Gwen to catch it."

"Be right there." I yanked loose and kept moving, smiling and waving all the way to Surly Wench.

Where I got in another line. "Free sample?" I delivered product to every patron leaving the counter.

Ten minutes later, I reached the register with a nearly empty basket. Sure, a fair share of the people tossed the samples in the nearest trash bin, but they saw me out smiling as if nothing was wrong because nothing was wrong. Our products were amazing and we were going to be fine. *I think I can.*

I think I can. "Hi. Remember me? Nate's friend? I came here the other day asking about John Francis."

Kenna smiled. "Sure. Are you here to talk to Lisa, too?"

"No. I really just wanted to take a look around the kitchen and maybe talk to you on your break. Wait. Did you mean, too, like in addition to speaking with you? Would I also like to talk with Lisa?" I rehashed the word jumble. Yeah, that was right.

"What?" Kenna's pirate costume was marked with condiments and sweat. Her brow wrinkled in confusion.

Hungry people complained behind me. "Hurry up, lady. Move your arse. Pick something already."

I craned my neck for a look behind her. No Lisa. "Did you mean to ask if I'm here to talk with Lisa, too, as in someone else is already here to talk with her?"

"Yes. That one."

"Excuse me." I dragged my basket through the swinging gate for employees only. Panic squeezed my chest. What if Lisa was in danger? What if the killer had her cornered out back? I couldn't handle two corpses in one afternoon. "Where are they?"

"Out back."

I made the sign of the cross and liberated my phone. I tapped 9-1-1 into the screen and hovered a thumb over the Send button as I opened the back door with a flourish.

The door banged against the side of the building.

Lisa squeaked and pressed a hand to her forehead.

Jake wrapped long fingers over his holstered gun. His smarmy stare sent fire through my veins.

I waved at Lisa before turning on Jake. "How'd you get here before me? You should be at Agatha's with the ME." Or waiting in any one of the hundred lines I was stuck in.

He extended a hand to Lisa, fully unaffected by my presence. "Thank you for your time. If I need anything else, I'll be in touch."

She zombied away, lighting a cigarette in a daze.

"How are you here?" I repeated.

He tapped the badge on his belt.

I let my head fall back. "Of course. You don't have to obey speed limits or wait in pesky lines like the rest of the world. You have a little badge and you just park in the no-parking zone and blow past everyone who obeys the rules. Is that it?"

"Pretty much. I used the maintenance entrance too. No line."

I fought the urge to roll my eyes. "Well, what'd Lisa say?"

He raised his brows and ran a thumb over his bottom

lip. "I'd tell you, but it's none of your business. Why'd you come barging out here like an animal?"

"Kenna said someone was questioning Lisa and it worried me. It reminded me of the vendors complaining earlier about two guys asking the same questions as me."

"What two guys?"

"I don't know. No one knew them."

"What'd they look like?"

"They didn't say."

"Why didn't you tell me this right away?"

I crossed my arms. "Why didn't you tell me who you thought was following us on our way to Horseshoe Falls? I saw you looking in your rearview fifty-seven times. Don't even try to lie."

"I called it in. My guys traced the plate to a rental car, paid for with cash by someone with a bogus ID."

"You think it was one of Bennie's goons?"

He stared. Apparently, I'd gotten as much from him as he was volunteering.

I went back inside and cornered the cook, a beady-eyed kid covered in grease and freckles. The grill in front of him was neatly lined with meat and veggies. "Were you here the day John Francis died?"

The kid dropped his spatula on the floor. "Yes, ma'am." He was my height and roughly three feet wide.

Ma'am? Did I look old enough for that title? "I'm twenty-nine." The words were more for my benefit than his.

"Mrs.?" His hopeful expression made it worse. Although not as bad as his red bandana and black leggings.

"No!"

Jake's chuckle curled fingers at my sides. Of course, he'd followed me in to gloat.

Kenna arrived in the kitchen with a notepad and arranged cups under the smoothie machine. "I'll help with drink orders, okay?"

Freckles nodded and grabbed a new spatula.

I watched Kenna. "Who usually makes the smoothies?"

"Anyone can. I'm pretty fast and I've memorized the recipes for everything on the menu, so I come back when I can and play catch-up."

"Are there recipes you don't list on the menu?"

"Sure. People make all sorts of requests, but not usually." She scooped berries into a cup with vanilla yogurt and pressed a button on the machine.

I turned to Jake. "We know John was poisoned. I heard someone tell you it was belladonna. Was the poison in the smoothie?"

"Seems that way."

I bit back a curse and grabbed Kenna's hand before she pressed the button on smoothie number two.

"Are you kidding me?" I growled at Jake. "Would it have killed you to say so without me asking?" I made a show of looking at my watch. "*Oh, by the way, the belladonna wasn't found in your wassail or hand cream.* Three seconds of dialogue. Three seconds. Was that too much to ask?" I turned my twitching eye on Kenna. "You were here Wednesday night. Who else made smoothies that night?"

"Me, Lisa and Moose."

"Who's Moose?"

Freckles looked over his shoulder. "Me."

Kenna snapped lids on the smoothies. "Moose is

training. Wednesdays are a little slower, so we practiced smoothies during the lulls."

She zipped back to the front with her drinks.

I slid into the space beside the trainee for a better look.

Moose slid a load of meat into a pita pocket and blanched. "Am I in trouble?"

"Maybe. Did you kill anyone?"

His mouth flopped open.

I swung my basket onto the counter beside him. "Were you paid or asked to do anything hinky on Wednesday night?"

"Kinky?" His voice squeaked.

"Hinky. Weird. Unusual."

"I have to wear this pirate costume and call ladies wenches. Does that count?"

"No."

Jake tapped my elbow. "I think you're done here. Let's get out of this nice boy's way."

I scanned the area, desperate for another line of questions before I was physically removed, but my mental well had dried up, and frustration was replacing my other emotions fast.

Moose loaded the grill with fresh chicken and kicked his forgotten spatula in the process. "Shoot." He looked around in a panic.

I ducked down and scooped it up. "I've got it." I tossed it into the sink. Excitement bit my spine and I dropped back onto the floor. "Jake, I have an idea."

He groaned. "Don't make me arrest you again."

"Kenna?" I projected my voice over the drone of impatient customers. "Who cleaned Wednesday night?"

"Me and Moose."

"Excellent. Did you do the floors?"

"Sure."

I turned to Jake. "Can we move the grill and cabinets, maybe the refrigerators?"

He eyeballed the appliances. "These are industrial-size appliances. I'd need half my team and a forklift to budge these."

I jumped to my feet and dusted my palms. "How about me and one Moose?"

Jake huffed. "I know what you're thinking, but Lisa said they clean the place top to bottom twice a day, open and close. There's no way evidence has withstood two days and four cleanings here."

I unlocked the wheels on the mobile cabinets where smoothie supplies were stored. "Maybe, but this isn't the Ritz Carlton. It's a temporary sandwich shop at an outdoor Craft Faire and the workers probably don't even clean their bedrooms. No offense."

Moose scraped the grill and shrugged. "I do sometimes, if Mom reminds me."

"Help." I motioned to Jake. "We can start with this, it's the smallest. We only need to move the refrigerators as a last resort."

Jake stepped forward. "What do you think we're going to find under there?"

"Everything. Be prepared." When I'd changed apartments, I was horrified and embarrassed by the amount of crap under my stove and fridge. I mentally gagged, recalling the shriveled food scraps and possible tooth I'd found under there. No one I knew had lost a tooth, so there was a previous tenant story I never wanted to hear.

Jake leaned his palms against the counter, and I put my weight into it. The piece rolled forward with an ominous creak and groan.

Moose swore. "That's hella gross."

"Like I said." I pulled on a fresh pair of gloves and fingered through the dirt and leaves, probably blown in through the back door. Dried food adhered to the floor on months of old grease. Dried crumbs and blackened fries circled one misshapen berry. I lifted it overhead. "Bingo."

"Well, look at that." Jake said.

Moose tipped forward at the waist, bracing dimpled hands on bent knees for a closer look. "Blueberry?"

Jake whipped his phone to his ear. "For the business's sake, let's hope it's not belladonna."

I did a mental fist pump. "For *my* business's sake, let's hope it is."

SIXTEEN

THIRTY MINUTES LATER, Surly Wench swarmed with activity and I'd made calls to Grandma's attorneys, Petal at Earth Hugger and Nate with my good news. Dan arrived along with others in navy jackets and undeniable authority. I slipped past Dan questioning Lisa at the front door. He gave me a formal nod, and I curtsied.

Fairgrounds security corralled a growing crowd of onlookers snapping photographs with their phones. Ugh. I pulled my cape up to my eyes. I didn't need my face included in their crime scene collection. Grandma would kill me with her bare hands.

I picked up the pace and skirted along the storefronts toward Guinevere's Golden Beauty. I was officially late but with excellent reason.

"Mia." Jake's voice echoed in the crisp fall air behind me. He caught up before I had time to turn and seek him. "Hey. Good work back there."

"Thanks." I pinched my lips to keep from babbling. Compliments weren't Jake's thing and they were certainly never sent in my direction. "This is my stop."

"Right." He nodded absently at my family's booth, scanning the area and avoiding eye contact.

Bree leaned her elbows on the counter and dropped her chin into waiting palms.

I spun my back to her and straightened to my full height of five-four. "Hey, I was wondering…"

"No more investigating. You did a good job finding

that berry. Your family's company is off the hook, now it's time to let me handle this."

We were off the hook for murder, but I still had a PR firestorm going, six weeks before Christmas. "Fine, but that's not what I was going to… Listen…" Nerves coiled in my tummy. Why was I sixteen in zit cream and braces with him? I shook it up. *Woman, up, Connors.* "Tonight's the big finale of Pioneer Days at Horseshoe Falls. Everyone will be out enjoying the weather and the games and there are usually fireworks."

He tilted his head slightly, as if he was trying to pick up a signal. "Yeah?"

"Yeah. The fireworks are pretty good, if you can take the cold. It'll be chilly by then. So, I wondered, maybe, if you aren't busy…" I motioned in the direction we'd come. "I mean, obviously you're busy, but if you have some time or get hungry later, I could buy you a lemonade and a kabob. You know, as an apology for making you so crazy all the time."

He narrowed his eyes and turned his lips down.

My heart sputtered frantically. It was stupid. I was stupid. The creeping sensation in my hair was probably the IQ points leaking from my brain. "Never mind."

"I could eat later." The expression on his face was fatal. He'd told me once it was his thinking face, but from where I stood, it looked like he wanted to smash something.

I probably didn't want to know what he was thinking. "Okay. Good."

"When?"

"I'll be home at seven. Bree's staying here until nine for me so I can be at Horseshoe Falls for the finale." *Stop talking!*

He didn't ask why.

He asked when. "I'll have to change. I'm out of clean pioneer costumes, so I'll have to wear jeans." *Shut up!*

He doesn't care. "You probably don't mind that. Costumes aren't your thing anyway." I pressed cold fingers to my lips.

"I'll be there at seven. I'm wearing jeans. I don't mind costumes. On you."

"You hated the Mary Poppins."

"That wasn't Mary Poppins."

It had most definitely been a Mary Poppins and, honestly, one of my better impromptu ensembles. I'd worn it to Comic Con not long after we'd met. The stilettos and fishnets probably didn't fit the traditional Poppins image, but short skirt and corset aside, it had been a kickass Poppins. Kind of brilliant, actually. "There was a steampunk twist."

"You were barely dressed."

My mouth fell open.

Bree bounded between us. "Time for work." She gripped my shoulders and steered me away. "She'll see you at seven."

Jake turned on his heels and waved. "See you later."

We made it to the gypsy wagons and leaned against the backside together. Tom smiled when he saw us.

Bree's wide brown eyes twinkled with mischief. "That was fantastic." She scribbled something on a little notepad and worried her bottom lip. "He's not what he seems at all. Is he?"

"I'm not sure."

Tom rocked on his heels. "I saw the whole thing. Nice work. You got yourself a date."

"It's not a date. It's meat on a stick and some lemonade."

Bree sighed. "Finally, my baby sister has a date."

I trailed Jake's silhouette in the distance. Did he think I'd asked him on a date? Surely not. I never said *date*.

If he did think that, what did it mean that he'd said yes?

I DRESSED IN my softest jeans and long sleeve shirt, then pulled a fandom T-shirt over top. My hair was down, and I had mascara on. Date or no date? The struggle was real.

Never mind. I didn't want to know.

I slid a lip gloss wand around my lips, just in case.

The doorbell rang, and I made a dive for the foyer. Finally, time to get on with it. Whatever would happen was better than the number of insane things I'd concocted in my mind. Nip it in the bud. Jump in. Get going. All great philosophies.

I hustled to the door and swept it open. "Hi."

Jake looked like I'd slapped him. "You're ready? I thought you'd need more time to change."

"Bree covered me so I could leave a little early. There wasn't much business, so they didn't need me."

"It was nice of your sister to cover for you anyway."

"You'd think so, but it means I owe her, and that's never good."

He stuffed his fingers into the pockets of low-slung dark jeans. His brown leather coat hung open, revealing a navy T-shirt beneath. Maybe I was projecting, but Mr. Cocky Pants looked a little nervous.

My tummy twisted stupidly. "Let me grab my boots. It's cold, right? I'll get a coat, too." I stuffed my feet into brown riding boots and headed for the coat closet. Taking a cue from Jake, I grabbed my cropped leather jacket, threaded both arms into the sleeves and freed my hair from the collar.

Jake read my shirt and smiled. "'Winter is coming.' Hey, I get that reference."

I controlled the shock on my face as much as possible. "And I get *that* reference. You read *Game of Thrones*? Wait. You're a Marvel fan?"

"I'm a Captain America fan. Who isn't? He's Captain America."

"Solid argument." I zipped the coat and stuffed everything I needed into my pockets—cell phone, keys, money, ID. "I should've guessed as much, coming from a military family where everyone serves in law enforcement afterward. Love for the Cap is probably in your genetic makeup. He's the personification of your hero complex."

"I don't have a hero complex."

"Of course." I locked my door and pushed the elevator button, then pretended to collapse.

"Mia!" His arms were around me before my knees fully bent. He straightened me and looked me over.

I smiled. "Like I said." *Point, Mia.*

He frowned. "That was ridiculous on your part and common courtesy on mine. What would anyone else have done? Let you fall on the ground?"

"I'm just saying."

The doors parted, and he motioned me on board first.

Thanks to the over-polished interior walls, Jake was everywhere. "Did you find anything more on the car that followed you here?"

"Security footage at the car rental company caught the men who used the fake ID. Dan's looking into them. We think they came down from Jersey."

"If they're associates of Bennie and came here to

kill John, they wouldn't still be in town, right? Maybe they got wind of his death and whereabouts and came to confirm for themselves?"

"We don't know, and we haven't found them. They returned the car before we got there."

I chewed a nail until we reached the ground floor.

"How about your PR thing. Did you get anything straightened out when you got home today?"

"Not really. I sent the good news out to consumers in a press release. Our products don't kill. Only time and sales will tell if consumers are over the accusations they heard. I really wish Petal would call me back. It's been days and she's completely AWOL. Not a good sign."

"Petal?"

"Never mind. I'm sure it's fine." I hoped.

Outside, the night was alive with community spirit. Horseshoe Falls residents filled the streets dressed in period costumes. They laughed and chatted, enjoying the night. Horseshoes and cornhole games were played on lawns lit by lanterns hanging on shepherds' hooks. A line of men waged a tug-of-war battle over blue tarps doused in mud.

Joy percolated in my chest. "I love these events."

"You don't mind all the people?"

"No. I love the people, especially from afar. People-watching is one of my favorites. The interacting is where I muck up."

"You do better than you think."

We moseyed past a line of street vendors hired for the weekend. I could get vinegar fries and kettle corn at the county fair, but only one weekend a year could I get goodies made over an open fire by local residents. The thick tang of barbecue sauce and campfires filled the air. "We have to get Bernie's kabobs off the fire. I don't know where the recipe came from, but it's heaven on a stick."

"Bernie's cooking tonight?"

"Every year. She wins the Campfire Award for her excellent food. She makes chicken, shrimp and steak kabobs that melt in your mouth." My tummy growled on cue.

"Deal." Jake sauntered beside me, matching his pace to mine and looking like the hero of a rodeo movie. Everything about his stride and disposition screamed *cowboy*. The marshal badge didn't hurt.

"Do you ever take off the star?"

"Nope. The job never ends."

"I'm not sure if that's sad or just really cool." I led him to Bernie's campfire. "We'd like to try all three, please."

"Mia!" She hopped to her feet and pressed me against her chest. "No costume?" Her bottom lip rolled out. Her bonnet and apron were adorable.

"Not tonight. I wasn't feeling the Hester Prynne and butter's rough on satin."

"Don't I know it. I nearly broke my bonnet in that slip-and-slide fiasco." She loaded kabobs onto a paper boat and squirted her secret sauce into the corner. "Nice to see you again, Jake. Hope you're planning to make this a habit."

We traded food for cash, and I handed Jake a basket.

He pushed a money clip back into his pocket and frowned. "I was going to pay."

"I invited you. It's my treat."

He turned his phone over in one palm and balanced the kabobs in the other. "Looks like the medical examiner confirmed that berry as belladonna."

I nibbled on a piece of charred chicken and headed

away from Bernie before we ended up on her blog again. "Excellent. Now there's no way anyone can point a finger at Guinevere's Golden Beauty for this. Even if Mindy Kinley tried placing doubt on whether or not the belladonna could've actually been in the wassail before, now we have the poison at the place he bought his smoothie. I'll send another round of letters and draft a new press release in the morning, if that's okay. It's not a marshal secret about the berry's whereabouts. Right?"

"No. Go ahead. It's thanks to you I'm a step closer to finding John's killer."

I didn't bother hiding the smile parting my lips. I bumped gently against his arm.

The night was beautiful. Storefronts were lined in white twinkle lights, and a full moon hung brightly overhead, surrounded by stars and a nice view of Venus. Somewhere in the distance a harmonica lamented and a banjo agreed. Horseshoe Falls loved Pioneer Days like I loved Comic Con.

Jake turned for the Sweet Retreat where Steve Kubicka manned a lemonade stand on the sidewalk. "Drinks are on me." He paid Steve and handed me a tall white cup. Pretty pink paper with images of ice cream treats covered the window where his butter sculpture had been.

I tapped a nail against the window. "I'm sorry about the butter horse. It was really good."

Steve rubbed his hands into a cloth and sighed. "Thanks. I'm just sorry for the way it ended. There were a lot of injuries that day. Butter's dangerous. Not just to your cholesterol."

Jake chewed on a kabob. "Amen."

Tennille King, my new friend, zipped across the street in our direction, towing a man the size of Jake's truck. "There you are." Her smile widened until a dimple caved in. "Mia, this is my husband, Ty. Ty, Mia and her… Jake."

Ty extended a hand to Jake and then me. "Nice to meet you."

Tennille dug a manila envelope from her bag. "These are yours. I'd planned to email them, but my laptop didn't do them justice. You want print copies. Trust me."

Someone called her name.

"Oh. Okay. Hey. We're going to go. Call me, Mia."

A smile spread over my face. I hadn't gone through with contacting her for a casual get-together yet, but the idea of having a girlfriend sounded amazing. There were some things Nate just never needed to hear.

Ty waved overhead as he followed her into the crowd. "Enjoy your date."

Jake went rigid at my side. "Should we sit somewhere?"

Before I fell over dead from nerves? "Yes, please."

We settled onto a bench near the waterfall and watched a group of men and women in brightly colored outfits clap and spin. They'd turned the empty clubhouse parking lot into the perfect place for a square dance.

I slid a shrimp off my stick. "Fireworks will start soon." A bonus of fall fireworks, no need to wait until ten for nightfall.

Jake inched closer. "What's in the envelope?"

"Pictures from the other day." I opened the flap and slid them into my hand. My face heated. I stuffed them back into the envelope and grabbed my drink.

"Wait a minute." He rocked me sideways and snagged the envelope from where I'd hidden it under my thigh. A long whistle crept from his lips. "Damn."

"I didn't know she was making dirty pictures until the last one." I peeked at the photos as he flipped through them. Slowly.

The shot where she'd asked me to feign shock looked like Jake was pinching my bottom. The pose where she'd asked me to pray looked like I was giving him a reason to. When I'd propped my leg onto the bench and peeled back my skirt, I looked like a pinup girl. Bree would have loved it. My hoisted leg didn't look bad in the black-and-white filter Tennille had added. She'd colorized the blue waterfall behind us and Jake's eyes, which were hooded and intently focused on my thigh. The lilt of his mouth and jut of his chin made him look sexier than anything I'd ever seen and, based on that photo, my thigh had caused all that.

I crossed my legs and shoved the lemonade straw between my lips.

Jake tucked the envelope into the inside pocket of his jacket. "You can get copies?"

"Mmm-hmm."

People filtered into the grass around us, settling onto blankets for the fireworks. Jake and I shared an awkward silence as we finished our kabobs.

He set the empty basket of sticks aside. "Can I ask you something personal without making you mad?"

I dared a look in his direction. "Try me."

"Why not Nate? When I met you, I figured you were a happily-ever-after waiting to happen. Three months later and nothing's changed. You have everything in common. I can't find anything wrong with him, and he meets your brains and brawns requirement. I don't get it. People are pretty predictable, but this has me puzzled."

"We're friends. That's all it's ever been. I don't understand everyone's fixation on this subject."

"I find *just friends* hard to believe."

I guffawed. "You were serious when you said men and women can't be friends? I was sure you were trying to prod me."

Jake swiveled on the bench beside me and hooked a knee between us on the wooden slats. "That's been my experience." He lifted a hand. "Boy likes girl." He lifted the other hand. "Girl likes boy." He clapped them together. "Sex."

"Oh, jeez. Are you serious?" I nearly choked on my lemonade. "You sound exactly like Bree."

A wide grin split his face. He shook his head and chuckled. "Maybe there's more in the middle, but that's how it goes, right?"

"No." A laugh bubbled out. "That is not how it goes. Good grief, man."

"It's been a while since I dated. Maybe I'm confused."

"Yes. You are confused. That or you watch too many dirty movies. When was the last time you dated?"

"I don't watch dirty movies. Who calls them dirty movies?" He laughed. "I haven't dated since high school. I met the one I wanted for life during my first tour in Kuwait. That was it for me, but she didn't make it home."

A little gasp caught in my throat. He'd said something like that to my family when Bree asked if he'd ever been in love. He'd said she died but didn't say how.

"I'm sorry." It was lame, but something needed to be said. What else was there? Darkness aside, I was unveiled beside him. Everything I said felt weighted, too important.

"Don't be sorry. Soldiers know what we're in for. It's a risk we take. Roadside bomb. I did three more tours before coming home. I couldn't bring myself to leave her there, but she wasn't coming home. One day I had to let go." He anchored an elbow over the back of the bench and heaved a breath. "Anyway. That was a long time ago. More than ten years."

"You didn't call me after you left. Was it because you thought I was with Nate?"

"No." He shook his head and looked into the night. "I don't know why. I just couldn't."

"Couldn't or wouldn't? I thought we were friends. You know I'm not great at understanding people or interpreting motives. It hurt when you didn't call. I assumed it was something I did."

He turned solemn blue eyes on me. "I lied to you for weeks about who I was and why I was in your life. I hadn't earned your trust. You had every right to hate me."

"I don't. You came clean, and we moved ahead."

"Well, while I was lying, I had some trouble separating the job from my personal thoughts and feelings. Undercover can get complicated, and you made it hard to see you as the criminal I was investigating. You were funny and quirky and charming." He cleared his throat. The scowl returned. "Bottom line, you had everything you needed, and I wasn't part of that equation."

"You took yourself out."

"It was no way to start a friendship."

"Isn't that exactly what happened?" I twisted on the bench to face him. "Aren't we friends?"

Fireworks sizzled into the inky sky and exploded into a kaleidoscope of colors.

His brooding face was almost too much to bear. Part of me wanted to flee, run for my apartment and lock the door behind me. The other part disagreed wholly with that course of action.

"Why not Nate?" He exhaled the question like his life depended on understanding my answer.

I blinked, recognizing this moment as one I'd live to regret. "He's too easy." There. I'd said it. "Not *easy*. He's...painfully agreeable." Bree swore the doting type of man was pure gold, but Nate took it too far. "He's never stood up to me or challenged me to try harder or be anything more than I already am. We get along perfectly at all times. I can't live like that." I laughed at the ridiculousness of my complaint.

Jake's brows lifted slightly. "No fire."

I shook my empty head. "Yes." Nate and I had no fire. No passion.

Jake leaned closer. Wow. He smelled amazing.

Spectators cheered for the fireworks illuminating the night.

He cursed under his breath and lifted his hand to my cheek. His thumb drifted over the tender skin beneath my ear.

A soft gasp popped out of my mouth.

His phone buzzed inside his jacket pocket, drawing his attention and breaking his unsettling gaze. He pulled away like I smelled of rotten cheese. "Archer."

I flopped against the backrest. Holy crap.

He was on his feet. "I've got to go. We've got a warrant for the apothecary's shop and storage facility. If this was a murder-suicide, we'll get the case closed tonight."

I jumped up. "Okay." My brain begged me to follow him on this excursion, but my ratcheted nerves said, *Go home and do not leave.*

Ever.

Nerves won.

SEVENTEEN

I COULDN'T SLEEP, but I did get an email I'd been waiting for. A local contractor had an opening in their schedule and could get started on a new booth for Guinevere's Golden Beauty right away. I emailed the specs, dressed for the Faire, and met him an hour before opening.

We reviewed the situation, haggled on pricing, then shook hands.

He pushed a clipboard in my direction. "We'll rope the perimeter off and get a solid foundation started today. I'm gonna make a trip downtown for the right permits, and have you back in business this time next week."

I scratched my name on the bottom line. "Thank you." I didn't miss the fact his sudden availability co-incided with the fact I had proof we didn't kill John. Even third-party companies didn't want to be associated with that kind of press. No wonder Petal was non-responsive. I'd made up my mind on her while I stewed over the number of things I couldn't control. She had until Thanksgiving to tell me where we were on our deal. After that, I'd assume she was out, and find another way to get our products onto retail shelves. I didn't want to work with someone who couldn't be bothered to return my calls, anyway.

Bree arrived fifteen minutes before the gates opened. A wool cloak whipped around her ankles in the cool morning air. She dropped two lidded coffees and three supply bags on Grandma's makeshift checkout and stared. "Are you okay?"

"Yes." I unloaded the bags with caffeine-enhanced nervous energy. "We'll have our booth back in a week. Oh, you brought muffins." I opened the plastic container and snagged breakfast. A fresh blueberry burst in my mouth. "This is amazing. Did you make these?"

She took over setting out cups and napkins. "Are we going to do this? Pretend you weren't the first one to work on a Saturday morning? As if there's no massive story behind your early-morning appearance?"

"I met with a contractor. You passed him on your way over here. Burly guy. Clipboard. Tool belt." Jeez. Scolded for being late, questioned for being early. "How about a 'good job'?"

Her eyes settled on mine, trying to extract the information she wanted, using her twin power, no doubt. "You look worked up. What's going on? Don't say nothing."

I crammed another bite of muffin between my lips and fluttered my eyes.

She took the container away. "Good job."

"Thanks."

"Now, what's wrong?"

I slid my fingers under my glasses and rubbed tired eyes. Jake's stinky-cheese look had haunted me all night. I'd called Nate to ask him for a guy's perspective but couldn't bring myself to tell him anything. Rejection was personal and painful. I was ridiculous for still thinking about it. Nate and I played REIGN, our favorite online role playing game, all night, until I came to meet the contractor. We made lunch plans for hanging out when my shift ended today.

I sucked crumbs off my fingers and smiled. "How's Gwen?"

Bree tapped her foot. "Talk, woman."

"Stop. You're making me crazy with that face." She swore we were cosmically connected because we were twins, and claimed to know when I was hurting, physically or emotionally. I wasn't convinced either way.

"Talk."

"It's been three days since John died, and I'm no closer to knowing what happened than I was the day he collapsed."

"I'm not buying it. You aren't a detective. You two weren't close. You saved our business. Try again."

The business part was still to be seen.

I smoothed my Guinevere dress and put on a professional face. "I'm working up a promotional campaign to smooth consumer relations after the nutball news allegations. The first round of coupons and sample invitations went out last night to our mailing list. I'm hoping they do the trick and we can get back on track for holiday sales."

"Nope."

I unlidded a coffee and leaned against the counter. She followed suit.

Jake's stink face popped back into mind. Why didn't I have any girlfriends? "Fine. I'll talk, but you can't. Promise?"

She lifted a three-finger salute. "Promise."

"I just need to say it all aloud so I can process. Then I'll move on and be done with it."

She waited. No talking. Keeping her promise.

I couldn't do it. I needed friends who weren't blood related or male. "Never mind."

Adam arrived with perfect timing, carrying a clipboard and pen. "Bree. Mia." He tipped his hat. "We're practicing in ten. If you want to warm up, now's the time, Bree." His black tights and green vest emphasized his small stature. He leered at me and then my married sister like a man in need of an eye-poking.

She set her cup aside. "I'll be right there."

He gave us another long look before departing.

I turned to Bree. "Do I want to know what you're warming up for at the brothel?"

She did a silent clap. "Adam put together a cabaret for us to perform. It's delicious and the absolute perfect addition for our grant work. Tom's helping backstage and overseeing everything, including crowd responses. I'm the lead." Her happy eyes turned pleading. "Which is why he made muffins. We hoped you'd watch Gwen for us during rehearsals. There are only a few, and they won't take long, I swear. Plus, Mom and Dad already agreed to cover you anytime you're helping with Gwen. Linus will take over as soon as he's feeling better."

As if watching my twin in a cabaret wasn't asking too much. "I get to play with Gwen and watch rehearsals? Nothing else?"

Her head bobbled. "Please. Please. Please. I haven't been onstage since high school."

"You were a cheerleader in college."

"Cheerleading's different. No one paid any attention to us on the sidelines, and everyone abandoned the stands for the bathroom at halftime. Please? It's all in the name of research." She drew an X over her heart.

"Fine, but only because I refuse to make Dad sit through your cabaret practices. I assume that's why he passed. Okay, also because my niece is wonderful and I don't see her enough."

"Excellent! Tom will bring Gwen to you when he's

needed backstage. I have to run. I'll be back to relieve you at lunchtime. I'm staying until close."

She bounded away.

I finished the coffee and muffins feeling duped somehow.

By lunchtime, I'd spoken to hundreds of shoppers, answered questions about the false news reports as diplomatically as possible, and explained the benefits of every item we carried at least as many times. Overall sales were shoddy, but at least people were stopping and seemed interested in what I had to say.

When Bree returned at lunch, I shoved off, eager to get home after a quick trip to the privy.

I sauntered along the dusty path, taking in the scenery. The fairgrounds made a perfect setting for Ye Ole Madrigal Craft Faire. The Renaissance Faire happened every summer in an apple orchard, but fall was the busy season for Ohio apples and the dead season for county fairs, so the Craft Faire had a separate locale. Passersby carried shopping bags and steaming cups. Their red cheeks and rosy smiles looked a lot like the commercials for holiday shopping.

Despite the crowd, the privy was empty. I washed up at the foot-pump water station and dried my hands slowly, not quite ready to go home. How sad was it that the Faire had lost two members in four days and no one seemed to notice? There wasn't even a memorial for John or a remembrance painting on display. Nothing.

A chorus of laughter echoed behind the fence. Business as usual for workers in need of a little nookie. The trilling giggle mixed with a heady and failing Scottish accent I'd recognize anywhere. I inched closer, pretending to dry between each finger and around the nails. The florist's accent fell away on some descriptive word choices about her cleavage and his tongue. A rough New York accent took over a moment before the talking ended. Ew. He was as bad as the rest of them.

My heart sank. He was also just a guy enjoying his life, like John. Like my best friend Baxter. They hadn't deserved to die so young or so senselessly. Much as I wanted to stick around and get a look at the unlucky woman with the florist, I had renewed purpose. This ordeal meant more to me than seeing my company's business back in order. A shopping bag with a silver horseshoe caught my attention. I wanted justice for the victims, and I knew where to go next.

I had a few more questions for Adele. I climbed the hill to the blacksmith's shop, planning my inquiry and hoping she'd talk to me again. The jousters were lined up for a tournament. Hopefully, the Action News team wouldn't be back. I wasn't at the wagons to help hold Grandma back.

Adele was busy showing a pair of wizards a birdcage, so I poked around, waiting my turn. She was my best resource so far. Though, I couldn't help wondering if she'd been jealous enough to kill both of them.

"You're back." She found me near the weapons where we'd first met.

"How are you?"

"Good." Her swollen eyes and splotchy complexion said otherwise. "Better." She heaved a sigh. "I'm working on it. I was mad and a little in shock when we talked before. It's bothered me. I must've seemed like a callous bitch. I'm not usually. Maybe I'm still in shock. I'm glad you came back so I can say sorry if I acted like a maniac before."

"You were fine. I know what you're going through. I lost someone over the summer. I still pick up the phone

to text him when a favorite show or song comes on…
then I remember."

She blinked glossy eyes. "Life, right?"

"Yeah. Life." I toyed with a line of leather whips on
the wall. "The last time I was here, you told me John
was seeing the apothecary. Did you hear about what
happened to her?"

Creases gathered over her forehead. She pulled a
handkerchief from her corset and dabbed her nose. "No.
Was she arrested? She hasn't been back to her shop
since he died."

"She's dead."

Her mouth popped open. "How?"

"Poison."

Blood drained from her cheeks. Panic widened her
eyes. "Do you think someone's targeting the people in
John's life?" She turned her gaze to a cup on her counter. "Was it something she bought from the Faire? Surly
Wench was closed today. Did she buy something poisonous there? Did Lisa do this?"

"We don't think the poisoning happened at the Faire.
What do you mean about Lisa? Was she seeing him,
too?"

"I don't know. I mean, she's over eighteen and not
using a walker, so she's in his age range. She's not ugly
and she's accessible." She found a chair against the wall
and fell onto it. "Am I next?"

"We don't have any reason to think that. Do you?"

"Do you have any reason to think I'm not next? What
if I'm targeted for being in his life?" Her long black
skirt dragged on the straw and dirt floor as she writhed
to get comfortable and catch her escalating breath.

"That's terrible logic. I don't have any reason to

think *I'm* not next. You can't look at it from that perspective or you'll be afraid of everything."

She flailed her arms. "I am afraid of everything." The heavy liner and raven hair dye suddenly seemed more like a cloak of protection than a statement of hard-assery. Her rapid breaths became shallow.

"Hey." I crouched before her. "Look at me. I'm here to see if you have any other names you can give me. Was he seeing anyone else that you know about besides Melanie and the apothecary? Also, did he ever say anything about his business? Do you know if it was doing okay?" The whole money situation didn't sit well with me. "I might talk to the partner next."

That got her attention. She straightened on the seat and settled herself. "I think business was good, but his partner was a real thorn. They argued all the time. John would come here some nights and drink after hours, just trying to escape. That's how we got together."

Interesting. "Any other women you can think of?"

The bird-cage guys were back at the counter. "Not really. Nothing more than a quickie hookup. Sorry. I've got to get this. Will you keep me posted if anything else happens?" She swatted her cup into the trash and gave her customers an apologetic smile.

"Yes."

I exited the shop and inhaled fresh country air. This had nothing to do with her or me. Whatever was going on had everything to do with John and nothing more. Except the apothecary, but I'd figure out how she got sucked in.

I turned for the castle gates and my waiting car. A pair of horses in dress armor rode into my path. A knight wearing a red coat of arms removed his helmet and smiled. "Milady." He dismounted his horse with a flourish and bowed at my feet. "May I be of service to you this fine day?"

I curtsied. "No, thank you, sir."

He stepped toward me as I moved away. "Might I buy you a cup of ale or coffee? Lunch, perhaps? Anything you'd like."

"No, thank you."

His used-car salesman grin gave me the creeps. "Your number then? Perhaps another time?"

"No." I widened my stance. No meant no, whether the topic was coffee or something more. "Kindly remove yourself from my path." Three ways to land him on his back, if necessary, ran through my mind.

He snorted and stepped away, palms forward. "Excuse me, Miss Priss. You're dressed for the Faire. I assumed you might want to play the part. A little knight in shining armor might be what an uptight princess needs."

Why were so many men pigs? This was why I didn't date. Where was Bree when this stuff happened to me?

"Hey!" Adele hollered from her shop. She had a broom in one hand and a pail in the other. "You want to hear me play drums on your head again?"

He scowled.

"No? Then shove off!"

The jerk disappeared without another word.

I spun in shock. I could've dropped him, but her effort was appreciated. "Thank you."

"Bloody jousters."

EIGHTEEN

I ARRIVED LATE to the concierge desk at work Monday morning, apparently not long after a pack of wild animals. "Good grief." I collected empty sugar packets, fallen swizzle sticks and stir paddles and stuffed them into the trash can. Did people have no respect for coffee?

I made a quick tally of things to accomplish and general time frames. I had a pile of emails to send and graphics proofs to approve for Guinevere's Golden Beauty. The accusations had been made and disproven in the span of a few days, but if I didn't act fast and stay on top of things, there could be long-reaching negative results. I'd contacted the news station and requested an interview with Mindy Kinley or at the least a timely on-air apology.

The clubhouse buzzed around me. Staff and residents hustled in every direction, chatting on phones and toting bags. Gym bags. Computer bags. Shopping bags. With Pioneer Days behind us for another year, Horseshoe Falls was back to business as usual, which meant a full inbox for me. Residents and IT problems were a package deal. Fortunately, most of the problems were solved by turning their machines off and back on again, but no one liked to hear that, so I'd volunteer to drop by and take a look. Score points for customer service and a little local gossip. Double win.

The door to my office swung open as I reached for

the knob. Fifi stopped, wide-eyed in the threshold. "Oh, glory be! I was on my way to get coffee and a pastry for you." A line of bangle bracelets jangled on her thin arm.

"Uh-huh." I slipped past her, raking my mind for the reason I'd asked her to come back. "You don't have to do that. I'm fully capable, but thank you."

She bit her thick glossy lip. "If you say so. I logged in to clubhouse email when I got here this morning. I used the password you gave me Friday, and I responded to all the messages and questions. There are two residents who need someone to come out and take a look at their machines. I called and tried to verbally walk them through the problem, but they didn't like that very much."

"The residents like knowing tech support does house calls. It's one of the perks here. They itch. We scratch." I set the coffee on my desk and turned back to Fifi. "Not really. Not literally."

She blinked long false lashes.

"I didn't mean to touch them if they asked."

She sniggered. "I like you. You're funnier than my last boss."

I slid onto my seat and logged in. The IT inbox was clean, aside from two marked with blue flags.

Fifi went back to her seat and tugged the hem of her floral mini dress. "I flagged the ones who want us to come to them."

"You did all that this morning?"

"I like to make a good impression and stay busy."

Maybe an assistant wasn't the worst thing that could happen to me. "Thanks."

"No problem. Can I have a voice mail passcode? I couldn't check those messages or I would have."

I got Fifi started on the voice mails, then I ran a

quick diagnostic of the system and double-checked the security. I'd made a routine of vigilance after the issues of this past summer. I released a breath. No one had tampered with the network. No hackers. No homicidal lunatics. I worked steadily through the morning on a pile of pet projects I hadn't had time to look at in months.

By lunch, I was running on fumes, mental and physical. "I need food."

Fifi jumped to her feet and pressed the phone receiver to her chest. "Can I get you anything?"

"No. I'm going to make those house calls you flagged. I'll grab something from Sweet Retreat on my way back. Can I pick you up something?"

"No thanks. I don't do lunch." She returned the receiver to her ear.

"Right." Well, I did lunch, dinner, breakfast, second breakfasts, the whole hobbit-inspired gamut. "Water then?"

"That would be amazing." She marked notes on paper and hung up the phone. "I checked the voice mail. Just repeats of email messages."

"Sometimes residents think the email might not make it, so they leave a voice mail as backup."

She crinkled her nose. "How do they know the voice mail gets here?"

"They trust what they know." I hoisted my bag over my head and secured it cross body. "Text me if you need anything. I shouldn't be long, and I won't be far." The walls around Horseshoe Falls guaranteed it. House calls were manageable on foot, but I preferred the golf cart mode of transport. It preserved my pedicure and designer heel addiction.

"Be back in a jiffy." I thrust the door open, ready to test my best time on two house calls and lunch. "Ah!"

Jake stood inches from my face. Alarm raced over his features before settling in quiet amusement. His hand moved to the gun at his hip before dropping nonchalantly at his side. "Afternoon, Mia."

Fifi hummed. "You should really get a window on that door."

I huffed to catch my breath. "What are you doing here?" *Why haven't you called since Friday?*

Why'd you make a stink face at me and flee?

What is wrong with you? I sidestepped him.

Unfortunately, he followed. "I thought you could use some help."

"With what?" I slowed to look him over. Jeans, boots, gray shirt, black duster. Gold star at his hip. "Missing the cyber-crime team? Need a little time at the keyboard?"

His lips parted slightly. If I didn't know him so well, I'd have expected a smile to follow.

"I spent some time online this weekend. It helped."

I headed for the door. "I knew it. Once a techie, always a techie." I swung the maintenance door open and I slipped into the sunshine.

Jake climbed onto the bench seat of the employee golf cart. "I played REIGN a few times. It looks like someone else is running your kingdom."

He played REIGN again? I hid the shock racing through my veins and revved up the cart. Apparently, I'd have company on my lunch ride. "I joined Nate's kingdom after the thing with Punisher last summer. Normally, I play at his place, but there's a Furry convention in town and Carl and the crew were in costume." I shivered. "I loathe Furries."

"You just handed your kingdom over to Faerie Fiend? She's arming the townspeople."

I hooked a right onto the main drag and headed for Sweet Retreat. Maybe I could eat before I made the stops. Who knew how long Jake planned to visit. Leaving him in the cart while I worked on a desktop seemed rude. Of course, climbing into my cart without asking was also rude, but that was to be expected of one of us.

"Faerie Fiend is a strong player," I hedged. I didn't like the thought of arming the peasants, but I'd needed someone to step up fast and take over the kingdom after my attack, and she'd been willing. "Wait a minute." I stopped at a crosswalk for a Segway and two women on horseback. "You haven't played REIGN in three months."

He lifted and dropped one shoulder by way of explanation.

"Why now?"

A green Prius rolled up behind me, and I pressed the gas. I waved at the Segway operator and horse riders as I pulled ahead. Horseshoe Falls had never been so beautiful. The trees were out in full autumn foliage. Fallen leaves in shades from crimson to amber dotted the roads, still damp from an overnight shower. The sun shone as if it hadn't gotten the message. Winter was coming.

Thanks to another day of blessed Indian summer, Dream Bean and Sweet Retreat were hopping. I snagged the last spot at the curb outside their doors and twisted on the seat for a better look at Jake. "Why now?"

"Why not?" His rounded shoulders and tight jawline indicated something was wrong. The stern set of his lips said he wasn't up for sharing, but he came to see me, so he should've expected a few questions. He ran the pad of his thumb absently over the shield on his belt. "It's a nice escape. Helps me think."

"Okay. Why so glum?"

"What?"

"You look a little pouty, like someone stole your pony. So, spill."

He guffawed. "I'm a grown man. I don't pout." His thumb brushed the marshal star again.

He'd called marshals the "ultimate lawmen" when he took the job. He'd made it sound like a life goal to wear that star. Seemed to me he should be ecstatic.

I hated to start a fire, but I'd taken a devout interest in studying human body language last summer, and Jake's body was screaming of tension and misery, exactly the opposite of what he should feel, having accomplished his life goal. "How's the new job going?"

He turned fiery eyes on me. "Fine."

I nodded, slow and steady. "Yeah?"

"Yeah."

"Or maybe it's not everything you made it out to be and you miss your FBI job? Maybe it's a little like that saying, never meet your heroes?"

He narrowed his hot gaze and worked his jaw side to side before climbing out with a huff.

I bounced to his side, obviously on the right track. "You miss the FBI? Marshalling isn't so great?"

He stared straight ahead. "'Marshalling' isn't a word, and I liked it fine until I lost my first witness then found him dead."

I mulled that over. "You know, I can relate to that. My sophomore year of undergrad, I landed a spot on Les Quizerables, the best academic team on campus. They were the smartest juniors and seniors in the state, and they weren't interested in adding a sophomore, but my record spoke for itself. I nailed the tryout and they reluctantly let me in, but our first debate was with Les Quizerables' biggest rivals, and I buzzed in on the tie-breaker with a wrong answer in overtime. I lost the game for us. I didn't hear the end of it for two years, until everyone on either team had graduated. It was humiliating. I got what I wanted, and I blew it. I didn't want to go back."

He turned his chin my way, without meeting my gaze. "But you did."

"Yep. I led Les Quizerables to nationals senior year. We lost eventually, but not without a hell of a fight, and I took two sophomores with us."

"Congratulations." He pulled the door open and followed me inside.

WE BROUGHT FIFI a fruited water back from lunch. Jake set it on her desk. "Hope you like apples and cinnamon. Bobbie Kubicka says it's great for cleansing toxins."

Fifi accepted the gift with enthusiasm.

I stuffed a big green straw between my lips and sucked down the iced vanilla latte to keep my mouth busy. Why was Jake still here? Had he come back to my office to visit with Fifi? "Don't you have investigating to do?"

"Actually, I got a call from Dan and came by to tell you about it."

I guffawed. "Well, what have you been waiting for?"

"He said several vendors over at the Craft Faire fingered you as a snooper. They said you were creeping around all weekend asking about John Francis and George Flick. Dan thinks you're interfering with a police investigation and I should bring you in. I assured him you were done with that. You have the situation with your company business to keep you busy."

My jaw dropped. Dan was supposed to be the nice brother. "That's ridiculous. I'm allowed to talk to other vendors. They're my friends." Kind of. I knew some of their names. "It's a free country."

"Nope."

"Nope? What does that mean? It's not a free country?"

"It means when your expression of freedom impedes an official police investigation, we win and you knock it the hell off. Plus, I've told you to get away from this thing before it runs you over."

"Fine."

"Promise me."

Was I twelve? "No."

Jake lumbered away from Fifi's desk and into my personal space. Hands on hips, frown on lips. "I'm serious as a snake bite, Mia. This isn't some jaded computer hacker." He gave a pointed look at our captivated audience. Apparently he didn't want to say much more. "What were you pestering folks about all weekend anyway?"

I lowered my voice and leaned closer. "I'm not okay with John's death, and his financial situation bugs me. He was a brilliant painter. I saw dozens of his pieces hauled out in shoppers' hands every day. All summer at the Ren Faire and again once the Craft Faire opened. How was Flick doing well if the painter was broke? It doesn't make sense. Then I heard they fought all the time about money, so I wanted to see what Flick had to say about it, except the gallery was closed all weekend. So, I asked around about him. Talked to vendors with neighboring booths and women I'd seen hanging around the gallery. I learned John did a lot of boudoir paintings, but not much about the partner."

Jake pressed his thumb and fingers against his eyes. "I'll take another look at the partner, but you have to stop. Dan's not joking about this. You can be charged with obstruction, or worse."

I swallowed long and hard on the last two words. "Fine, but if Flick's not there again today, I think you should check on him at home." I stepped closer until our shoes touched. My voice was barely a whisper. "In case he's like the apothecary, if you know what I mean."

Jake backed away. "Maybe, but I don't like him for this. He had too much to lose." He shifted his weight. "I'll check in on him if he doesn't show today. I will. You won't. Got it?"

"Got it."

"Did you hear anything else I can pass on to my team and Dan? Might win you some points with Dan if you at least gathered some useful intel in the process."

I slumped into my chair, exhausted from his close proximity and giant attitude. "No. That's all I've got. Well, that and a brain full of images I can't erase. I watched my sister prance around in fishnets and shake her behind for two days. The brothel's drama company is putting on a short cabaret this week. Clean Fun, Dirty Woman."

Jake's deep laugh startled me. His chest bobbed with the rhythm of the sound.

"I'm sorry. Are you laughing? I didn't think you did that."

He toned it down to a handsome smile. "Your sister's funny. My family would love her."

"Everyone does." I sighed.

"How's your company doing? I saw another clip on

the news with your booth in the background. It's coming together well."

"We'll weather the storm. I've got multiple balls rolling to maintain customer trust and encourage new sales. Grandma has her lawyers on standby. We'll be okay."

I shot Fifi a look, and she turned back to face her screen.

A voice in Jake's pocket repeated his brother's name. "Eric. Eric. Eric. Eric."

He freed a cell phone and swung it to his ear. "Yep." After a long pause, he shook his head and disconnected. He tapped the screen and cocked a hip. Lines raced over his forehead. "What in the world?"

I inched to his side, slow so he didn't startle, and peeked at the screen.

He turned the phone toward me.

Jake's younger brother, Eric, and his fiancée, Parker, stood side by side in blue jeans and white button-downs. He had a shotgun in his hand and the barrel crossed her middle. She had the tiniest pair of cowboy boots seated on her palm.

I clamped a hand over my mouth.

"Aww." Fifi looked over my shoulder. She patted Jake's back. "That's the sweetest thing I've ever seen. What a fun way to announce a pregnancy!"

Jake's eyes widened. "They aren't married." He turned to face me. "The wedding isn't until Christmas."

I pointed to the phone. "Shotgun wedding."

His expression waffled as he processed my words and the photo.

A grin the size of all outside spread across his usually somber face. "I'm going to be an uncle?"

Fifi clapped.

I nodded, feeling much the way I had when Bree announced her pregnancy with Gwen. "Looks like."

He shoved the phone in his pocket and smacked his palms together. "Should I get them a gift?"

"Go for it."

Jake swept through the office door.

Fifi and I ran into the hall behind him. "What are you going to get?"

"Fishin' pole." He disappeared through the club-house front door with a spring in his step.

Baby's first fishing pole. Well, at least it wasn't a shotgun.

NINETEEN

I ARRIVED AT the Faire Monday afternoon with my mind in splinters. Hard as I'd tried not to fixate on what really happened to John and whether or not his business partner had gotten away with murder, I couldn't help it.

I'd made every effort at distraction. My apartment was clean. My bookshelves were alphabetized, and my efforts at recouping lost trust in Guinevere's Golden Beauty products were paying off. Online sales were buoyed by a fresh promotional campaign I'd launched late Saturday night, when analytics showed our website traditionally had the most traffic.

Nonetheless, I wanted to talk to Flick. Where had he been all weekend, if not fleeing town with a guilty conscience? I'd find out the minute I could get inside and past Bree.

I still had that other thing on my mind, too. It wore a grim expression and a marshal badge.

I tugged my heavy wool cloak across my chest and ducked my head against the wind. Mondays were slow at the Craft Faire, so at least I didn't have to park in Timbuktu. Still, my boots and hem were heavy with mud by the time I reached the castle gates.

I flashed my most magnanimous smile and curtsied at the familiar guard as I passed.

Thousands of twinkle lights lined vendor signs and wrapped mammoth oak trees. Minstrel music and laughter danced in the cider-scented air. The effect was enchanting.

Bree danced around the wagons with Gwen on one hip. She twirled and cooed, clearly enjoying herself.

One look at my face would ruin that. "Hey."

Her smile fell. "Hey. How was work?" Apparently, it was a ton of pressure being the proper grown-up twin.

"Good. How's the cabaret coming?" I shoved my bag under the counter and made silly faces at a smiling Gwen.

Bree knitted her brows together. "The cabaret's harder than I expected. I'm not sure I'm doing the slow dips right. My feet get tangled, and I look like an oaf."

I blew a raspberry. "You were a dancer for like twenty years."

"Cheerleading doesn't count, so erase about half those years. Actually, I'm not sure any of my dance experience counts. None of it was anything like what we're doing. I feel like a moron up there."

I made a show of looking over each shoulder. "Am I being punked?"

"What? No." She handed Gwen to me and scowled. "I'm asking for your help. Not to be teased."

"I'm not teasing. Since when are you insecure?"

She rolled her eyes in true drama queen fashion. "Oh, yeah, right. I'm the totally confident perfect one, and you're the neurotic, uptight freak show. Is this opposite day?"

I settled against a big wooden wheel. What was happening? I'd never seen Bree lose her cool. That was my territory. She waited for a response. What could I say? I was a mess and she knew it.

I needed an escape hatch. I wanted off this ride. "No one says *opposite day*. Not since elementary school."

She flopped into a popup chair near the wassail and poured a cup. "I'm old and chubby."

Ah, fishing for compliments I understood. I'd seen this routine before. "Go on. Vent. It's my turn to listen."

"This costume is meant for a coed who hasn't carried, delivered and nursed a tubby little angel baby. The ruffles make my big ass look bigger and the corset barely makes a dent in this waist." She smacked her tummy. "If that's what you call the fresh roll around my belly button. I used to look like that." She motioned to me. "Why is this happening to me?"

I kissed Gwen and set her on her blanket with a line of well-chewed toys. "Bree. You're beautiful, and you know it. Your body looks different than mine now because it did a powerful, miraculous thing. You pushed an entire princess from your loins."

She chuckled.

"I'm serious. What have my loins done lately? Nothing. And look how huge your boobs are. The corset might not cinch your waist, but look what it does to your cleavage. I have to put tube socks in my bra to get that effect."

She ran a finger over the curve of her breast. "Tom seems to like them."

"They're nice. Everything about you is nice. You are a total MILF. Not to me because DNA but you know for other people."

"Thanks."

I filled a cup with wassail, enjoying the moment of sisterly peace. "Your feet get tangled on the dips because you need to cross your ankles before you turn. Then you can just swivel on your toes. You're making it harder than it is." I'd watched enough practice sessions this weekend to see the differences between Bree and the other dancers. That was one of the big ones.

I lifted the cup to my nose and inhaled the steam before taking a deep pull of the rich cinnamon drink. "Whoa!" I hacked. "Who spiked the wassail? I can breathe fire."

"Dad. Sorry. I forgot you don't drink."

Yeesh. It was Monday dinnertime, not Saturday night happy hour. I caught Bree's self-important stare. "Sometimes I drink." Wine sometimes. A little. "Not absinthe or whatever's in this. I like my inhibitions intact."

She cocked a brow. Swirled her cup and finished her drink. "Your turn. I didn't mean to tell you all that so now you have to tell me something."

Tit for tat. We never shared without proper repayment. This way no one had the upper hand. It kept us from tattling when we were younger. Leverage.

I sniffed the drink and set it aside. "Jake came to Pioneer Days Friday night."

Her smile widened. "Yes. I remember you inviting him. And? How'd it go?"

"It was nice. During the fireworks, he touched my cheek, looked at me like I had a booger in my nose, and snatched his hand away before it incinerated from my disgustingness."

"Oh." She nodded.

"Well, don't nod!"

She shook her head. "Sorry. Of course I shouldn't. Men are stupid. Not Tom, but the rest for sure. Don't give it another thought. He probably just remembered at that moment he'd forgotten to put on underwear that morning or something."

"Seriously. You get paid to study human sexuality

and that's what you've got for me? You nag me end-lessly to dish about my love life and this is what I get? He forgot his underpants?"

"Mia?" A small voice stopped my rant.

Bree jumped to her feet. "Hello!"

Parker, Jake's brother's fiancée, smiled sweetly at Bree. "Wow. That is one…small…costume." She looked at the older woman beside her. "It's nice. Isn't it, Mrs. A?"

Mrs. A? Mrs. Archer? I pulled in a quick breath and grabbed Gwen off her blanket. We'd met briefly at Parker and Eric's engagement party, but that felt like years ago instead of only a few months. I barely recognized her out of the context of their family farm. "Hi. Hello. Hi there." I scooted into the space beside Bree. "Hi." Why did I keep saying that?

Parker parted her lips and looked from Bree to me. "Um."

I pushed a hand in her direction. "It's so nice to see you again." I shook Parker's hand and then Mrs. Archer's. "Bree, this is Parker, Jake's brother's fiancée, and his mom. This is Bree, my older sister."

Bree shot me a sour look.

"This is Bree's little girl, my gorgeous niece, Gwen."

Gwen opened and shut one dimpled fist in greeting.

Parker's hand fell to her narrow waist, resting protectively over her abdomen. "Sorry. I only met you once. I guess I'd forgotten what you looked like."

"It's fine. We're twins. Bree's older."

Bree made an ugly face. "Stop saying that." She scooped Gwen from my arms.

Mrs. Archer looked relieved. "It's so nice to see you again, Mia. The boys didn't tell us you had a twin."

"Well, it's not something I'm terribly proud of."

Bree bumped me with her hip. "It's really nice to meet you both. Mia and I were just talking about Jake."

"No, we weren't." I shook my head and tried to be less uncomfortable. "We were talking about cheese." *Cheese?*

"So, what are you guys doing here?"

A smile touched the corners of Jake's mom's mouth. "Shopping. I love your lotion. Nothing soothes my tired fingers like Camelot's Chamomile Cream." She lifted her hand for my inspection.

"You use our lotion?"

"For years now. I had no idea it was a locally owned company. I received it as a gift about five years ago, and I reorder online as needed. It's brilliant. I bought a half dozen as gifts for friends." She swung the bag on her arm. "Imagine my surprise to learn all my kids know Guinevere."

I patted my huge gown. "It's our grandmother's company. We just help out."

Parker beamed. "I have to admit I'd hoped to run into you while we were here. This is probably weird to ask, but we do this thing every year right before Thanksgiving."

She handed me a card. "It's no big deal, just a tradition of ours, and honestly, we could use a few more women in the group. We call it Friendsgiving. We get together at Jake's and play cards, board games, video games, whatever. It's a night away from all the hoopla and holiday prep to be silly and relax and reconnect. Jake and Dan started it when they were in college and away with the military. It was as a way to see everyone in one night instead of making a bunch of little stops when they were home on leave or vacation."

She shrugged, nonchalantly, but the pep in her voice

worried me. Instinct said this was a much bigger deal than she wanted to let on. So why invite me? And why hold back on the enthusiasm? Social cues flew around me, missing the mark by miles.

Bree stole the card from my hands. "Cool. Why didn't we think of this, Mia? We need Friendsgiving."

I whipped the card from her grip and grabbed my phone. Thankfully, Grandma had yet to see me to confiscate it. "Let me put the address into my phone." I secretly texted Bree to knock it off. This was hard enough without her meddling. "There."

"So, you'll come?"

Was no way, José, an option?

"Maybe. As long as nothing comes up between now and then, I don't see why not."

My phone dinged. Bree responded to my text with a little devil face emoticon.

I shoved the phone into my pocket. "Okeydokey."

Bree bounced Gwen on her hip, regaining their attention. "Should Mia bring anything? A dish to share? Cookies? Maybe a guest?"

I scowled. Where was laser eye technology? Why weren't laser eyes a thing yet?

Parker tipped her head. "No. You don't need to bring anything. Friends are always welcome, though. The more the merrier."

I loosened my cloak. Surely someone else knew this was awkward. "Sounds fun." For someone who didn't mind a party or group settings where they knew no one.

Bree took over the conversation, and I went to my happy place where I pulled it together when things got weird. Why was Parker inviting me to Friendsgiving? Why was Mrs. Archer watching me? Why did my twin have to be dressed as a harlot?

A familiar face came into view through the dim evening light. George Flick sauntered along the path toward the art gallery. His dark attire and the black plume in his hat implied a state of mourning. Was it all for show, or could he have hurt John? His slow crawl toward their booth seemed morose and authentic, but maybe that was a result of regret for his actions.

"Mia?" Parker sounded nervous. "Are you okay?"

"Hmm?" I examined their faces. What did I miss?

"Do you feel all right?"

"Oh. Yes. Sorry. I need to check on something. Excuse me." I slid between the women, thankful for an escape and only mildly horrified by my less-than-graceful exit. "Thank you for the invitation," I called, waving the little envelope overhead as I hastened away.

Leaving Bree alone with two members of Jake's family was unfortunate but unavoidable. She loved to gab. There was no stopping her. If I'd stayed to moderate the conversation, I might've missed the chance to ask my main suspect where he'd been for the past two days.

I followed a trio of women into the small wooden building decked out in John's artwork.

Every square inch of space was adorned in art of every shape and size. Paintings hung in rows from the ceiling, on hooks and on walls. John must have painted around the clock to accomplish so much.

Near the back of the shop, George waved at an oil portrait on an easel. "This was his final work." He pressed a hairy knuckle to his eye and shook with emotion.

A group of women swooned and patted his arm. "We're so sorry."

Oh, brother.

"Hi." I scooted into the mix. "I'm Mia Connors. I

work the Guinevere's Golden Beauty booth with my family."

The man removed his knuckle from his eye and stroked his bushy beard. "I know you."

"Right. Good." I rubbed my palms together, wishing the women would go away. "Your partner was a friend of mine. I've learned he was poisoned, and I was hoping you might be able to help me find out who would do something like that to him."

"Are you suggesting I did it?" His booming retort brought the enormity of his size into pinpoint focus. He hadn't seemed dangerous before, curled in on himself and weeping. However, standing fully erect and looking like an angry Paul Bunyan changed things.

I took an eensy step back. "No. I thought since you worked directly with him, you might know who would want to hurt him. Did he seem troubled during his last few days?"

"I've already answered these questions when the actual police asked them. I don't have to talk to you." He glared down at me.

"No. You don't, but you're certainly worked up for a guy pretending to mourn. I thought you'd want to help him. I thought you might explain why you're doing well financially and John was broke, or maybe where you were all weekend?"

His face burned pink, then scarlet. He turned slowly toward the women. "Would you kindly excuse me for just a wee moment?"

He hustled me outside, jerking his head to the left. He released me as we moved alongside the gallery's exterior. I curled my fingers around a fresh can of pepper spray in my pocket.

Shrouded in shadows, the man collapsed against the

side of his shop, tears welling in his blue eyes. "I can't believe he's gone." He wrenched himself forward and braced both hands on his knees. "Who would hurt such a talented and tenderhearted man? It's senseless."

Not what I'd expected. "Well, that's what I'm trying to find out."

He sniffled. "He was my best friend, you know? We hit it off right away. We've been partners ever since, almost a year now. He was a master. He could've painted anything. Even the greats would be green with envy in his presence. He wasn't just a brush and beautiful face, either. He had heart." He grabbed handfuls of wild brown hair and pulled it, clearly stricken.

"Word around the fairgrounds is the two of you fought. Often. Is that true?"

He nodded. "I thought he should put his talent to work on greater things. Enter contests. Accept big commissions. Have a fancy show downtown where everyone could appreciate him. He refused. Half the time he was here, he stayed in the back or wandered the grounds. It was like he avoided me. It broke my heart."

"Mr. Flick, where have you been the past few days?"

He blinked tear-filled eyes. "Mourning."

I ran over his words. His tone. His behavior. I sank my teeth into my lip. "I might be off base here, and I'm sorry if I am, but I'm on a time limit. Were you in love with John?"

Fire raced over his features, morphing them through a bevy of emotions. He jerked upright, towering over me in the darkness.

I grabbed the mace again. My cold fingers fumbled, unable to uncap it before he lunged at me.

His long hairy arms wrapped tight around my shoulders and pulled me against him. He tipped his scruffy cheek against my head and whimpered.

I froze.

His chest bobbed against mine. "I never told him how I felt. He died without a clue." Ugly sobs broke over my hair. "I knew the minute I saw him at a museum, admiring a Dali. He was the perfect man."

Oh boy. I wiggled a travel pack of tissues from the pouch at my hip and lifted one to him. "Here."

He accepted, and I jumped out of reach. "I'm not a hugger." I needed an antibacterial shower and all new clothes, not to mention shampoo. "I'm going to go. Keep the tissues." I backed away slowly. "Have a nice night. Don't forget those women looking at that painting. I'm sure John cared about you too." Not like *that*, but maybe. Who knew?

TWENTY

I LOWERED MYSELF onto the floor beside Nate, careful not to spill my chips, and stretched my legs out in front of me. "I don't know. Mr. Flick seemed really broken up. Maybe Jake's right. That guy had too much to lose." I set the chips aside and hoisted my laptop onto my legs.

"Maybe." Nate shoved another slice of pizza between his lips. His red Flash T-shirt emphasized the vast mop of Ron Weasley hair hanging in his eyes. "I still think it was a crime of passion. Never underestimate a jilted lover."

"You say love. I say money." I logged into REIGN and grabbed my virtual weapons for a short quest into the Luminous Mountains. "I still think his death has something to do with money. He used to paint for a crime family. Even if I'm not convinced this was a hit, I can't ignore the whole federal witness bit. Maybe I was wrong before. Maybe that comes into play somehow." The mysterious pair who rented a car and followed Jake and me to Horseshoe Falls came to mind. Where were they now? Who were they, really?

"You don't agree with the love angle because you've never been in love."

I sucked on a diet soda and made plans to beat the snot out of a few opposing huntsmen until I figured out where to take my investigation next.

Nate's character appeared beside mine on my screen. What'd those huntsmen ever do to you?

I stunned him with my sword.

"Hey!" His character drank a health potion and kicked dirt my way. Nate peered over his screen but looked away when I met his gaze.

I scooted on my backside, turning my screen away from him. My jeans slid easily across the cool wooden floor until my shoulders rested on the leather couch I'd bought for my new place. The old couch had been covered in memories I didn't want.

Nate's bright green eyes inched up to meet mine. This time I was waiting for him, but once again he turned them back to his screen.

"What?" I shoved my laptop onto the floor and folded my legs. "I see you staring. Are we flirting now or do you have something you want to say?"

"You think that was flirting? No wonder you don't date."

I tossed a chip at him. "Shut up. What do you want? Say it."

"No. Another time." He raised his knees to balance his laptop in front of his face. "It's nothing. Unimportant. No biggie."

The next chip I threw bounced off the back of his screen. "Say it. Don't keep looking at me with that face and not talking. There's obviously something on your mind. You've been quiet all night, and quiet isn't in your repertoire. If you won't tell me what's on your mind, then at least tell me you have advice on who I should question next about the murder."

He lowered his laptop. "I need business advice."

"Oh, geez." I rolled onto the floor, and faced the ceiling. "You don't want my advice. My company's in peril."

He set his computer aside and leaned toward me.

"You'll turn it around. You're great at business, Mia. Come on."

"Blah." A certain company called Earth Hugger didn't seem to share his faith. It was now Tuesday night and Petal still hadn't returned my calls.

"What if I told you I spent all my savings and I'm kind of excited about it?"

I snapped upright, careful not to topple my computer. "You did not." My chest tightened at the thought. "People don't get pensions anymore, Nate. What were you thinking? That was your nest egg. You needed to invest that money. How many times have I told you? Your life expectancy is almost one hundred. Do you have any idea the cost of medical care? Old people need lots of medical care, and you'll need it for decades after retirement. Assuming you ever get to retire, since you just made a colossally stupid money choice." I grabbed my drink and sucked it down. "I think I'm having an attack."

"Knock it off." He threw my chip missiles back. "I don't need money management or investment advice."

"I think you do."

"I need business advice."

"Don't start a business. Eighty percent of new businesses fail."

His jaw went rigid. "If you don't listen to me soon, I'm going to come over there and hold your mouth shut."

"Hey!"

He narrowed his eyes. All signs of his normally jovial disposition were gone. Only the stern-faced boxer who regularly scared the bejesus out of beefy men in silk shorts and robes remained.

I let out a long breath and nodded.

"Thank you." He brushed himself off and stood to pace along my wall of windows. "I bought REIGN."

What?

"Baxter and I talked about game creation for years. You know that. You were part of most of it. Last fall we started a bible of details and ideas. What worked and what didn't. Improvements on existing favorites. Reasons other games sucked. We spent entire weekends on it sometimes. I thought we'd hire a designer one day and start our own online role-playing game, but then Baxter died and I let it all go." He spun to face me, features alight, the expression I loved. "Then, something amazing happened."

I lifted my eyebrows as high as possible without breaking my promise of silence.

"REIGN went up for sale. All the rights, everything. I couldn't pass it up."

I raised a hand, no longer able to be still. Adrenaline burned through me like I'd just won a trip to space. On *Serenity*. With Mal.

"Yes?"

"You own this game?" I turned a nervous finger toward my open screen. Excitement pounded in my chest. "It's yours?"

"Mmm-hmm."

A little squeal escaped as I leaped to my feet. "And you can do anything you want to it? Add levels? Secret missions? Easter eggs? Character development? Expand the map and membership packages?" My business mind kicked into high gear. My gamer mind went berserk. "We can advertise to colleges, other online role players, Comic Con!"

Nate pinched his lips into a knot and rocked on his heels. "Yep."

I stomped my feet.

"I did good?"

"You own REIGN."

"Yeah, but I spent, like, all my savings."

The numbers scrolled in my mind. He'd bankroll this investment for decades. I could help. I had connections. Marketing. Investors. "You'll get it back."

"I spent all my savings," he repeated.

"It's okay. This was a fantastic investment." I paced beside him. Adrenaline zipped through my veins. "We should stop playing for the night and start making a proper business plan. There's so much to talk about, I might get an aneurism."

"Well, don't do that. Did I tell you I completely closed out my savings?"

I nodded, ready to reassure him with numbers. "Let me call my accountant."

"Mia." His giant mitt landed on my arm. "I was thinking I could use a partner to take Baxter's place."

I froze. "Me?"

"It was a lot of money. Even half is a lot. Too much to ask, I know, but…"

I jumped on him.

He caught me in his long arms and spun me around. "Is that a yes?"

"Yes!"

"Thank goodness. I spent all my savings." He finally looked appropriately concerned.

I laughed. A wild, cartoon-villain laugh. "I'll transfer half the amount back into your account in the morning."

"Thank God." He set me on my feet. "I thought I was going to throw up when I signed the check over."

"We're going to be rich, rich nerds!" I slapped him

a high five. "This is exhilarating. I own REIGN." I wandered to the kitchen and opened the freezer. "We need ice cream."

"You own half." Nate climbed onto a stool at the island. "Make mine a double. Do you have chocolate syrup?"

"Pft." I shook my head and lined toppings on the island. "Amateur."

"Nice. Hey, the other thing you asked, about the murder, I've got nothing. I counted on Flick to give you a new lead, and I think you should let it go. Focus on your business. Businesses." He smiled.

"Maybe I will. All I got from Flick was a shower in his tears." I shivered at the memory. "If I wasn't ready to stop, though…" I made wide pleading eyes at him.

He tapped his toe on my marble kitchen floor. "Flick exhausted our known sources close to John. You could try another avenue. Who can identify belladonna? Someone had to know what it was, what it could do and where to find it."

I filled two mugs with Moose Tracks and poured chocolate syrup on top of one. "I don't know. The apothecary could have, based on the pile of books in her kitchen. Didn't do her a ton of good, though. There's an argument to be made for internet access. Anyone can learn and acquire anything now."

"Could John and the apothecary have been a murder-suicide?"

"Maybe." I slid a mug across the island to him. "She died on a different day. I'm no expert on murder-suicide, but it seems like she'd have gone out right after him. Right?"

He spooned a heap of ice cream into his mouth. "I

can't even imagine what someone like that is thinking. I've got nothing."

"I feel like I'm missing something obvious, but I can't get my finger on it. There's more I can do. I just can't think of what it is."

"Could she have been researching his death? Could she have known he was poisoned and had time to get books on the subject?"

"Maybe, but then why'd she die the same way?"

"Testing the theory?"

I poked my dessert, losing my appetite and enthusiasm simultaneously.

Nate set his empty mug in my sink. "What do the Archers think of your continued pursuit in this matter?"

"Dan wants me arrested for obstruction and Jake threatens me daily."

Nate smirked but didn't comment.

"Their mom and Parker, Eric Archer's fiancée, came to the Faire tonight."

He slid back onto his stool with a cat-that-ate-the-canary look. "Shopping?"

"Yea, but Parker gave me something." I ran to my cloak and bag in the foyer and grabbed the invitation. "This."

Nate flipped the envelope open and wrested the invite free. "Friendsgiving."

"She asked me to go."

"And you said?"

My laptop began a familiar tune. Someone was attempting to video chat with me.

I exchanged confused looks with Nate. "I told her I'd try to make it. Assuming nothing came up."

He jogged into the living room and returned with my computer. "Oh, really? Friendsgiving is tomorrow, and you're a liar. We're not done with this conversation. Answer this. It's making me crazy." He set my laptop on the island.

I pressed the Accept button and Fifi's face appeared.

She waved. "Hi, Mia!" Her gaze traveled to Nate at my side. "Hi. I'm Fifi, Mia's new assistant. You must be the boyfriend."

Everyone made assumptions.

Nate slung an arm around my shoulder. "Business partner, actually. Are you a gamer?"

I suppressed a laugh. She looked like a Victoria's Secret model. I hardly saw reason to suspect…

"Absolutely!" Her face filled the screen as she leaned into the camera. "I prefer online role play to system games, except Zelda because duh Zelda, but for sure."

"Wh-what?" I stammered.

She frowned. "Did I interrupt anything? I hope it's okay I called."

I lifted a hand to slow the conversation and pace my thoughts. "Why did you call?"

"Oh, because I finished cleaning up all the community files on the network, made some flyers for events I saw coming up on the calendar, and ordered business cards. I wanted to ask if you needed anything before I went home."

"Home? You mean you're still at the clubhouse? Who's locking up when you leave if you're there alone?"

"Um. I don't know. I thought the door would lock behind me."

"Why are you there?" Panic seized my chest. Baxter had gone to the clubhouse after hours and got murdered. I hadn't stayed late intentionally in months. "You need to leave. No, wait. I'm coming to you. Don't go anywhere." I shut the laptop and grabbed my coat.

Nate followed me onto the elevator. "Did you grab your work keys or your car keys?"

I shook them between us. "Work."

"She seemed nice. You were a little rude."

"Sorry."

The doors parted at the ground floor, and I hit the pavement at a clip, moving across the darkened street toward the trail around the falls to the clubhouse. The moon loomed low in the sky. Lightning bugs and whippoorwills had stilled for the winter. Silence hung heavy over Horseshoe Falls. I hastened across the empty lot to the front door and screamed when a silhouette emerged.

"Hey." Fifi opened the door for us. "I didn't mean to upset you. I didn't know the door wouldn't lock automatically."

Nate rubbed my back. "It's not you. We lost a friend recently and the effects are still fresh. Forgive us?"

Was he flirting?

She blushed and tossed platinum hair over one shoulder.

Yeesh. "Come on. Let's get your things." I led the parade down the hallway to our office. "I'll get you a key and passcode for the alarm in the morning."

She lifted a coat and bag from her desk, eyes wide. "Does this mean I can stay? You aren't firing me?"

Grief and regret pooled in my tummy. "No. How can I fire a hardworking gamer?" Maybe I needed to stop looking back and start looking forward. Maybe it would be nice to have a girlfriend to work with.

Nate smiled. The future was shaping up, thanks to his secret purchase and surprise offer. Good things still happened.

"Excellent!" Fifi pulled me into a hug and bounced. "You won't regret it, I swear. I get a little flighty sometimes, but it's because I'm so creative, not because I'm not paying attention. I hear everything, and I'm a quick study. I have dual degrees in botany and ecology, and I'm a Juris Doctorate. I'm amazing at research and organization."

I glanced at Nate and stepped out of her embrace. "You're a lawyer?"

"Oh, no. No. I never took the bar. I don't practice or anything. I just thought it'd be fun earning the degree, and it was."

Nate whistled. "Brains and beauty. You must owe your firstborn and all your plasma with those kinds of student loans on a temp's salary."

She smiled. "Not at all. My family's loaded. I'm kind of the black sheep."

The smile on my face grew so large it hurt a little. "You're the black sheep in your family?" *Me too.*

"Oh boy." Nate waved us back through the door. "Come on. Let's all go be besties at Mia's place. She has the best games and ice cream. She and I just bought an online role-play game, REIGN. Have you heard of it?"

"No. Is it good?"

"It's fantastic, and it's going to get better."

She looped her arm in his. "Do you live here, too?"

"No. I live downtown in the old bank building. My place is crawling with Furries this week, so we're hanging here."

"I love Furries." Fifi knocked into Nate, who passed the favor on to me.

Well, no one was perfect.

We boarded the elevator to my apartment in awkward silence.

Fifi was quiet for a long beat. "So, if Nate's not your boyfriend, who are you dating?"

"I don't date." I slid onto my floor at the next stop and opened the door for my guests.

"What about the marshal? He's cute."

Nate palmed his forehead and pressed my front door shut behind him once we'd all entered. "What about Friendsgiving?"

"What?" Fifi laughed.

I handed her the card and crossed my arms.

She read the card silently but moved her lips. "You don't want to go?"

"She wants to go," Nate answered.

I grabbed the invite. "I haven't decided."

Nate gave me a knowing look. "The invitation says you can bring a friend. We can come if you're supposed to go."

We? They met five minutes ago and they were *we* now?

Fifi nodded slowly. She dug in her bag and retrieved a Magic 8 Ball. "First, let's ask the ball." She closed her eyes and rolled the ball in her hand. She smiled at the little window and turned it to me. "What do you think we should wear?"

Nate turned her hand for a look at the answer.

"What does it say?"

He grinned at the ball. "Absolutely."

Absolutely.

Fifi handed me the ball. "Ab-so-freaking-lutely."

TWENTY-ONE

WEDNESDAY WAS BEAUTIFUL but chilly. One of those days photographers of the rural Midwest capture for postcards and tourism. The morning frost had burned off slowly, leaving tiny crystal blankets over the earth until lunchtime. I'd arranged a half-day at the office to cover Bree's dress rehearsal and hustled over to the fairgrounds. When I arrived, the brilliant costumes I loved were mostly concealed by cloaks and various other outerwear.

I headed for the wagons to let my folks and Grandma know where they could find me, and stopped several yards short.

The rebuilt Guinevere's Golden Beauty booth was finished early, and it looked amazing. The canopy roof was covered in thatch and lined in twinkle lights. Four intricately carved posts rose from the ground at each corner and stretched into the air. Majestic sapphire and emerald flags stood atop each pole, undulating in the breeze. It was impossible not to stare at the master-piece. Even the wood shone with fresh stain and oil. I owed those contractors a bonus. Most vendors wouldn't have been back this season after the damage Melanie's tantrum had delivered upon us. This crew had pulled it together in under a week. I loved them.

Grandma hugged me and kissed both my cheeks. "You did great! People are stopping left and right to ask about the new booth."

Mom sauntered to my side. "I agree. Fabulous work, Mia. Now, get over to the stage before Bree comes looking for you. She's called me twice."

Grandma frowned and opened her palm to my mom.

Mom cursed and handed over her cell.

I nearly skipped to the stage, still in possession of my phone.

The cabaret moves were simple, and Bree wasn't tripping on her feet anymore during the dips. Gwen and I danced in the empty front row, shaking our money makers as needed to coax a fresh giggle lose from her chubby cheeks.

I used Gwen as a puppet to mime Bree's moves. She and I knew the routine as well as anyone onstage, better than a few, but we didn't like to brag.

A handsome figure in jeans and a brown leather coat caught my attention as I spun. Jake rounded the stage, examining the general setup and taking a hungry look at the wide buffet awaiting the dancers.

I waved Gwen's dimpled arm and lifted her to block my face. "Hey! Over here, Marshal!"

"Hello, Little Miss." He took the empty seat beside me and hoisted Gwen onto his lap.

I smiled. "What are you doing here?"

"Your grandma said I could find you here."

"Oh, did she?"

"Yep. She said I should sit close and make Adam jealous so he'll try harder because you're a touch obstinate."

"Grandma wouldn't say that."

He tugged Gwen's bonnet over her ears and gathered her white wool jacket around her bulging tummy. "The last part might have been me. It's nice to see Gwen, but what happened to Lionel the manny?"

"Linus. He has the stomach flu, and they admitted him to the hospital for dehydration."

"Yuck."

Onstage, Adam called a wrap, and the dancers lined up to praise him, jogging in place to stay warm in their too-tiny costumes. Fishnet hose, corsets and ruffled underpants did not make an outfit. I had lingerie bigger than that.

Well, not lingerie as much as cotton pajamas, but I still wore those indoors.

Jake arranged Gwen over one knee and bounced her while clicking his tongue in an easy rhythm. "So, Adam, huh?"

"Shut up."

"He keeps looking over here. You aren't even smiling. You'll never get a date like that."

"You're lucky you're holding a baby."

Jake passed Gwen to me and stood. "I'll run a background check on him. Does Bree get special treatment for being your sister?"

Adam handed Bree a basket with wine and roses. He caught me staring, and I mentally kicked myself.

I angled away, pointing my back in Adam's direction. "No. I think he likes Bree and I'm an obvious substitute for the married twin. The whole thing is very unfortunate and weird."

"Bree, huh? I thought they said he's supposed to be smart?"

My chin dropped "Oh, I'm sorry. Was that a compliment?"

Jake walked away, crossing the space to the stage. He shook Tom's and Adam's hands.

"Did you hear that?" I asked Gwen. "That was definitely a compliment." No one preferred me over Bree.

Ever. Except Nate, but he was biased and Bree was already married when they met.

Gwen slapped my cheek with a spit-soaked hand. "No."

She was right. I was overthinking.

Jake returned to my side, a crooked smirk wound across his face. "I can't get over the resemblance. It's like talking to a pod person."

"Thank you."

He ran his gaze over Bree in her tiny outfit, then me in ten pounds of heavy woolen skirts. "She looks like you and sounds like you, but nothing she says is remotely you."

"Pretty much how twins work. Two separate people."

"Ever think of joining the cabaret? Adam said he could use another dancer. He also asked who I was and if we were dating. I sensed jealousy."

I ignored his nonsense. "I will never get on a stage and do burlesque, or get on a stage, period."

"Ah, but to clarify, you're not opposed to a private showing?"

I laughed and bumped him with one hip.

"Never say never." The hint of a blush darkened his cheeks.

I ran my mind over scenarios where I could potentially end up dancing burlesque. "No. I'm pretty certain *never* is accurate. I don't do stages." Private dancing was also out, but in case we were flirting, I decided to leave the possibility out there. I'd read men were eager voyeurs.

Tom and Bree shook Adam's hand and headed our way.

I smiled widely when they were in earshot. "Nice

job today. The dancing was great and the lighting and props were perfect, too."

Tom bowed dramatically. "I stayed up all night painting set pieces."

"Of course." I scrutinized the basket hanging in the crook of Bree's arm. "What's with the gift?"

She beamed. "Adam says we're the most dedicated couple he's ever worked with and he couldn't pull this off without us."

Tom chuckled. "Schmoozing the family is also good practice when courting a reluctant damsel."

Jake shot me an appropriate look of fear and stepped away.

No one called me a *damsel* without a pinch.

"Ow!" Tom jumped.

Bree scowled. "Mia! How old are you?"

"Too old to be called a damsel."

"Touché." Tom rubbed his arm and moved on to Jake. "Bree tells me tonight's Friendsgiving. That sounds like fun."

I blanched, shoving my hands into cloak pockets before I pinched Bree for blabbing. I'd hoped I was off the hook when Jake didn't mention it right away.

I'd never been so torn in my life. I wanted to go, but I didn't want to actually go. Parties stressed me out. Strangers did, too. Acting normal in front of Jake's family and friends seemed flat out impossible. Which was why I'd asked Nate and Fifi to come along. They could be my safety blanket. My distraction. My shut-it-down crew when my babbling veered into ugly territory.

Jake shifted his weight. "It's not bad. Parker sent me to offer Mia a ride."

I forced my gaze away from Bree's judgmental stare. "Nate and Fifi said I can ride with them." I tacked on

"Parker told me to bring a friend" by way of explanation for my added guests.

Jake inclined his head slightly. "Are they a thing now? What happened to Kenna from Surly Wench?"

"She's a little young for Nate. I don't think they have much to talk about."

"Tough to find brains and beauty," Jake mused.

"You're not kidding."

Tom wound an arm around Bree's middle. "They can't all be Connors women." He wobbled suddenly and his smile faltered. "Wow. I'm not feeling very well."

Bree wiggled free and collected Gwen from his hands. "Well, don't breathe on Gwen. You've probably caught whatever Linus has. The last thing we need is a sick baby the night before our show. Matter of fact, let's go home and get you in bed." She looked my way. "It was only a matter of time before one of us became contaminated." She pushed his shoulder, directing him toward the exit. "If it wasn't Linus, maybe it was something you ate. You inhaled half the buffet table while I was dancing. Two trips. Don't think I didn't notice. This is why we don't do complex carbohydrates."

I bit my tongue.

Bree's little family swept away with signature dramatic flair. She swung her behind gregariously out of sight.

Jake dusted his palms. "Give your friends a call. We can meet them at your place and they can follow us to mine. My family's already there setting up."

I shot Nate a quick text and got pizza and cow emoticons in response. "They're eating pizza. They'll be busy a while."

"No problem. My family likes to drink, play cards and make stuff up. They'll be there until dawn."

We walked in amicable silence as far as the castle gates before curiosity got the best of me. "Is it okay I invited Nate and Fifi?"

"Sure. The more the merrier."

"That's what Parker said. Are you sure it's not weird?"

"Why would it be?"

I stopped to get a bead on his facial expression and body language, but this was Jake and my mission was impossible.

"Hey!" A boy in a dragon mask darted into view, waving a rolled piece of paper in front of me. "Are you the girl from the stage? Are you the one who was dancing?"

Jake laughed.

I sighed. "Close enough, I guess. Why?"

He pressed the scroll against my hand and ran away, legs pumping.

Jake snatched my gift and unrolled it with hasty fingers. "What the hell?"

"What?" I grabbed it back.

Jake didn't answer. He flew after the kid, while I stared stupidly at his vanishing back. I fumbled with the scroll, which wasn't paper after all, but some kind of weird substance, like a leaf. Black ink lined the curved sides. Adrenaline thrummed through my veins as I read the words.

End this quest or your Wee one is next to sample my work. Below the words was a red 3.

My wee one? Fresh memories of dancing with Gwen came to mind. The kid asked if I was the one from the stage. A fiery mix of fear and disgust throttled me, striking panicked feet into motion. I flew across the dusty path at full speed, blindly racing in the direction

Jake had run. *What kind of animal threatens a baby?*
Tom's pale face flashed into mind. Someone had poisoned my sister's husband. Maybe Linus, too. Was that
possible? Bree had scolded Tom for making two trips to
the buffet. Who had access to the buffet? Anyone. My
tummy filled slowly with ice as I skipped over fallen
foods on sticks and twigs carrying crimson leaves.

I pressed my phone against my ear before I had the
sense to make a plan.

"Bree?" I squeaked.

"What's the matter?" Her tone slid from a cheery
hello to big-sister mode in the space of a heartbeat.
"Mia? Are you okay? Are you hurt? What's the matter?"

"I'm fine."

Jake's silhouette appeared in the distance, shaking
someone by his shoulders.

I found my voice and forced it through clenched
teeth. "I think Tom was poisoned. You need to go to
the emergency room. Don't go home first. Get him
checked out."

"What?" Shuffling and thunking noises burst
through the receiver. "Wait! I dropped the phone. Turn
here!" She barked orders at Tom. "Just do it. Mia said
so. Pull over. I'll drive. Mia? We're headed to the hospital. Start the phone tree. Wait. Tell me what happened.
Then start the phone tree."

"I got a threat on a leaf." I skidded to a stop beside
Jake, now on his phone. The kid was pressed against
a raked fence. "Bree? Did you eat anything from the
buffet tonight? I think something there was poisoned.
Maybe the berries. Did you feed anything to Gwen?"

Tires squealed through the phone line. "No!" Bree

swore like Dad at a football game. "Start the effing phone tree!" She disconnected.

Jake stuffed his phone into his pocket and jerked the kid away from the wall. "Tell her what you told me."

The kid's wide blue eyes were glossy with fear, likely instilled by Jake before I'd arrived. His dragon mask lay in the dried mud at his feet. He shoved a long swath of jet-black hair from his eyes. "Some guy paid me five bucks to deliver the note. He said it was for the girl on the stage. I thought it was a love note or something."

"Who?" I asked, stuffing fingers into my cloak pockets so I didn't grab him and shake the answers loose or pepper spray them out of him.

"A guy in costume. I don't know."

"What kind of costume?"

Jake palmed his shoulder. "Tell her."

The kid swallowed long and hard. He was young. High school, maybe, and cocky. I hated cocky.

He snarled at Jake's hand on his shoulder. Apparently they'd had this conversation already. "Just some guy. I don't know who. He was old. I don't know how old, like thirty. He had a stupid puffy shirt on and brown pants like a dude from the past. Like him."

I followed his accusing finger to a line of men in exactly that ensemble eating giant turkey legs and drinking ale. A hundred other identically dressed men surrounded us, shopping, working, cleaning. Dudes dressed in outfits from the past were everywhere.

"Dammit!" I rubbed my eyes hard enough to dislodge my glasses.

"That's what I said. Sort of." Jake turned in a small circle, scanning the area. He addressed the kid again. "Do you see him now? Could you identify him in a lineup?"

I huffed. Was he planning to haul in a hundred men? Could he do that?

The kid pulled his shoulder free of Jake's clutch. "No, man. I don't know these people. I'm from Pennsylvania. I came with my mom as punishment for sneaking out to see my girlfriend. I've never been here before. I don't know anyone. What kind of loser do I look like?"

"Hey." I whacked him with the note. "Someone threatened my family with this leaf. Shape up and take it seriously, would you?"

"It's papyrus."

I turned the note over in my fingers. "What?"

"The leaf. It's papyrus. You know, a big-ass leaf from Egypt or something. Can I go now?"

Jake nodded and looked at me. "Yeah. He doesn't know anything."

The kid yanked his mask off the ground and pulled his hood over the back of his head before strutting away like the punk he was.

I tapped the note against my free palm. "When do we have to be at your place?"

"You don't have to come. You should probably be with your family."

I wrapped my arms around my middle to steady my shaking limbs. "I need to talk to the florist. Do you think it's really papyrus?"

"Maybe."

"I'll text Nate to take his time. I want to ask about the leaf, stop by the ER and change into jeans. I can ride with him and meet you later."

Jake moved steadily at my side, providing strength where mine was failing. "I'm the marshal. I was already planning to ask the florist about the leaf before that kid said it was papyrus. Why don't you go home and change? I'll come by later and let you know what I find out."

"No way!" I screeched. "Some insane person threatened my family. He threatened a baby!"

"Fine. You can come with me, but I'm following you to your place afterward and driving you to mine. Nate and Fifi can follow us."

"Fine." I tapped my phone screen and blinked back boiling emotion. "I have to start the phone tree." The phone tree consisted of my parents and Grandma, plus Bree and me. Tom was fair game if Bree was unreachable. Small but effective and used liberally.

We sidled into the florist shop like a normal browsing couple, minus my scowl and slight tremor.

I pretended to thumb through a book of bouquets, while watching the clerk for any signs of guilt. I raised onto my toes after a minute and whispered to Jake. "He's not acting like someone who just poisoned my brother-in-law."

He turned his lips to my ear, grazing my cheek and sending flames through my core. "Sociopaths never do. They don't have actual feelings. Just schemes."

My brain flailed with mismatched emotion.

He untwined our arms and moseyed through the shop.

I shook off the goose bumps and strolled up to the register. "Hi, Duff. Remember me? Mia. Do you recognize this leaf?"

The florist rubbed the leaf between his thumb and first finger. "Papyrus?"

"Yeah. Papyrus." I forced a droll expression. "Do you carry it here?"

"Nah. It's impractical and expensive. People come

here to order flowers. Pretty ones, not leaves. You can probably get it online. Try eBay."

"What will it cost me?" I waited for an exact figure or some other indication he was a sociopath and liar.

"I don't know, lady. What do you want from me?"

Jake met me at the counter. "It's true. I don't see anything like it here."

I made a peace sign with my fingers and pointed them at my eyes before turning them on Duff.

"Come on." Jake tugged me toward the door. He extracted the note from my white-knuckled grip. "Dan's at my place. We'll hand this off to him tonight."

I nodded stiffly, craning my neck to glare at the florist until he was out of sight. "Can we swing by the hospital?"

"I wouldn't have gone home without stopping. Your family needs an explanation."

Local security breezed past us, moving double time. Each man and woman had a freezer bag of food or a tray in hand.

"Is that from the buffet?"

"Yep." Jake tugged me along. "I called them while I chased the kid. They bagged everything for analysis. Someone's questioning the other dancers and stage hands. EMTs are responding for basic health checks. Everyone will get a non-specific spiel about potential food poisoning and advised to seek medical attention if they suspect they're getting ill after they leave here."

I released a shuddered breath. "A lot of people could be sick because of me."

"Doubt it. This guy's calculating. Your family was targeted." He squeezed my fingers. "My team's on their way. I need to speak with Dan. I'd rather do it at my place than the crime scene."

"Why not call him? Maybe you should stay. See what you can find out."

"Nope."

The moon loomed low, like my spirit, casting an eerie glow on the world. Unease washed over me. The killer could be anywhere. Anyone.

I inched closer to Jake as we made our way to my car. "What if they find a clue and you aren't here?"

He wiggled his cell phone. "Technology."

"Right."

"Let's get you changed. Visit your family and head to Friendsgiving. There's nothing to do here. My responsibility's with you and your family now."

I beeped Stella's doors open and hesitated. "Why aren't you more worried about Tom and Bree? They could...be like John."

"No. The note was a threat. Meant to scare. Nothing more. Besides, you're obviously the target, not them. Not yet. Whoever wrote the note wanted to rattle the weak link. They're a family with a baby. If there was a perfect person to scare, it was Bree. As a bonus, she has influence on you. The killer didn't want to end them, just motivate them to stop you."

I dropped onto the driver's seat and stuffed my key into the ignition. "Okay."

He braced his hands on my roof and leaned in on me. "What about you? Why aren't you more upset?"

"Me? Oh, I'm numb. I think I'm in shock. Ask again in an hour."

"Will do." He shut the door and walked away, presumably to his truck.

I swiped a hot tear sliding over one cheek. The shock was wearing off.

TWENTY-TWO

THE HOSPITAL WAS a nightmare. By the time we got there, Mom was hysterical. Dad had Dan in a corner, growling about his role in the situation, and Bree was in the bed beside Tom. Grandma played peek-a-boo with Gwen in the waiting room. Apparently, Bree got sick after arriving and the staff had admitted them both. Dan had called ahead and filled the doctors in, so they were treated to couples' stomach pumps and a regimen of fluids.

Results weren't in yet, but I could guess what they'd find in those stomach contents. Belladonna. Nightlock. Hemlock. Maybe even some other whacked-out medieval poison. Seeing her helpless did things to my heart. Bree wasn't helpless. She was fierce. I'd seen her battle through a fifteen-hour labor and natural childbirth, but someone had broken her. Someone who wanted to punish me.

I apologized every way I could imagine until she kicked me out, insisting I attend Friendsgiving and tell her about it in the morning. She would be fine. I wasn't sure I would be.

Dan assigned a detail to my family and promised to meet us at Jake's in a few hours.

I pressed the elevator button to my floor and rubbed the chill of stress from my arms. "You're positive she's fine? There aren't any slow-release poisons working their way through her blood right now? No chance something went unseen by the doctors? What if she's worse in the morning?" A wedge of pain clogged my throat.

Jake held the door while I stepped into my apartment foyer. "I heard her ask the doctor how much her stomach contents weighed. You're worried she might die. She's worried about her dress size."

I hung my cloak and zombied down the hall to my room. I pulled on my softest jeans, a fitted vintage blouse, appropriately in black, and stuffed my feet into penny loafers. A swipe of lip gloss and two doses of mascara later, I replaced my glasses and went to the kitchen with purpose.

Jake pivoted in front of my window wall as I passed. "You look nice. What are you doing?"

I whipped a fresh trash bag into the air and opened my refrigerator, dropping cartons of berries and packages of cheese into the receptacle. Condiments. Leftovers. Yogurt. Gone. I lined beverage cartons, bottles and containers along the sink, unlidded them and turned them upside down over the drain.

A warm hand landed between my shoulder blades. "Mia. Hey. Look at me."

I turned tear-blurred eyes on him. "He poisoned my sister."

Jake pried my fingers off an orange juice container and pulled me against his rock-solid chest. He stroked my hair and folded his free arm protectively across my back. I'd never imagined him as the comforting type. That was Nate's natural talent, but Jake's instinct to guard and protect was there in every fiber of his skin against mine.

An ugly sob built in my chest, ready to erupt. "He hurt them and threatened Gwen. It's my fault."

His hand froze. He gripped my biceps and pushed me off him in a swift, jostling move. "Hey."

I blinked the heavy tears loose and dared a moment of eye contact.

"This is not your fault. There's a monster out there hurting people, and that has nothing to do with you."

"I'm meddling." My lips quivered in betrayal.

His brows dove together. "My grandmother meddles. You think someone should kill her?"

A sudden laugh spouted from my lips. "No." I pressed a hand to my mouth, settling my rampant emotions.

"No?"

I shook my head. "No, but I also provoked him." Or her. Women could be psychotic, too.

"You provoke the daylights out of me. Maybe you have a point."

I shoved him and walked to the counter where I kept tissues. "Shut up."

His hands were back on my shoulders. "This is not your fault. I need you to trust that we will catch whoever is behind this. You've got two Archers, the local PD and a marshal unit on the case."

I ran a tissue under each eye and turned with a nod. "Okay."

"Now, can you do me a solid and let us handle the investigation for a few days?"

I returned to my trash bag and emptied my cupboards. "Yeah."

"Now what are you doing?"

"Same thing I was doing before. How would I know if someone poisoned my food? Security here isn't that good." I pulled a painful breath and imagined someone in the shadows of my closet or guest room. "The killer might have already been here. He might be here now."

A knock sounded on the door and I squeaked.

Jake's posture stiffened as he walked into the foyer, right hand on his sidearm. One look into the peephole and he dropped his arm. "It's your friends. How'd they get in the building?"

"I gave Nate the code."

My front door sucked open, and Jake greeted Nate with his usual booming enthusiasm. I released a long breath that had felt like the only thing keeping me upright.

Nate strode into the kitchen and leaned one broad shoulder against the doorway. His retro Space Invaders shirt peeked through an open jacket. "Whatchadoin'?"

I loaded the last of my plates, cups and bowls into the dishwasher and opened the silverware drawer. "Washing dishes."

"Weren't they clean when you put them away?"

I stopped to stare, a fist full of cutlery in each hand. "Who really knows?"

"Jake," Nate called, pushing off the counter. "What'd you do to her?"

Fifi bounced to my side. "Here, let me help." She opened cupboards until she found something to wash and turned hot water on at the sink.

Jake groaned into a fist. "She's taking precautions against poisoning."

I snapped the dishwasher shut and set it to annihilate mode, or pretended as much. Surely, no poison could survive my high-end bowl blaster.

"Okay. Let's go."

Fifi shut the water off and dried her hands. No questions asked. "I can finish this when we get back."

My heart swelled into my throat and tears pressed the backs of my eyes. "Thanks."

Now, for the truly scary portion of my evening.

JAKE'S HOUSE WAS lined in twinkle lights and pickup trucks. Country music poured from closed windows, and a pair of four-wheelers raced through the field like really loud ghosts in the night.

He parked in the loose gravel outside his garage and gave me a look. "I'm not responsible for anything you see or hear tonight."

"Got it." My turn to see his family at its best. I slid off the seat and into the gravel beside him.

Headlights bobbed along the pitted drive in our direction. Nate, no doubt, was doing his best to preserve his glossy white paint.

Time to meet the family again. My heart thundered and roared in my ears.

Nate stepped close to my side. "Nice place you've got here, Archer. How much land is this?"

"About ten acres. Our grandparents divided their estate and distributed the land to the grandkids at our high school graduation parties. I think the plan was for everyone to follow grandpa's love of farming, so he'd grow old in a rocking chair, looking over one hundred and forty acres of farms."

Jake's front door swung open, and Parker jumped onto the porch. "Jake!" She bounced into his arms and a twinge of emotion pinched my lungs. What must it feel like to be so comfortable with him?

Eric lumbered into view behind her, and the porch light flicked on. "Hey. Come inside. Pizza's getting cold."

At the word *pizza*, Nate was through the front door. Fifi followed.

I brought up the rear, with Jake's hand at the small of my back, impossible to ignore. He was quiet, even for him.

He stopped at the oversized porch swing and motioned me to have a seat. I gladly accepted. The swing groaned on an oversized spring and creaked under our weight.

Jake pushed off with his boot. "My family's big."

I bundled my coat tighter at my middle. "And?" My breath lifted into the air on a cloud of crystals.

He looked out at the land. His land. Trailing the four-wheelers with his eyes. "I thought you might need a minute to mentally prepare before going inside."

"Thanks."

"Those two knuckleheads turfing my field are Boston and Phoenix, siblings named after their places of conception. My aunt and uncle are the family hippies. Your folks would love them."

I mulled that over. "Probably."

The four-wheelers roared past the porch and disappeared into the side yard.

"Inside, I expect to find all my cousins. Their spouses or dates. My brothers and their ladies. Neighbors. Friends. People I grew up with and possibly a face or two I don't know. A few are probably gaming. Some are playing poker. Most are already swapping stories based partially on fact and heavily on alcohol."

I smiled, imagining the scene he described. "Do you mind having a full house like this?"

"Nope. I'm used to it. There's no privacy in Archer life. There are only endless lines of people who want to give you advice and casseroles, the homemade all-fat kind. They cook with lard and cow's milk from our family cattle. They use full-fledged cane sugar and no substitutes."

"Bree would die."

He nodded. "Yep."

"Okay. I'm ready."

He pulled his gaze to mine and lifted a brow. "You sure? They're going to have a lot of questions for you."

"I've got Nate. I'll be okay."

He pursed his lips before moving to the door.

I didn't attempt to guess what that was about.

Inside, a fire warmed the busy room. Circles and crowds of people filled every inch of space. He'd nailed every scenario, though he hadn't predicted the duo singing country karaoke by the fire. The house was small but inviting and made of logs. His furniture was nice, but worn, and a line of boots rode the carpet next to his door.

Fifi waved from the rug beside the fireplace. "Mia!"

I took a seat with her and absorbed the activity around us. Jake made his rounds, clapping shoulders and accepting hugs. There was easily a thirty-year age range from kids in high school letterman coats to others clearly old enough to be their parents. Maybe they were. Everyone nodded and welcomed me. No one asked questions. I had a feeling I could thank Parker for that.

After his hellos, Jake folded himself onto the rug with us. He settled a paper plate piled with pizza on one knee. "You doing okay?"

"Yep."

He dug in his jacket pocket and freed his phone. "Fifi, you studied plants, right?"

"Yes!" She took the phone. "I love plants." Her expression of peace and reverence at the sight of the thing morphed into something scary after she examined the little screen and took a minute to absorb the wretched words. "Oh my goodness."

Jake dotted his lips with a napkin. "What can you tell me about it?"

"It's a threat. The leaf looks like papyrus, but I can't be positive from a picture. The ink is probably stuff you buy at the store." She traced her pointer finger over the screen. "I bet this has something to do with what happened to Mia's sister. Nate didn't go into details, but this would explain a whole lot."

I nodded. "We know. I checked with the Faire florist and he said you can order it online. Do you know anything about that?"

She returned the phone to Jake. "You can get anything online. It's probably on eBay."

I made a mental note to shop eBay more often. Apparently, they had everything. "What do you think the three means?"

"I don't know, but it's weird, right?" Fifi mused. "The whole Faire theme is Renaissance times. No one used papyrus during that period, so why didn't the person sending this just use paper?"

Jake tipped a beer to his lips. "Dramatic effect? Maybe to make a point."

"What point?" Fifi and I said in unison.

Jake set the bottle aside and squinted at his buzzing phone. "Dan's here."

The door opened, and Dan swept inside. He headed for the fridge and helped himself to a beer before scanning the room for Jake. He distributed handshakes on his way to the fireplace. Shockingly, he folded himself beside me. "Your sister and brother-in-law were discharged. They're both fine. I put a detail on your family and debriefed the lot of them. Everyone's staying with your grandma until this blows over. Those big old walls over at Horseshoe Falls will come in handy."

Unless the killer knows about the path through the woods. I pushed the thought aside. What were the odds of two killers knowing that little tidbit?

Fifi repositioned herself closer to Dan. "What happens next?"

"We're retracing our original leads tomorrow. See if we missed something."

I stiffened. "No new leads?"

"I'm afraid not."

"Ever find the goons who rented the car?"

"Nope."

The door sprang open and two women covered in mud strode inside. They kicked off their boots and shucked their jackets before sliding out of camo print coveralls.

The taller one smiled at Dan. "They're all yours." She chucked a key, and he caught it in midair.

The other girl did the same, throwing her key to Jake. He spun the key on his finger and leaned my way. "Boston and Phoenix."

"Gotcha."

Dan stood slowly and arched his back. "Not me. I'm beat. Eric? You and Parker want to go muddin'?"

"Hell, yeah!" Eric folded his cards and vacated his seat at an ongoing poker game to collect the keys.

Jake grabbed my hand and shoved onto his feet. "Come on. I've got coveralls from junior high that might fit you."

I stumbled across the room, seeking Nate for a speedy escape. He smiled and waved, cheerfully sliding onto the seat Eric had abandoned.

What the heck were we doing? Going mudding? What was that about? I didn't know, and I didn't want to find out. I liked it by the fireplace. "I don't know how to mud."

Jake laughed and shoved me into a bedroom. He slid the closet door open and tossed black coveralls my way. "Pull them on over your clothes and I'll find you a hunting jacket."

"We're going hunting?" I squeaked.

He left without answering and dragged the door shut behind him.

This was why I avoided parties.

PARKER GAVE ME the rundown as we walked onto the front porch dressed for combat.

Jake and Eric climbed aboard the two mud-soaked four-wheelers and waved us over.

Jake scooted forward and smiled. "Climb on."

"I'm not sure I can do this."

His normally stormy eyes twinkled. This was his turf. His land. His good time. "Swing your leg over and have a seat. It's like riding a horse."

I shook my head. "Uh, not at all."

He barked a laugh. "Correct. Now, hurry up so we can chase them."

Eric and Parker raced through the dark field beside Jake's house, watched by a sky full of stars.

I sucked it up and lowered my body behind Jake's. There was nowhere to hold on. "Um." I placed my palms gingerly against the sides of his coat.

In a lightning-quick move, Jake grabbed my hands and pulled them tight around his middle, bringing my body flush against his. "Hold on." He released me in favor of the handlebars and revved the engine.

Every muscle in my body tensed. I squeezed his hips with my thighs.

The machine jumped into gear and we tore through the night. Brisk autumn wind whipped against my face.

"Ahh!" I screamed and laughed and bounced over things I couldn't see in the dark, secure and fearless in Jake's care.

When we got back to Jake's, my beanie hat was soaked in mud, along with the rest of me. The tension, however, had dissipated. The wild ride had shaken my inhibitions loose. Who needed alcohol when there was ten acres of farmland to destroy?

Mudding was my new favorite.

IT WAS AFTER one when Jake pulled into the lot outside my building. The night was different in my world. Peppered with traffic sounds and generally well lit. Nothing like the place we'd left behind.

I walked slowly to my building, stretching each leg as I moved. "I don't think I'll be able to walk straight tomorrow."

Jake snorted. "I'm going to leave that statement alone."

I unlocked the door and waited, but Jake didn't budge. "Do you want to come up?"

He looked at his feet, the sky and then me. "Nah. I'll catch up with you tomorrow."

Disappointment and rejection blazed stupidly through me. "Okay. If you're sure."

"Unless you want me to. I mean, I can if you need me to check the rooms for you."

"No. I'm fine." I slipped inside the building with my shoulders, back and chin up. "Talk to you later."

I rounded the corner to the elevator and bounced

the heel of my hand off my forehead. The drive to my place from his took an hour. He'd driven me all the way home just to leave.

My phone buzzed with a text from Jake as I stepped out of the elevator on my floor. Text me after you look in all the rooms. I won't leave until I get the all clear.

I ran through the rooms, peeping behind curtains and under furniture. All Clear.

No. No one waited in my apartment.

No one waited for me anywhere.

TWENTY-THREE

NATE ARRIVED AT my office an hour before I finished work. He greeted me with a wink and coffee. "Don't mind me. I've got plenty to keep me busy." He produced a smart water from his bag and set it on Fifi's desk. Small pieces of fruit floated inside.

She smiled.

He set up his laptop on the printer table and stuffed earbuds into his ears before I could object.

My mind wandered ruthlessly over a list of possible culprits and ways to inflict extensive pain on the one who hurt my sister.

"Come on." Nate slapped my desk. "You're daydreaming. You haven't touched your keyboard in ten minutes, and it's five. Let's go. The sooner you get to the Faire and see Bree gleefully shaking her bottom onstage, the sooner you'll believe things are better than you think."

He was right. I wanted to see Bree. Let her sass me. Complain about my life. Whatever she wanted. "Fine."

We walked Fifi to her car before heading to my place.

I unlocked my apartment door and held it with my hip for Nate to pass. "Did you drive all the way to Horseshoe Falls so I didn't have to walk home alone after work?"

He pulled a face. "No."

"Ah, then this visit was planned. You're coming tonight to watch Bree perform."

"No again. That's an image I don't want in my head. I have an appointment with a financial planner tonight. Spending all that money on REIGN has given me nightmares. What if this venture fails and I end up with no savings, living in one of those old age homes for people without money? Do you know what happens to those people?"

I let my head fall forward in bad friend shame. "Life keeps distracting me. I'm good for half. I promise. I'm so sorry I haven't gotten it to you yet."

"Don't worry about it. I need to get my finances in order anyway. I've been putting this off for over a year, and I finally have sufficient motivation. Do you know I've been out of grad school for six years? My student loans are paid off, and the money's accumulating. Banks only offer a half percent interest on savings accounts. It's insane. There must be a better way to save." He peered into the empty fruit bowl on my island and frowned. "My stock portfolio isn't bad, but it could use a professional eye."

I opened the freezer and tossed him a bag of frozen pizza rolls. "Make sure the planner doesn't screw you. That happens way too often. Nuke those if you're hungry. I don't think the bag's been tampered with, but eat here at your own risk. Don't make any for me." I zoomed to my room for a quick change.

The microwave hummed to life.

Nate's voice carried down the hall. "Friendsgiving was fun."

My cheeks warmed with memories of roaring through the dark with Jake. "Yeah. You and Fifi seemed cozy." I thumbed through a row of fresh-pressed Guinevere gowns in my closet in search of my favorite, a crimson-and-gold velvet number with a square neckline and billowy sleeves. Bingo. I hoisted it over my head and yanked the zipper between my shoulder blades. My curling iron heated on the vanity as I twisted my hair into the elaborate updo I preferred with this dress.

"I like her. She's fun and not at all like anyone would expect by looking at her." His voice was closer.

I pulled my door open. "Is this zipper stuck?"

"No. It's all the way up."

"Oh, okay. I have to finish my hair. Come on in."

He collapsed onto my bed, and I got to work with the iron. Nate sighed. "I miss Baxter."

"Yeah. Me, too." I still talked to him when I was alone. I'd sent emails to his account for weeks after his death. The process of letting go was slower than I'd expected, and the guilt was crushing.

A few curls later, I jammed a dozen extra bobby pins into the style for good measure and wiggled my head. Nothing moved. "Okay. Done."

Nate turned his head to face me but didn't get up. "Is it like we're replacing Baxter, if we let Fifi into our little group?"

"No. Can you even imagine what Baxter would say if he saw her? I take a hit on my self-confidence every time she walks in the room."

Nate didn't argue.

I did a mental raspberry and headed for the kitchen. "Your pizza rolls are probably done."

He beat me to the quiet microwave and hauled out the steaming plate. "Have you talked to Bree today?"

"Yeah. She's fine. The doctors said the doses she and Tom got weren't lethal, not even enough to do real damage. Whoever poisoned them knew what they were doing." I poured a glass of water from the sink.

Nate straddled a stool at my counter. "What about the manny?"

"They're testing him for plant-based poisons now."

"Did you know belladonna means beautiful lady?"

I scoffed. "Duh."

"How about the fact it was used in Italy during the sixteenth century to open a woman's pupils? They thought it was pretty. It's been used for everything from asthma to hemorrhoid suppositories over the years." He shoved a pizza roll into his mouth.

"I think I just threw up a little."

"What? Hemorrhoids happen. Wait until you have kids."

I choked on my water and shoved my palm between us like a traffic cop. "Shut. Up."

"I read articles on *Web Doctor* all night. I'm thinking of getting my MD. It's not that many more credits and MCATs seem easy enough."

"Who says that? Do you know how many people plan their entire lives around becoming a doctor but they can't pass that test? You're such a narcissist."

"Oh, right, and you think they'd be hard? You think you couldn't pass?"

I walked away. "Hurry up or I'll be late. I have to watch Gwen so Bree can do a quick run-through before the cabaret. This is opening night."

He carried the plate with him to the door. "I can't believe she's still performing."

"Are you kidding? It'd take the apocalypse to keep Bree off a stage."

Nate looked pensive when we boarded the elevator but didn't voice whatever bothered him.

I eyeballed the plate of pizza rolls in his hand. "You have to give that back, you know. Wash it first."

We stepped into the day together and he stopped at my car. "Hang on." He dug his phone from one pocket then stuffed it back. "Kenna."

"Jake asked about you two. What's going on there?"

"Nothing. She's young. Hot, but young. We had nothing in common. Do you know she prefers the new *Star Wars* movies? Hasn't even seen four, five or six."

I clucked my tongue, appropriately dismayed. "Kids these days."

"I know. Right? Anything new with you and your marshal?"

"Nope. You know how it goes. There's no love for a geek girl."

He opened his mouth to argue, but "Flight of the Bumblebee" buzzed though my phone, and he closed his lips.

I pressed the speaker button. "Bree? I've got you on speaker. Nate's here."

"I need a favor."

Nate smiled.

I pulled in a long breath. I could feel the request coming. She wanted me to go out with her little weirdo director. "The real Renaissance man." *Yuck*. Then again, it was the least I could do after the mess I'd gotten her into. Thirty minutes on a bench with Adam, some coffee and a hot pretzel should make us even. "Yes. I'll go out with Adam. If you say he's my perfect match, then who am I to argue?" He wasn't even close to perfection, but I owed her.

She squealed. "That's amazing! I'll call him. Wait. No. You tell him. That's why I'm calling, actually. I got dressed for the show and when I got in the car, I started crying. Don't you dare tell anyone that, Nate. Ever."

He leaned through my open window. "Of course not."

A wave of nausea stole my breath. "Are you okay? You're not sick again, are you? Did you eat anything today?"

"It's nothing like that. It's probably PTSD. I think

I've mentally associated what happened with the performance, which I realize is nuts, but you know what that's like."

I exchanged a look with Nate. "I do."

"Great. Then, it's settled. Mom picked up my costume and will meet you at the Faire. Dad will help her at the booth, and you'll go on for me tonight."

"What?" I screeched. "Nononononono."

Nate disappeared. He landed on the ground, pulsating with silent laughter.

I opened and shut the door to bonk him. "I cannot do that, Bree. I can go out with Adam for you. I've been on my share of crappy dates. I can do that. I can't perform a burlesque routine in front of an audience in that little slip of silk you call a costume. No."

"Mia!" Her voice snapped from sweet and cordial to I-will-pull-your-hair. Hard. "Yes, you can, and you will. You have an eidetic memory. You've seen me practice the routine multiple times. You can do this."

"I'm not a dancer. You're the dancer. You do. I watch. It's how we survived adolescence."

"Exactly. Just switch places with me like we used to. No one will ever know. If you make a mistake, everyone will think it's me. What do you have to lose?"

My mind? "No."

"Please?"

"Uh-uh."

She huffed into the phone. "I didn't want to have to do this, but I can't let the whole cabaret down, Mia. I wouldn't be experiencing this panic if it wasn't for you drawing some lunatic's attention our way. Lots of people knew John. Lots of people were there when he died. Only you jumped in feetfirst like one of *Charlie's Angels* and pissed the killer off!"

I sucked air. "That's low."

Nate peeped over the edge of my door before straightening himself and making a replica telephone with his thumb and pinky finger. He mouthed, "Call me later," and got out of Dodge before I exploded.

I fumed at the phone in silence. Did I owe her? Was it my fault? Jake said it wasn't, but did it matter what he thought? At the moment, it seemed to matter what Bree thought, and she thought it was my fault she was poisoned.

"Mia?"

"Fine, but I hate you."

She made kissy noises and disconnected.

Jerk.

Nate texted me five times on my way to the Faire.

Break a leg!

Wait. You said yes, right?

I can't believe I'm missing this for financial planning.

Please ask someone to tape it for me.

Call me when you're done.

IN KEEPING WITH Murphy's Law, my life and other things that sucked, Dan and Jake Archer were front and center when I arrived at practice in the world's smallest, most ruffled ensemble.

Dan noticed me first. "Hey, Bree. You sure you're up for this?"

Jake turned my way. His gaze drifted over my figure before hopping back to my face. Instant recognition dawned.

Dan's smile faded as he waited for my response.

"Yep. Yeppers. Yepp-ee?" I ducked my head and walked around them.

Dan matched my stride. "I wondered if you have time for a couple questions before the show. You were a little out of sorts at the hospital, and I didn't want to bother you. Now that you're back at the scene, do you recall anything unusual about last night? Maybe someone delivering the food was different than who you'd expect? Maybe someone was lurking around the table during practice? Anything at all."

"No. Nothing I can think of."

Jake chimed in. "How are you feeling?"

"Nervous."

He curved his lips into a smirk. "That's to be expected."

The unspoken *for your first time onstage* loomed between us.

I focused on Dan. "Why are you here? You aren't staying for the performance, are you? I'm certain a cabaret isn't an appropriate way to spend your work hours."

Jake interjected again. "Actually, we're planning to speak with everyone who was here last night, then stay for the show. In case anything else happens."

I swallowed hard. What else might happen? Besides me falling off the stage in a black-out face-plant. "You don't need to stay." I scrambled for a good reason they should leave immediately. "You assigned me a detail. They'll keep watch and let you know if they need you." Thank goodness for that dumb detail.

"Right. Right." He rubbed his chin. "Where are they? I'd like to leave some parting instructions."

They were at Grandma's, watching Bree and her family like they were supposed to do. "Backstage."

Dan gave Jake a long look and headed backstage. "I'll go talk with them."

Jake turned heated eyes on me. "What are you doing in that outfit?"

"Bree's claiming PTSD. She's afraid to go on tonight, but she didn't want to ruin it for all the others who worked so hard. I agreed to take her place, but you can't tell anyone."

He pressed both oversized palms to his face and groaned.

I adjusted the ostrich feather in my hair and gave the girls a boost. The extra ten pounds Bree kept after having Gwen made her costume roomy up top, which was a bad idea in something already so revealing. One wrong move and I'd be exposed.

Dan called from backstage. "Hey, Marshal. Can you come back here a minute?"

Jake leveled me with a curious stare before walking away. "Stay put."

I grabbed my cloak and checked the time. Something had played at the back of my mind for far too long. An idea ignited like a medieval torch. The florist would have an understanding of the belladonna plant. He'd be the most obvious one for ordering papyrus. And when I'd seen him with a woman at the privy, his Scottish accent had slipped into something more Jersey than Ohio.

What if he was the killer?

TWENTY-FOUR

THE PATH BETWEEN booths was crowded with holiday shoppers taking full advantage of the final tolerable days before ice and snow encapsulated Ohio for the winter.

"Excuse me." I skirted through clusters of women with bags and festive parkas until I reached the florist.

The door was locked.

"Bollocks." I kicked the door gently and scanned the crowd.

Two doors down, Melanie rubbed her abdomen and smiled at a lady twice my age.

"Melanie!" I waved a hand overhead and hustled in her direction. "Have you seen Duff the florist today? Did he just leave or has he been gone all day?" Did he close up shop after poisoning my sister and Tom last night?

"Mia?" She tipped her head in confusion at the giant red plume in my obnoxious headpiece.

I rolled my wrist in the universal sign for get-on-with-it.

"He was here earlier. He's probably at the privy or getting a bite to eat."

My tummy churned at the mention of food. I took another look at the teeming paths of shoppers. "Okay. All right. I'll try back, then. Wait. Do you know anything about papyrus? Have you ever seen him with it? Does he usually carry it in his shop?"

"Papayas?"

"No. Papyrus. They made scrolls from them in ancient Egypt."

She scrunched her face. "But this is the Renaissance."

Right.

"Okay. Thank you." I broke into a jog and made my way up the hill to the blacksmith's shop before the show started. I asked the blacksmith's daughter about papyrus and the florist. She wasn't any help either.

With ten minutes to go, I dashed back to the Tilted Tulip. Bingo!

The lights were on when I tugged the door. "Hello?" My muscles were warm from the run and my heart raced with nerves and hope. If Duff was the killer, he couldn't attack me in a crowded place like this, and I'd have beaten Jake to solving the puzzle. I'd text Jake to arrest him. My sister, John and Martha would be vindicated, and everyone could relax again.

Duff was crouched behind the counter, restocking bags. "Good even. Oh, it's you."

"I'm in an enormous hurry, so can you tell me where you're from originally? I heard your brogue slip a few days ago. You were with a woman near the privy."

His shoulders slumped and he puckered his lips slightly, apparently deciding what to do with me. "I'm from Jersey. What's it to ya?" There it was. The ugliest accent on earth. One that gave him common ground with the mobster who'd wanted my friend dead.

"Do you know Bennie the Bean?"

"What?"

"Do you know the name? Does it mean anything to you?"

"Yeah."

I stumbled backward. "Did you kill John Francis to collect on some bounty from Bennie or any of his known affiliates?"

"What? Hey, lady. Are you drunk or something?" He looked over both shoulders. "Is this a hidden camera show? Am I on television?"

"No." My fingers curled into tight fists.

"Oh, I see. Then you're flat-out crazy?"

"Don't think I didn't notice you avoided my question. I'm a student of human behavior. I'll know if you're lying."

"I didn't kill nobody. I moved here from Jersey years ago. I got a work transfer. I finished college in Cleveland."

"How do you know about Bennie?"

"All my family's in Jersey. I still visit every summer. Hit the shore. Get a tan. Come on." He plucked the collar of his shirt.

"Where were you ten minutes ago?"

"Bathroom."

"What about last night? Did you poison my family? Write a creepy note on papyrus?"

His eyes widened. "That's why you came in here asking about papyrus? Someone hurt your family?" Fear changed his expression. "You think Bennie's after you?"

"I don't know. I'm trying to find out." My voice hitched with each word. "I've got to go."

I ran all the way to the stage and apologized profusely to Adam before jumping behind the curtain as it rose.

Spotlights illuminated the dancers. Tinny music blared through hidden speakers, and I swallowed my pride for Bree.

I refused to look into the audience. Jake and Dan were out there somewhere, and there was no doubt Jake had filled his brother in on my impersonation by now.

This wasn't a fair trade for her mild poisoning. This was the definition of awful.

I plastered on a fake smile and struck a ridiculous pose. All there was left to do was smile and plot my revenge on Bree.

TWENTY-FIVE

THE RED LIGHT cue flashed across my legs, and I froze. A cold breeze flapped my skirt ruffles against my thighs. My cleavage skin pulled tight in gooseflesh, and I was certain everyone saw. My traitorous eyes scanned the restless crowd. Bodies filled every seat and formed a semicircle around the back row. Burlesque might not have been a traditional Renaissance performance, but it was certainly a crowd creator. With any luck, the local news wouldn't show up like they did to cover the jousting. The last thing I needed was video footage of the travesty about to take place.

A tremor played over my fingers, and my tongue dried out. The flames of tiny candles trapped in mason jars flickered along the stage lip, casting strange shadows on the polished boards, taunting me. Dan and Jake sat in the front row, captivated by my inability to move. Tears blurred my vision. This was not me. I couldn't do this. I wasn't a performer.

"Bree," Adam hissed from the space offstage. "Bree! It's your cue. They're waiting."

The music stopped and silence boomed louder than my pounding heart.

A tiny white flag caught my attention down front. Jake whipped it overhead until I turned his way. He stilled the unfolded napkin and held it open with both hands. COSPLAY.

Cosplay.

Fear roiled in my core, morphing slowly into something wonderful and familiar. *Cosplay.* I loved cosplay. I turned to face the stage crew, hidden among shadows, and I squinted against the blinding spotlight. "One more time."

The music began anew and a smile crept over my lips. I gave a stiff nod to Jake for saving my life. As far as anyone besides him and possibly Dan knew, I was Bree.

My hip bounced with the steady beat of a low bass drum. The high hat joined its brother, and I began a slow catlike walk to the mason jars, fanning my arms wide. As the instruments joined in, I added the choreographed arm motions to my swaying rump. One hand on the back of my head. The other playfully covering my cleavage. I synched the memorized moves to the music with ease. I was dancing! On a stage! I dropped into the quick squat Bree normally fumbled, whipping my knees open and closed before going bottoms up. I dragged gloved hands, fingers wide, up the length of my legs.

The crowd went wild, and I let loose. I rolled my head in large circles, arms wide. I spun in quick turns across the stage, stopping between each to make an exaggerated Betty Boop face and pop my bottom or arch my back. The rhythmic pounding of heels behind me increased my bravado. I wasn't alone. I was part of a show. Energy pulsed through me, filling every cell and fiber. We marched in a broad circle, one hand on the girl ahead of us, before breaking into a knees-high, Rockettes-worthy kick line.

I belonged onstage.

People clapped and whistled. Shoppers poured into the audience, unable to walk past when they saw the show. My crazy heart tap danced a rhythm against my ribs. A bass voice down front barked in approval, feeding the fire in my limbs.

I closed my eyes, embracing the moment, strutting toward stage left for my next pose and shimmy combo.

Three fast cracks erupted, shocking me from my high. Pain ricocheted through me. I grabbed my chest to stop the searing ache. Cabaret music nearly swallowed the sounds, but I'd heard them. I'd felt them, collapsing my lungs. A spotlight found me. Girls squealed and fled the stage. I peeled tight fingers from my damp corset and found them coated in thick red liquid.

I screamed long and loud enough to earn a job in Hollywood. My life flashed before my eyes, beginning with my family and how this was Bree's fault. Her guilt trip had literally killed me.

I did not belong onstage.

The crowd burst to life like kindling caught fire.

Dan's voice boomed over the chaos, barking orders into the void.

My knees buckled. I landed on my backside with a graceless thud.

Jake sped onto the stage and dove over me, shielding me with his body and rubbing my chest and ribs with both hands. It shouldn't have felt so good to a dying woman. I squeezed off a prayer for forgiveness and made pleas for survival on conditions of immediate confession and unlimited Hail Marys.

"Sit up." Jake hefted me into a seated position and pulled me to my feet. "Come on."

I scurried behind him, dragged by the tight grip of his hand over mine. Every breath pierced my chest. "Hey!" The word burned a trail up my throat. *Never move an injured person.* Girl Scouts had taught me very little, but that was a rule. "Jake! Stop!" I grabbed my throat and sipped oxygen into straining lungs.

He pushed me into the shadow of the rear stage wall and unholstered his gun. "Paintballs."

"What?" I dragged my hands over the red stains and turned my palms in the dim light. "Paintballs?" I croaked.

I dropped to the floor and put my head between my knees. I was alive! Why couldn't I breathe?

"Someone's toying with you," Jake growled. "You're like a mouse in a giant, demented cat's paws."

The image was horrifying. But I was alive. "What do we do now?"

"Did you get a look at who shot you?"

"No. It was too dark. They were in the shadows behind the curtain at stage left."

His jaw pulsed in fury. "I'm going to kill him. If you see it happen, keep your mouth shut."

"Okay."

Jake paced the space before me, coordinating via cell phone with other members of his team and local law enforcement.

Two shiny black shoes came into view. I tipped my head slightly for a look at the newcomer. Dan. He squatted before me. "You okay?"

I gave him a thumbs-up.

Dan slid the tan duster off his shoulders and handed it to me. "What on earth were you doing onstage? I thought Bree was nuts for going on tonight. Taking her place was incredibly stupid. What's wrong with Connors women?"

I rubbed hot tears off my cheek. "I can't breathe."

Jake turned for a long look at us. "Stand up," he told Dan. "Turn around."

Dan obeyed and Jake moved behind me. He loosened my corset until I nearly lost it, and he handed me his cell phone in flashlight mode. "Take a look at the damage. Just paintballs. If the shooter was within a hundred feet, you'll be sore for days. If he was closer, who knows? He could have bruised your ribs. It's unlikely your ribs are broken."

Dark blue and purple circles marred the pale skin beneath my corset. My windpipe opened a bit.

Jake wrapped the duster around me and rubbed his palms up and down my arms. "You'll be fine. You've probably had a lot worse damage from your horse."

He remembered my horse? I'd shown him a picture of me on horseback once, but I'd assumed any memories of our summer together were lost to him. Another closed case. "I have." I'd fallen from Lancelot my sophomore year of college and broken my collarbone. That was true misery.

"Can you breathe or do you need to sit back down?"

Dan gave a quick glance over his shoulder. "Panic attack?"

"Yeah." Jake answered for me. He gripped my forearms and watched me intently with fierce eyes. His Adam's apple moved slowly up and down before he spoke. "When I came home from the service, I had panic attacks. I know what you're feeling. It's going to be okay."

Tears spilled over my lids. How stupid was I? This man had been to war. He had reasons to panic. I'd survived an hour with an assailant last summer and a couple paintballs. My mind reeled with the idiocy of it all. "I'm sorry."

A troop of Faire security guards arrived with giant flashlights and anxious faces. Jake led me toward them. "These guys are going to escort you to my truck. Your dad will bring your car to you later."

"What about you?"

"I'm coming along. You aren't leaving my side again. Got it?"

"'Kay." My shallow breaths slowly deepened. Jake had a plan. I was okay. My family was safe. This was a vicious joke, nothing more. No one was hurt. I turned the thought around in my mind. "Do you think the shooter knew it was me up there and not Bree? Does he know I'm a twin? Was the poisoning also meant for me, or do you think they poisoned Bree so I'd take her place?" *So they could shoot me.*

Jake nudged me forward. "I don't pretend to know what these sickos are thinking. There's a whole division for that. I'm here to capture criminals and bring them to justice. Profilers wrestle with the why. Personally, I don't care why as long as they get what's coming."

His philosophy seemed harsh but, at the moment, I couldn't argue.

We entered the parking lot as a unit. Jake took point. Staff security stood on every side, nestling me in the center. Shoppers were corralled at the gates for questioning.

"Jake? I need to get my laptop from Stella. I locked it in the trunk."

He waved a hand overhead and the security on his flanks headed into the field ahead of us.

Headlights bounced through the grass in our direction, coughing a bark of a siren as if an afterthought. The car rolled to a stop in our path, and a uniformed officer spilled out. "Where do you need me, Marshal?"

Jake inclined his head in greeting. "They could use help taking statements at the gates."

The cop waved two fingers near the brim of his hat and left us.

I hurried to catch up with Jake. Stella came into view several rows away from Jake's truck. A colony of bats swooped through the inky sky, bathed in moonlight before disappearing into the shadows. Something dark flipped in the breeze over my hood. "Wait," I whispered. "There's a flag tied to my antenna."

"Officer," Jake called.

The new arrival changed direction, heading back our way at a jog. "Sir?"

"Get an evidence bag." Jake crossed the last few feet to my car. The grim expression on his face stole the oxygen from my lungs. "We've got another one."

Another note.

I forced the obvious question through trembling lips. "What does it say?"

He turned the makeshift flag my way, shining his phone screen over the thick red image. A large 2 filled the space.

"What does that mean?" I croaked. "Two what?" Two attempts to hurt me or Bree? "Is it a code? Is that papyrus?"

"Toss me your keys."

I did as he asked while working an endless stream of possible meanings for a number two in my head.

The officer snapped on a pair of gloves and dropped the note in a baggie.

Jake opened the trunk, tossed my bag over his shoulder and motioned the security guards to fan out. "My truck. Now." He pressed his cell phone to his temple and relayed information about the note to someone, while heading toward his truck at a clip. It was papyrus.

The same man who'd sent the kid to deliver the first note had tied a number to my car. He knew my car. Did he know where I lived?

I jog-walked to keep up. Stress chattered my teeth and iced my veins. Two threats in an hour was my all-time record. I didn't want to know what came next.

Jake stuffed his phone into his pocket and slowed to stare at me. "Where did you go before the show? I told you to stay put, but you disappeared. Where'd you go?"

"I went to see the florist. I remembered he had a Jersey accent. Plus, a florist is the obvious person to order papyrus and he'd know about plants like belladonna. I had to ask him if he killed John."

Jake swore.

"He said he didn't do it."

Jake raised both hands skyward and let them fall hard against his sides. He made another call. "Bring in the florist."

I forced a supportive smile. "Thanks. I believed him, but…"

"But?"

"He was gone when I first tried his shop, then he turned up a few minutes later. He probably had enough time to leave the note if his plan was already in motion."

Jake ground his teeth. The phone rang and he slid back to marshal mode. "Get in my truck. I need to get you away from here."

"'Kay."

Even if he was mad at me for interfering, I'd trade a dozen officers for one Jake. There was no doubt he would protect me or that he was capable. I moved my feet toward his truck, one after the other, entranced by the hypnotic cadence of his tone. The moment of safety evaporated without warning. Curses dripped suddenly from his lips. He slammed a palm into the hood of his truck and wrenched a square of papyrus from his windshield.

This one said 1.

"Oh no." A countdown.

TWENTY-SIX

THE RIDE HOME took hours. We stopped at the local police station, where I made an official statement, then at the Marshal's office, inconveniently located several towns away. My disposition wavered incessantly between irritation at being paraded around in Bree's ridiculous costume, cloak or no cloak, blinding anger at whoever did this and overwhelming relief I'd survived.

Sometime during an EMT's evaluation of my mental state, annoyed, and physical damage, general bruising, I formulated a new life purpose. As long as I had breath and mobility, I wouldn't stop hunting the animal torturing us. An invisible ogre hoped to scare me off his trail with some paintballs and hate mail? Foolish. If he'd taken time to study his prey, he'd know I was far too hardheaded to let this go now. I wouldn't be a plaything, despite my current getup. There were no perfect crimes. Everyone got caught sooner or later. Sooner worked better for me.

I'd kept in touch with the phone tree every step of the way via group texting. Grandma had everyone at her place and pizza on the way.

Jake waved his badge at the guard gate. The young part-timers on night shift weren't as friendly as Bernie or as vigilant as Jake preferred. For once, I agreed with him.

He cleared the gate with a frown. "I'll drop you at your apartment to change then circle back to watch the gate. That guy at the booth has his eyes on his phone. A herd of elephants could get past him."

"What about pizza? My family's got ten thousand questions. You need to be there. I can't handle all that crazy alone after the night I've had."

He made a cranky face. "You'll be fine. There's a detail on the corner of your grandma's street. I've got to stay here. My team confirmed the identities of the men who followed us with the rental car. Both are confirmed associates of Bennie the Bean's son, Anthony."

"We were on our way here." Mob goons knew where I lived.

"They know I came here. That's all. I'm staying at the gate until I can get someone to cover me. Let your family know I'll come over as soon as I can. I'm going to walk, scout the way as I go. I'm sure the community's safe, but that seems the best course. I'll answer their questions when I get there, but safety trumps curiosity."

That was debatable in this family, but I didn't argue. "Fine."

I rode the elevator alone to my empty apartment. I had three minutes to perform a thorough check and text him or he was coming up. In light of the new revelation, I preferred he tend to the gate, so I quickly cased the place. Relieved not to find any lurking murderers, I texted him ALL CLEAR.

I watched his taillights disappear from my living room windows and dim in the distance. The ticking clock in my silent loft reminded me of scary movies, steadily counting off seconds until a pair of hands jutted from the shadows and dragged me kicking and screaming off screen.

I hurried to my room for a hot shower and fresh

clothes. The sooner I was enveloped in the hustle and bustle of my family's fussing and clucking, the better.

Bree's costume clung to my stomach, attached by sticky, partially dried paint. I winced as my ribs responded to the freedom of losing the corset. Bruising had spread like an ugly venom beneath my skin, changing the pasty white to varied shades of purple and brown.

I climbed, terrified, into the shower and washed the night down my drain. Tears. Fear. All of it, except my new mission. My mind reeled with possible suspects and motives. The killer taunted me because I interfered and got his crazy attention. I was a game to him. Was John his game before me? If I knew the motive, it would help narrow my suspect list. Who would kill John and why? The apothecary was close to him. She might have seen or heard something. Most crimes had something to do with money, but John was broke. There was no money to be made there. So why hurt him? Unless my original blackmail theory was right. John might have given all his money to this invisible bully. If I didn't have more money than I could use, I might have followed that theory longer.

I coated myself in a second lather, trying impossibly to wash the negative away and hone my thoughts. There was always Jake's hypothesis. Maybe it was a mob hit. I wasn't a mob expert, but hit sounded quick. Boom. It didn't make sense for the hitter to stick around like this, which took me back to the theory this had nothing to do with Jersey. Except the unnamed thugs in the stalking rental car were from there. Why else would they come to Ohio, if not for the man intending to put their jobs and freedom in danger?

After a thorough scrubbing, I exited the shower feeling solid. Strong. I'd hash this out with my family over pizza, and we'd find another thread to pull until the killer was in handcuffs.

Bree had texted three times while I showered. Once to tell me she parked Grandma's golf cart in the spot my car normally filled. Again to say Dad returned my car to the spot beside it, my designated visitor space. She also said to put on lipstick because she invited a friend.

I returned her text with a close-up picture of my unhappy face. She promised no matchmaking for a month, but I knew who she had in mind this time, and I'd already asked Jake to come. On business.

Outside my closet, I dressed in layers. A camisole, a paisley blouse and a V-neck sweater, plus jeans stuffed into boots. I'd never wear enough clothes again.

My phone buzzed with a text from Grandma as I boarded the elevator.

Marvin's at the gate. Will you swing by and show him the way?

On it.

I hopped into the night with vigor and boarded Grandma's cart. A few minutes later, I found Marvin in a sleek new Cadillac just inside the gate. Jake waved from the security booth.

Marvin stuck his head through his open window. "Should I follow you? If you're too cold in that, I could give you a ride."

"No. I'm fine." I motioned for him to follow and pointed to the empty clubhouse lot as we approached. I wasn't getting in a car with anyone I'd just met after the day I'd had and, to be honest, I didn't fully trust him to follow me and not mow me down with that giant car. I'd take my chances at hand-to-hand combat if needed.

Marvin parked in the first space and repositioned his rearview mirror. He ran a palm across a few white hairs on his head and climbed out, carrying a small potted plant. "Nice wheels." He patted the roof of the golf cart and climbed in beside me. His black pants rode up his calves, revealing navy socks with multi-colored music notes.

Would a killer wear such happy socks?

He whistled as we started down the road. "I used to have a cart like this. I bet these are handy in a closed community. Your grandmother loves Horseshoe Falls."

"Me, too. This cart belongs to Grandma." Hence the sporty royal-blue-and-emerald paint job. She'd wanted little flags to line the roof, but I advised against it. Too showy.

I pressed the gas a little harder and hoped to cut out as much small talk as possible. For all I knew, killers loved happy socks, specifically ones with music notes. I kept him in my periphery as we motored along. If he was the killer, he'd need real magic to take me down tonight. He was bigger, but I was younger, faster and currently meaner.

He ran milky blue eyes over me as we blinked in and out of sight in cones of light cast from meticulously planned street lamps. "I'm sorry about what's happening to you and your family."

"Thanks." My gaze slipped to the little potted flower in his hands. My mind itched with puzzle pieces scraping toward one another. "Is that for Grandma?"

His face brightened. "Yes. It's a zinnia. Magenta for lasting affection."

I swerved. My grip tightened on the wheel. "Like a coral rose means desire?"

"You know the language of flowers. Very good. Most young people pay no attention. Your grandmother has taught you well. She's a true Renaissance woman." His words turned to jumbled noise.

I veered off the road and stamped the brake, unable to release the wheel. *The language of flowers.* Plants and flowers were all over this case and I hadn't given them a single thought. Not in that aspect. What if this was the new lead everyone was waiting for? "Do you know the language? Do you know any other meanings?"

"A few. It's been decades since I took an interest. My mother loved zinnias, so their meanings and colors stuck."

Shivers rocked through me as I forced my hands from the wheel and into my pocket to retrieve my phone. I flipped through recent photos with bumbling fingertips. "Do you know any of these?" I shoved my phone in his direction.

I'd lied to Jake and saved pictures from the apothecary's murder scene. She was surrounded by flowers. John had a trash can full of flowers. What if they weren't romantic bouquets? What if John confided in her about the flowers and she discovered their sinister relevance? I felt the truth of it in my bones.

Marvin tapped the screen and pointed it my way. "It's hard to say without my glasses, but I believe this one is a geranium."

I blinked. "Yes. It's a geranium. Do you know what it means?"

He wrinkled his brow. "Well, I might be confused."

"What does it mean?"

"It's been a very long time, you understand?" His jovial demeanor turned awkward. "I think it means folly. It's a rebuff. Like saying you're stupid. I'm certain whomever sent you a geranium had no idea. Surely no gentleman would insult a lady that way. Most people have no idea the language exists. They simply choose what's pretty." He frowned at the ugly geranium. "Or practical."

"This wasn't a gift for me." I thumbed to the next photo. "These were sent to recent murder victims. What about this one?"

His eyes widened. "Oh, dear."

"Marvin, please." I turned to face him in the little cart. "Tell me about this one. What do yellow carnations mean?"

He nodded, giving the little screen his full attention. "Rejection. Maybe disapproval."

"Okay. You're doing great. And this? What about these little white flowers? They look like the shrubs that grow here."

Marvin cleared his throat and checked over his shoulders. "It's a mock orange. It grows everywhere. They mean deceit."

I spun in place, jammed the gas and gunned the cart toward Grandma's house. Marvin gripped the dash to stay on his seat. "What's happening?"

My phone buzzed. I tapped the screen.

Bree: Have you left yet? My special guest is at the gate. Pick him up and bring him over with Marvin.

I darted past the unmarked car at the corner of Grandma's street, clearly our family's security detail, and angled into the base of her driveway. "Go on. Tell them what you told me. Let Bree know I'm going to pick up Jake at the guard gate. I'll fill him in on our way back. They have the florist in custody. The new information will cinch this case."

Marvin nodded and hustled to Grandma's door.

I zoomed back the way I'd come. I slowed to wave at the detail, but no one was in the car at the end of her block.

I shot Bree a text: Your detail is missing.

Bree: Grandma called them inside to feed them. You're already? Come in.

My family was safe. The officers were with them. I had solved the case. I should've been ecstatic, but the weight over my heart hadn't lifted.

I powered back toward the gate, taking a shortcut through the grass around the lake, and down the walking path past the waterfall. There was no time for stop signs and intersections. Jake would finish the puzzle. I'd tell him what Marvin said, and he'd help me pull it all together. I rounded the falls and looped back onto the main road as something Marvin said niggled in my mind. He'd called Grandma a Renaissance woman for knowing the language of flowers. Since he also knew this language, did that make him a true Renaissance man? Where had I heard that phrase?

Jake's truck sat silently at the curb where I'd passed it before. A new car idled in front of it. His backup. I shot onto the road in front of it and stopped for a closer look, half expecting Jake to be waiting. The men inside appeared to be asleep. Their heads lulled forward. A pair of paper cups filled the holders. Crumbs covered their chests.

"Oh, no." I jumped free of the cart and pounded on

the windows. "Hello! Hello!" I jerked the driver's side handle to no avail. "Jake!" I screamed at the booth several yards away. "Jake!" I ran around the car to the curb. The passenger door was unlocked. I swung it open and the passenger rolled onto the curb headfirst.

I stuffed a fist into my mouth and texted Jake. Silently praying for a good reason he hadn't heard me scream.

The phone rang in my hands. "Hello?"

Jake's anxious voice filled my eyes with fresh tears. He wasn't dead. Not like the pair before me. "Mia? Where are you?"

"I'm at the car in front of your truck. Your men are…" What were they? I pressed two fingers to the man's neck at my feet, carefully probing the warm skin for signs of life. Blood poured from his head where the sidewalk bit a chunk of his scalp away. That part was my fault. I closed my eyes and concentrated. Slowly, a gentle thrumming registered through my icy fingertips. "Alive! His pulse is thin, but it's there. I don't know about the other one. Hang on."

Jake's voice flared into marshal mode. He ordered people around in the background.

I didn't see any movement at the gate. "What's taking so long?"

I scrambled over the fallen man into the car and shut down the engine. If whatever they ate didn't kill them, carbon dioxide wouldn't finish the job on my watch. I pressed my hand to the driver's throat, massaging the stubbled skin with my fingers, hunting the place where I'd find his heartbeat. "I don't feel a pulse on the driver, but my hands are shaking and he's got this crazy neck beard." Adrenaline rocketed through me. "I could use some help over here! Get your ass in gear, Archer!" I scanned the silent night again. Only road noise and personal panic tainted the calm. "Who are you talking to? I don't see anyone other than these two."

"I'm coming." His voice came in sharp jolts. "I'm leaving the detail with your family. I'm running to you. How the hell did I miss you leaving the house?"

"I took a shortcut. I skipped the roads and used the grass and footpaths." I'd missed him. If I would've stuck to the roads, I would've seen him. "The grass was faster!"

"Dammit, Mia! Get in the car and lock the doors until I get there. If you can get behind the wheel, come pick me up!"

I flailed as the multiple mental demands temporarily confused my limbs. *Get inside.*

Lock the door.

The killer is here. I double-checked the driver's door. Locked. Panic shot through me. "I can't shut the other door. The passenger's half on the sidewalk."

"Push him out."

I turned in the small space, climbing partially into the driver's lap and braced my feet against the passenger's. "He won't budge. I've got to get out and pull him."

"Do not get out."

"What else can I do? Hide in the backseat?" I climbed across the passenger's lap and onto the sidewalk, cell phone clenched between my ear and shoulder. I grabbed his hands and tugged, more carefully now, with a visual reminder he was nearly standing on his head. One shoulder held most of his weight. The slight rise and fall of his chest reassured me. "Come on, buddy. I need your seat." I turned him onto his back and dug my heels into the concrete to drag him from the car.

Footfalls echoed in the distance at a pace I couldn't imagine keeping. Jake was almost here.

"Mia!" His powerful voice echoed through the night, a barely audible life raft.

"I'm here. I'm at the car." My voice wasn't as big as his, but surely he heard me through the phone. I disconnected and wrenched my stiff neck upright. I shoved my phone into my pocket and gave another heave. The passenger slid free, and his bottom hit the curb. "Hallelujah." One more tug, to extract his legs from inside, and I'd lock myself in. I'd call an ambulance for good measure. Jake might have, but it couldn't hurt. Maybe he'd be here by then.

"Need some help with that?" a whiny voice erupted behind my ear. Sugar-sweet breath fluttered the hair at my neck, and cool round metal something pressed my spine. My tummy collapsed. I knew that voice, and he wasn't a mobster.

I released the poisoned man and turned slowly toward my assailant, Adam, clenching angry fists at my sides. "You're a real Renaissance man."

"True." He pointed the gun over the car's roof at Jake chewing up the distance, running at full speed in our direction. He turned the gun on me. Pressed the cold metal barrel to my temple and tugged my back against his chest. "If you make a sound, I'll shoot your boyfriend. Nod if you understand."

I bit the thick of my lip until I tasted blood. I forced one sharp dip of my chin in acceptance. The gun might be another paintball gun. Another ruse. It might also be real. Who was I to wager Jake's life after all he'd done to protect mine?

"Good girl." Adam dug hot fingers into my hair and pulled me into the shadows.

TWENTY-SEVEN

I AWOKE SURROUNDED by red lampshades and props from the cabaret. My head ached as if it had been split like a melon. I rolled onto my side and pushed into a seated position to get my bearings. Soft minstrel music floated through the brothel. I steadied my head and wobbled onto my feet. *How did I get here?*

"Hello, gorgeous." Adam strolled into the room, and the memory of him pointing a gun at Jake struck me back a step. "I wanted to wake you, but I know how you women like your beauty sleep. Not that you need it. You're perfect." He leaned a shoulder against the doorjamb, gun in hand. "How are you feeling?" He moved into my personal space and trailed a finger along my cheekbone. "All better?"

"No. My head hurts. I'm angry. How did I get here? Why were you at Horseshoe Falls?"

"Your sister invited me. I was her special guest. I'd originally hoped to win Bree's heart, but she's married and inflexible on the subject of fidelity, I suspect. I'm sorry if that hurts you to hear."

He pushed me onto a padded bench and sat beside me. "It must be difficult living in her shadow. I can't stand to think of it. In fact, when she pointed you out last fall, I was shocked. How could there be two of her when she's so fantastic? But here you are. You're thinner. More complicated, but I enjoy a challenge. When she said you were single, I realized fate had another plan for me. I didn't need to eliminate Tom. I was drawn in by Bree as an hors d'oeuvre. A little temptation to whet my palate, but she wasn't the one meant for me." He smiled gently. "You're the true main course. If that isn't proof enough of our destiny, I don't know what is. It's like the gods looked down and said, 'Hey, we want you to be happy, so we made another one. Here she is.'"

"I don't date." I did, however, let my stupid self be abducted by an oversized Chucky doll.

His smile faded. "You're stubborn. Resistant. It'll pass."

"My friend just died." I blinked through the haze. At least he didn't have the gun pointed at me. As long as he was talking, there was hope. Strangely, I felt ten times angrier than he looked. He seemed eerily at ease. Delusional? That was bad. I tried recollecting something from school about stalkers, but my mind squirmed away, distracted by the fierce throbbing of my head, which was growing audible. I touched my neck and scalp with tender fingers. "Did you hit me?"

"You wouldn't get in the trunk."

I rolled my eyes and winced. He needed a distraction. "Can I have something for the pain? Some water? A bandage?"

Shock blanked his face. "Oh. Yes, of course. I'm sorry. That was rude of me." He bustled around the little room, collecting items in the pockets of his smoking jacket, and slid back onto his seat. "Here. Everything you asked for. I can get anything you need."

How about the police?

I accepted the bottled water but refused the pills. Ingesting anything from him was out of the question. He'd already gotten the upper hand on me once. Water loosened the thickness in my throat. *Keep him talking.* All the websites I'd read last summer on abductions flooded back. I'd obsessed for weeks over what I could've done better. Different. *Keep him talking.*

"How'd you learn to use belladonna so efficiently? You managed to kill John and the apothecary, but only made Bree and Tom sick. That must take skill. A command of the plant." Hopefully, he didn't say he practiced.

"Trial and error. I used to be bullied." He scraped a hand through wild curly hair and rubbed his freckled nose. "Kids can be mean."

"Did you kill John because he bullied you?" I squeezed my eyes shut and peeled them open again. Nope. Still blurry. I needed an admission of guilt. Something to make sure I was his last prey.

Anger mauled his childlike face. "I'm not a child anymore, Mia. I killed John because he stopped paying."

His anger sprang memories of my previous abduction into mind, etching away my confidence. I needed to watch my mouth. A killer is a killer no matter how different their motivations. I wasn't sure yet if Adam's fixation on me would be my demise or saving grace. With a little luck and fast talk, I had a chance. Unfortunately, my luck wasn't great and my fast talk was mostly babble. Worse: Adam leaned toward the paranoid side of nuts. He'd see all my moves coming. I had to outsmart him with my brain scrambled.

"Take the pills." He lifted them to my mouth.

"No, thank you." I pressed my lips tight and forced a small smile.

"You don't trust me." His hard eyes narrowed. "Didn't I tell you we were fated? Take the pills. They'll help your head."

I contemplated my options. Pretend to pass out? That wouldn't help. Make a run for it? He'd catch me. I squinted against another bout of searing pain. "I think you gave me a concussion." Sweat slicked my hands and I ran them over my jeans, discreetly dragging my thumb across one pocket. My cell phone had saved my life the last time. The hard form of my phone was missing.

Adam growled like a furious kitten. With a gun. "I know what you're doing. Do you think I'm an idiot? Of course I took your cell phone." His voice hitched. "Do I look like an amateur to you? Like a joke? Like a clown who'd steal you away only to leave you with a lifeline?"

"No. I wasn't. I didn't."

"Don't lie!" He hopped onto little feet and paced, rubbing the back of his neck. "We're getting off on the wrong foot. Maybe we should kiss."

"What?"

"Or I could hold you. I want you to feel safe. I don't think you see the chemistry we have here or the full picture of what I have to offer you. You're too distracted with worry. There's nothing to worry about. I brought you here to fill you in on the escape plan. We're partners now. I'm no chauvinist. I'm a feminist. Like you."

"Escape?" That was the best thing I'd heard all night. "Tell me about the escape."

"If we're going to be together, we need a plan. I want you involved in the process. That's what couples do, right? Make plans."

"What?" I'd said it before, but either my concussion was worse than I thought or he was farther down the rabbit hole than I realized.

He rubbed the gun against the side of his head. "Why do you think I needed the money? You can't be the breadwinner. That's my job. Bree told me you own half your company, which makes you rich. I'm a CPA, and not a great one. The economy's rough."

"She told you I own the company?"

"Half the company. She told me everything about you. As much as I was drawn to her, she only wanted to talk about you. Turns out, you and I have a lot in common. We love the Faire. We love food and history and soon, you'll see we love each other."

I did a long blink. My questions were finally being answered, but at a faster rate than my aching brain could process. "You've been stalking us since last year?"

"Yes." He beamed. "I watch. I don't stalk. Bree and I are friends, but I keep track of you both. It's harmless and very responsible, if you think about it. You should know who you're dating before things go too far. I've spent the last few months getting my finances in order so I could officially ask you out. I'm a bit of a risk taker, and I didn't think you'd approve. Women who run companies don't take financial risks. It's a bad habit. What can I say? I don't have many, but everyone has something to improve upon, I suppose. You wouldn't have liked my account balance, so I placed some bets to double my money." He whistled long and loud, smiling ear to ear. "You should've seen the cash I threw down. The whales at the tables were shocked."

"You're a gambler?" I sorted through a multitude of blooming questions, mentally separating his crazy from the useful information. "John was broke. Was he a gambler, too? Did you say he stopped paying you? Did you kill him over a bet?"

Adam leaned forward at the waist and patted my throbbing head. He took my hand in his and resumed his seat at my side. "No, honey. He wasn't a gambler. He's broke because Duff can't play cards or hold liquor."

"The florist?" What did he have to do with this?

"You see, while I beat the coins out of him at Texas Hold'em, I noticed a familiar face in the paper."

"Duff had a New Jersey paper."

"That's right. There was a little picture of John in the bottom corner, only his name was different, and it said he was a known mob associate. His story didn't make it above the fold, but that was better for me. Duff didn't notice him. He's not real bright and he was easy enough to frame, but you wouldn't take the bait."

"The poison plants, flower threats…papyrus! That was all you, trying to frame Duff?"

"All me. I took his paper home with my winnings and did a little research. Seemed like a guy who painted for the mob should have had a lot of money. Plenty to spare, if you know what I mean, so I sent him some notes."

"Requesting blackmail money to fund my kidnapping."

"He had money. We needed money. He earned it by breaking the law. It only seemed fair he split it with us or we'd turn him in."

"Stop saying *we*." Emotion clogged my throat. "John didn't have any money. He was in federal protection, you moron. The government seized his assets. He didn't have anything. Not even his own place. He was watched all the time by marshals and mobsters." The reality of how awful John's life had become slapped me in the face. No wonder he was such a flirt. What else did he have outside the Faire?

Adam stilled. "I didn't know that."

"You blackmailed him." Anger boiled in my veins.

"Who did you say you'd turn him over to? The mob? To the local news?" A moment of clarity pulled the final clues together. "When he'd depleted his accounts and refused to pay any more, you sent threats with flowers."

"I wanted to encourage him to part with his money. I thought he was stalling. That he had more and was being stingy."

"That's not a reason to blackmail someone." My voice crept up a decibel, and I grabbed my head. "Why'd you kill him? If you thought he had more money, why not press harder? He can't pay if he's dead. Why not move on and find someone else to pinch? Anything besides murder." This was why his partner had money and John didn't. The business was thriving, but all John's money had gone to Adam's escape fund, i.e. abduction plan. A plan where I was unbelievably at the center.

Adam lifted his brows and a look of remorse settled over him. "He wised up. Figured out who I was. Confronted me. He threatened to turn me in unless I gave the money back, so I promised I would. He said he'd keep my secret if I kept his and we'd be square."

"You lied."

"Well, yeah. It wasn't like I could trust him. He worked for Bennie the Bean once."

I inched away from him under the guise of consideration. I rubbed my chest and put on my best thinking face. I gauged the distance to the door and took physical inventory. If I got a head start, I could beat him outside, but I couldn't run long with my head throbbing and my vision blurring. It was dark, but he knew the grounds as well as I did. If I could break free and hide long enough to formulate another plan, I had a chance.

"Are you angry?" he asked. "Can you forgive me? I did it for us."

"You killed him. Not just him, the apothecary, too."

"She wouldn't let it go. She kept nosing and digging." He turned a pointed stare on me. His moppy hair fell against his forehead, and he slicked it behind his giant Opie ears. "I tried to warn her."

"With more flowers. I saw them. You poisoned Tom and Bree. You threatened Gwen."

"I would never hurt them. It was just a game. A little belladonna can be beneficial when administered properly."

I doubted that.

He sauntered my way, erasing the small advantage of proximity to freedom I had on him. He rubbed my shoulder, dusting hair away from my neck. "They had food poisoning. No big deal. I would never hurt a baby. That was a joke."

"It wasn't funny. It scared me, but that was what you wanted, wasn't it? You wanted to scare me. That's why you shot me with paintballs, not bullets."

He smirked and wiggled the shiny black handgun. "Paintballs. I would never shoot you with bullets. I love you."

We exchanged a long look. He'd slipped, and he knew it. Paintballs. The gun in his hand might hurt like hell when fired, and give a serious concussion when used as a hammer, but it couldn't kill me.

I slung an arm over his neck and yanked him onto the floor. The gun clattered across polished wooden planks. I bolted into the night.

Darkness enveloped me immediately, and I squinted, begging my eyes to adjust. I ran left out of the brothel. Most people instinctively go right. Hopefully, he thought like most people, at least in this aspect. The world shimmied, and I ducked behind a wide oak to vomit. I wiped my mouth on one sleeve and reoriented myself. Long shadows crept over the grass, thrown from a full moon above the treetops. Sounds were multiplied in my head by fear and pain. Squirrels in trees. Distant traffic. A rattling trash bin. I pressed the heels of my hands to my temples and suppressed a cry. I needed a hospital. I doubted medical care was on Adam's list of approved stops for our escape.

I scanned the area for signs of a five-foot loon. The world was still.

I needed to reach the security office. There'd be phones there, but that was behind me. Beyond the brothel. I'd have to double back. Why didn't I think of that first?

A broad beam of light bounced over the grass near my feet. "Come out, come out, wherever you are." Adam's singsong voice soured my stomach.

More games.

I'd run, and it was exactly what he wanted.

"Mi-a." He dragged my name into two long syllables. "Isn't this fun? Think of all the fun we'll have together in Mexico. I have enough to get us across the border and into a nice little house, a *poco hacienda*, in a town where we'll be treated like king and queen."

I scurried on my backside around the tree, keeping my feet away from the beam of light. A little house in Spanish was a *casita*. He was such an idiot. I hated him. So much.

"You've always wanted to be queen, right? That's why you play Guinevere here and at the Ren Faire. I've seen you in action. You're glorious. Magnanimous." A kiss smacked the air. "Perfection." His voice carried from the other side of the tree.

I swung my hands forward and planted them on the

cold grass. In as swift a move as I could manage, my feet were under me in a runner's position, and I bolted forward.

"Ah, ah, ah," he called.

A loud crack split the night and my ankle rolled. Pain splintered around my sides, radiating from my back. He'd shot me again. Tears of frustration heated my eyes. The sting from close range was nearly unbearable. Hate simmered in my gut. I hobbled farther. He shot me again.

I collapsed with a grunt. The last of my oxygen. I lay still, like a wounded animal, sipping fresh air and pressing back the pain. I needed to catch my breath before I could fight or run again.

He approached with palms up. "I don't want to hurt you, Mia." Slowly, he crouched and plucked hair from my tear-stained cheeks.

I filled my chest with determination and whipped my aching head forward to connect with his. He flopped onto his bottom with a shout.

I screamed in pain, forced myself back into motion and ran into the night, slipping between darkened booths and moving steadily toward the security office. My head wailed in throbbing agony, and dots danced in my sight. I demanded my body stay upright and in motion. I had the rest of my life to pass out. A very long life without Adam. There was work to do first.

My body complied with reluctance. The whimpering was impossible to silence, but I did my best to lessen the impact of my steps and stick to the shadows. Pain sliced through my brain, lungs and back with every move, every breath. When the security booth came into view, adrenaline ran fresh. I grabbed the biggest fallen limb I could and marched at the office like the twenty-by-twenty foot piñata it was. I needed what was inside, and there was no time for trying the knob.

"Mia." Adam clucked his tongue from a few steps away. "Did you think I'd lost you?"

I swallowed hard and swung the limb, connecting it to the door's window with all the anger I had left. Glass fell from the top of the door in a twinkling cascade, glinting under the autumn moonlight. I stuck my arm inside and unlocked the door while Adam approached.

I opened the door and slunk around it, putting heavy aluminum between his paintball gun and my body.

He peered at me through the broken window. "Put the stick down, Mia. I don't want to shoot you again, but you're not cooperating. The gun is an incentive. This is called negative reinforcement. I tried positive reinforcement. I was friendly. I gave you a flower. You didn't respond to that, so I had to switch training methods."

I forced my mouth shut, despite the rage clawing to get out.

"Drop the stick, Mia."

"Stop saying my name."

"MiaMiaMiaMiaMiaMia."

"Stop." The tremor in my hands spread up both arms to my chest. Panic. My windpipe narrowed. My throat burned. I dropped the limb and yanked the receiver off the phone on the desk behind me.

Adam ripped the door open as my finger hit the final number. He shoved my sternum hard, and I toppled over folding chairs onto the dusty linoleum floor.

He pulled the phone to his ear and scowled. "Who is this? Who did you call, Mia? Your marshal? Your giant ginger? Your sister?" He shook the phone. "Hello?"

I'd dialed 9-1-1. Had the call not gone through?

He groaned, exhaling and swearing. He slammed the

receiver down repeatedly, growing angrier with each hit. His freckles disappeared beneath the bright crimson of his cheeks. "You called the police?"

I felt the floor for something to use as a weapon. There was nothing.

He launched himself at me, wrenching me onto my feet and hauling me out by my hair.

I screamed in pain as I stumbled along beside him. The black dots in my vision morphed into a tunnel, dimming my world. "I'm going to pass..." My knees buckled before I could finish.

Adam went down with me. I stayed down, barely conscious, formulating a new plan. He looped thin arms beneath mine and dragged me toward the lot. I dug my heels in, making the task as difficult as possible.

He grunted along at a snail's pace like an ant unwilling to put down the cookie. "We have to leave now. You've ruined our escape." His voice wobbled. "Why'd you have to ruin it, Mia? I had it all planned!"

Adam leaned me against the wheel of his car and popped the trunk.

I pulled my legs under me, preparing to run, knowing I couldn't.

"Get up!" He pulled my arms above my head.

I pretended to remain unconscious. Dead weight. I laid my head against the ground, unable to form another coherent thought, fearful I'd be out cold soon. The hard-packed earth rumbled beneath my ear, and I winced.

Adam swore.

Blinding light crossed my closed lids. Someone was here.

He slammed the trunk and tripped over my legs, scrambling for his car door.

I swallowed dirt as Adam shifted into drive and tore

away from me in the large earthen lot. Scents of mud and grass and exhaust choked me into a coughing rage, which splintered my head in ragged strips of pain.

Strangers surrounded me, talking gibberish and rolling me onto my back. I floated in the air, tears streaming. The empty field was suddenly thick with lights and people. Jake's truck blocked Adam's car only a few yards away. Adam was splayed across the hood like a girl in a nineties rock video. Jake held him there by his face.

Satisfied I'd won, I let my eyes fall shut.

TWENTY-EIGHT

I GOT DRESSED on Thanksgiving morning for the first time in nearly a week. I chose a vintage wrap dress in taupe, with my black patent leather heels and clutch. If I'd spent another day in yoga pants, I'd have lost my mind. Marcella had checked on me every afternoon, delivering her rich homemade meals and pastries. The Lindseys kept me in coffee, and the Kubickas made sure there were endless pints of ice cream to go with Marcella's desserts. Horseshoe Falls had rallied around their fallen IT girl, and Fifi had handled things at the clubhouse in my absence. In summary, I was well rested, plump as the turkey in Grandma's oven and spoiled rotten.

I spent the morning curling my hair and dressing. According to my doctors, a whack on the head like mine could slow me down for weeks. Maybe, but it wouldn't keep me from Thanksgiving with my family. We had good cause to celebrate. Earlier this week Grandma had told Petal where to stick the Earth Hugger offer. Bailing on us at the first sign of crisis wasn't what our company needed. Instead, she'd signed with Earth Hugger's biggest competitor, Berry First, a global conglomerate I'd assumed was out of our league. I'd sent them a sample basket after a recent convention, and Grandma nudged them when she'd had enough of Petal's despondency. Score for Grandma. Berry First offered her a deal no one could believe, including Petal.

I applied false lashes and two coats of Kiss Me Not

fuchsia nail polish with a smile. Our family was going to be just fine.

The ride to Grandma's was short but precious. Large oaks dripped with rainbows of autumn leaves and blessedly shaded the streets. I inhaled my final few minutes of quiet until bedtime. Thanksgiving with the Connors was a marathon. We had appetizers out all day, ate dinner early, played board games and watched movies, while routinely making our ways back for leftovers throughout the evening. The fun didn't end until Bree passed out from her twelfth cup of eggnog and I had meat sweats.

Grandma's drive was packed. Cars spilled from the black asphalt onto the street. Dad's Plymouth, Tom and Bree's minivan and Grandma's Mercedes claimed the driveway. I parked Stella at the curb behind Marvin's Cadillac and shut my door gently so as not to encourage a headache.

Rich, buttery aromas wafted from her home, curling around me and cupping my face with flavorful promises of foodgasms to come.

Christmas music and garland filled the rooms. Marvin and Grandma played Monopoly in the living room. He waved as I passed. She cackled. "I win! Give me all your money!"

Mom and Bree buzzed around the kitchen island, setting the hors d'oeuvres on trivets and tiered trays, shoving dishes in and out of oven doors and shooing Dad away from the candied bacon.

"Mia!" Mom hugged me with enormous oven-mitted hands. "I'm so glad you're here. Look at you! You look amazing! How do you feel?"

"Thanks." I pulled up a seat at the island and relaxed. "I feel a lot better."

Bree slid a glass of eggnog my way.

I made a crazy face. "It's noon."

"No. It's Thanksgiving." She spun toward the radio, where "Jingle Bell Rock" had started, and turned it up. Her headband had a turkey on it, wearing a Santa hat.

I laughed. "How many have you had?"

"None for me." She winked. "Can't I just be happy?"

"Not that I'm aware of."

The doorbell rang. I did a quick head count and groaned. Bree shoved me off my stool. "Get the door."

"Geez." I shoved her back. "You're acting weird. This had better not be an ambush. You promised."

"I invited a guest. So, what? Now go. It's for you."

I bit back a thousand reasons her statement was ludicrous and stormed toward the door, determined to save my day. Whoever was out there could come back tomorrow. When I wouldn't be here.

Gwen beat me to the door on Tom's shoulders.

"Must be nice to fly." I tugged one of her tiny pigtails when Tom set her on the floor. He hid behind the door again, pulling it open as he retreated.

Jake rocked on his heels outside. Dark jeans, blue plaid button-down and what looked like a Captain America T-shirt underneath. The familiar red-and-white rings of his shield peeked above a button left open at his collar. "Hey."

"Hi."

Gwen slapped a chubby palm against the glass door. "Bababadoo!"

I scooped her up and opened the door. "Come in."

Jake obliged. A big white gift bag swung from one wrist. Gwen strained against my grip, reaching for him. He poked her round tummy. "You look beautiful in pigtails. Ever heard that before?" He dug in the bag and produced a stuffed turkey. "This is for you."

She grabbed it in both hands and kicked her feet until I set her on the floor. She shoved the turkey's head in her mouth and clapped. Her feet were invisible beneath the giant green dress as she swept away, eager to show off the prize.

Tom shut the door and offered his hand to Jake. "Glad you could come. I know your family has plenty to keep you busy today."

He tucked his chin in agreement. "True, but I can't turn down dinner at Mary's."

Mary's? Since when was Jake on a first-name basis with Grandma, and when had Tom had the chance to invite Jake for Thanksgiving? "Did I miss something?"

Tom turned toward the kitchen. "Yeah. About a week. A lot can happen in a week."

"Like what?" I smiled at his Thanksgiving shirt. He wore it every year for tradition. Mom bought it for him while he and Bree were dating. A cartoon pilgrim, hiding a knife behind his back, motioned a turkey to join the feast. The caption read: *Come on.*
Get Stuffed.

He rubbed his palms together like he always did when he had gossip. "Nate asked Jake and me to play REIGN as test subjects. He wanted us to challenge some existing aspects of the game and look for ways to optimize usability."

Smart. "But you aren't gamers."

Tom wagged his chin in disagreement. "Nate says everyone's a gamer. We just don't know it yet. He wants to introduce future gamers to REIGN. Bring them in with your game. Like a gateway drug. He thinks it's a good way to create brand recognition and loyalty."

I gave the men my best angry eyes. "You've been testing REIGN while I was laid up watching Netflix? No fair. Why didn't anyone tell me?"

Jake dug in the bag. "We were working. You were supposed to be resting, and I am a gamer. This is for you." He handed me a file.

I turned it over in my hands. "You brought me paperwork? I think I'd have rather had the turkey." I worked uselessly to smooth the confusion on my brow.

Jake sighed and flipped the cover open. He tapped the papers. "It's information on gun training and a membership to the local range. You get lessons, practice time and the test for a concealed carry license when you pass. I already spoke with your dad about it, and he's on board. You can practice at my place anytime, and there might be a gun in it for you at Christmas if you play nice."

Aww. I took it back. My heart did a goofy flip thing. He'd be around at Christmas? "Thank you."

He scrutinized me. "I don't like it and I wish you'd stay out of trouble, but I'm beginning to see that summer fiasco wasn't a fluke. You're a habitual offender. Pepper spray and some college self-defense courses won't do the job forever."

I stepped forward on impulse and looped an arm around his middle for a squeeze. I generally adhered to the no-touching-without-an-invitation rule, but the gift did something to me. He trusted me with a gun. He accepted me, faults and all. I had no plans to ever carry a gun, but it was the thought that counted and, coming from Jake, this was huge. The moment my cheek hit his chest, I regretted it and leaned away. "Sorry."

He attempted to hug me back at the last second, and the whole thing was arms and awkward.

We looked at each other until I thought I'd combust from the pressure. I loathed silences like these. My tongue nearly vibrated with the need to yammer about anything that would end the moment.

Jake reached into the bag again. "I brought you something else. This one's not from me."

I smoothed my skirt and gave the file another look.

He handed me a large white envelope with embossed rings in the corners. "It's from Parker and Eric. They want to invite you to their wedding. Parker had your old address. She called me for the new one, but I told her I'd see you today so…"

"Oh. Thanks. I'd love to." I grabbed the envelope, but he didn't let go. "What's wrong?" Maybe he'd hoped I'd say I couldn't come. Maybe attending his brother's wedding was too much, too soon? The last time he closed a case in my area, he hadn't called for three months. Had I read into the gun thing too much? Maybe keeping me alive was a basic Archer instinct and nothing personal. Parker's invitation probably ruined his plan to avoid me until someone else I knew dropped dead. So, hopefully never. "Oh." I reduced my grip on the invitation.

He dipped his head. "The thing is, the reception card has a place to mark your plus one. I'd hoped you might come as my plus one."

"As your date?" My cheeks heated. "I mean…" A headful of words fumbled over one another in my mouth. "It's okay if not. I just need to know what I'm dealing with. Either way is fine. I still want to go. Parker's great. Your brother seems nice, too. Eric, I mean. Also, Dan." I forced my mouth shut and prepared to slap a hand over it if it opened again.

His charming smirk frustrated me. "It's my fault. I should've been clearer. I'm asking if you'll be my date to Eric's wedding."

"I have to check my calendar."

A belly laugh rumbled through him. "Well, all right. You'll let me know?"

"Mmm-hmm." I pressed the invitation to my chest and turned on my toes toward the kitchen. "You hungry?"

"Little bit."

Dad handed us empty plates upon arrival. He had his sweatpants on. Ready for the marathon. "Gwendolyn says we can have appetizers. Good to see you again, Jake. Tell your brother I'm sorry for chewing him out at the hospital. I was out of line." He clapped Jake on the shoulder and looked at me. "Where's Nate?"

I smiled. "Meeting Fifi's parents for a pre-dinner, totally casual, non-date afternoon. I think it's more. He won't admit it. He's eating dinner at his mom's this evening." I checked my family's faces for appropriate levels of shock and awe at my most excellent gossip.

Jake set his plate on the counter and dug into the bag again. "Knew it."

I scoffed. "You didn't know it."

"Did too." He discarded his now-empty bag and placed an apple pie on the counter. Plastic wrap clung to the cinnamon-dusted face and tiny apple-shaped cutouts in the top. "Nana sent this. I told her you'd have plenty, but she called me a freeloader."

The room chuckled.

Mom uncovered the pie and set a serving knife beside it. "Thank your Nana very much for us. It smells like heaven." She squeezed past me to pat Jake's stubbled cheek. "I'm glad you came."

My heart did another dumb flip. Maybe there were other side effects to a concussion, like irrational attachment disorder. That had to be a thing. He glanced my way, and I turned my head.

Bree caught me. Her lips were puckered up and pulled to one side. She thought she knew things she couldn't know.

I filled my plate with tiny sandwiches, veggies and Mom's dip, careful to leave room for all my favorites, still baking in the ovens. I took a seat beside Jake at the island. "What happens to Bennie the Bean with no one to take the stand now that John is gone?"

He tapped broad thumbs against the marble counter. "I guess we trust the legal system to do its job and hope the feds have built a solid prosecution."

I huffed. "He's getting off."

"Probably. How's your head?"

"Okay. Thank you for asking." The hair on my arms stood at attention. The kitchen had stilled around us. Humility crept over me. "What?"

My family jumped to attention, reverting to whatever they'd been up to before they were caught staring.

I angled toward Jake and lowered my voice, despite the fact we were on display like puppies in a store window. "And Adam?"

"Not going anywhere for a very long time."

I released a thankful breath. "So, what's next for you now?"

He wiped his mouth with a turkey-shaped napkin and turned my way. The creases on his forehead deepened and released before he spoke.

I braced myself for what would come. The air around us thickened with tension.

He shook his head slightly. A small smile played at the corners of his normally grouchy mouth. "Turkey, I think."

Whatever he'd considered saying, he'd changed his mind.

Lucky for him I'd given up sleuthing, or I might have been tempted to figure that one out.

* * * * *

ACKNOWLEDGMENTS

I can't stop thanking Carina Press and Harlequin for their amazing support and encouragement. I'm frequently awestruck by the obvious love they have for their authors. Their endless patience and enthusiasm put me on track to become a proper mystery writer. I hope I'll make them proud. I'm also amazingly thankful for my blessed editor, Deborah Nemeth. I think I owe her a bottle of wine, or perhaps, a pledge of my fealty. She's basically fantastic, and I love her. Huge, humongous thanks to Jennifer Anderson, Dawn Dowdle, Melinda Crown and the rest of my girl crew who keep me going when I want to give up. Finally, big bear hugs to my precious parents for believing I can change the world, and to my colossally fantastic husband and offspring for loving me while I try.

ABOUT THE AUTHOR

Julie Anne Lindsey is a multigenre author who writes the stories that keep her up at night. She's a self-proclaimed nerd with a penchant for words and proclivity for fun. Julie lives in rural Ohio with her husband and three children. Today, she hopes to make someone smile. One day she plans to change the world.

Learn about Julie at:

Julieannelindsey.com
Find Me on Facebook!
Tweet Me!
Read with me on Goodreads
Pin with me on Pinterest
Blogging at Musings from the Slush Pile
Capturing life on Instagram

Get 4 FREE REWARDS!

We'll send you 2 FREE Books plus 2 FREE Mystery Gifts.

Harlequin® Intrigue books feature heroes and heroines that confront and survive danger while finding themselves irresistibly drawn to one another.

FREE Value Over **$20**

Get 4 FREE REWARDS!

We'll send you 2 FREE Books plus 2 FREE Mystery Gifts.

Harlequin® Romantic Suspense books feature heart-racing sensuality and the promise of a sweeping romance set against the backdrop of suspense.

FREE
Value Over
$20

Get 4 FREE REWARDS!

We'll send you 2 FREE Books plus 2 FREE Mystery Gifts.

Love Inspired® Suspense books feature Christian characters facing challenges to their faith... and lives.

FREE Value Over **$20**